LAST CHANCE COWBOYS

THE OUTLAW

D1013956

ANNA SCHMIDT

sourcebooks
casablanca

Published by Sourcebooks Casablanca, an imprint of Sourcebooks, Inc.
P.O. Box 4410, Naperville, Illinois 60567-4410
(630) 961-3900
Fax: (630) 961-2168
www.sourcebooks.com

Printed and bound in Canada.
MBP 10 9 8 7 6 5 4 3 2 1

With love and appreciation to the amazing trio—Natasha, Mary, and Melody—you know who you are and what you have done for me and this story!

One

Arizona Territory, Spring 1883

AMANDA PORTERFIELD GAZED OUT THE WINDOW AT the endless landscape where cattle grazed and wild-flowers were in full bloom—this beautiful place where she had spent the entire twenty years of her life so far. Even with all this natural beauty surrounding her, she was quite sure she would go stark raving mad unless something exciting happened to break the sheer monotony of her days.

Practically everyone else in her family had found love, or at least adventure, but here she sat with no prospects, either romantic or adventurous—preferably both—in sight.

Amanda sighed and drifted toward the sounds of her mother and the family's housekeeper, Juanita, talking as they sat in the courtyard. "I think I'll go into town," Amanda announced after pouring herself a cup of coffee and flopping into a high-backed chair.

"That's a good idea," her mother replied, setting aside her mending. "I'll come with you."

Amanda swallowed another sigh. The point had been for her to be off on her own. If adventure did not find her, then perhaps she needed to seek it. But with her mother along for the ride, it was unlikely Amanda would be successful in her quest.

"It's been weeks since we went shopping," her mother added with a sly smile designed to let Amanda know that she understood exactly what was behind her daughter's sudden announcement. "Perhaps a new dress is in order for the fandango the Johnsons are hosting next weekend?"

"Perhaps," Amanda agreed, and she couldn't hide the smile she gave her mother in return. As much as she tried to mirror her sister's maturity and sophistication, the truth was that Amanda loved shopping and parties. And who knew? There might just be someone interesting to meet at the Johnson gathering. It was spring in Arizona, and ranches were hiring to handle the branding and other tasks involved in getting the cattle ready for market in the fall. She felt her spirits lift.

"Perhaps we might visit the Wilcoxes as well," her mother continued. "It occurs to me that you need something meaningful to occupy you. Doc Wilcox mentioned a friend of his in Tucson—a banker whose wife died several months ago. The man is looking to hire a tutor for his children. I think you would make an excellent candidate. We could stop by and speak with him about how you might go about applying for the position." As usual, Amanda's mother was planning her life for her.

"I don't want to be a teacher, Mama."

"And I didn't choose to be a widow," her mother

replied bluntly. "We make the best of our lives, Amanda, and right now, you need to find some direction for yours. So go fetch your bonnet—that sun is going to be fierce today. And ask Chet to hitch up the wagon."

Reluctantly, Amanda did as she was told.

Amanda's brother-in-law was a quiet man and a good listener. "Mama thinks I should apply for a position in Tucson tutoring some rich man's children," she groused as she stood by the corral and watched Chet select a team of mules and lead them to the wagon. "She thinks I need *direction* in my life."

"And what do you think?" Chet asked.

"I think…" What did she think? "If it were up to me…"

Chet quirked an eyebrow as he harnessed the mules. "If you got that job, it just might lead to something more to your liking."

"I don't see how. I mean, how would spending my days going over spelling and reading and such, and my nights preparing lessons and exercises, possibly lead to—"

"Of course, you'd have to move to Tucson," Chet interrupted, as if she hadn't spoken. "That would be a big change from living out here with a bunch of rough cowboys and your family." He wrapped the reins around the brake and gave her a hand up to the seat. "Sometimes, Amanda, what seems like nothing special turns out to be just what you didn't know you were looking for in the first place."

She grinned. "Like you winding up here and married to Maria?"

Chet winked at her. "Exactly like that."

Amanda snapped the reins, and the wagon rolled forward toward the house. Why couldn't she find a man like Chet? Smart and strong and good-looking as all get-out. Of course, in the time Chet and Maria had been married, Amanda had realized that looks weren't everything when it came to being happy. Chet was content to be a rancher and had settled into a routine. He had little taste for adventure. While that suited Maria, Amanda was pretty sure she wouldn't last a year as a rancher's wife. On the other hand, there was much to be said for a handsome cowboy. If only she could find one who shared her urge to try new things.

It was nearly noon by the time they reached Whitman Falls. The ever-efficient Juanita had packed a full lunch for them to share with Eliza McNew, owner of the town's general store. "No need to go spending money eating at the hotel restaurant," Juanita had said as she set the hamper in the back of the wagon.

Of course, Amanda had been looking forward to eating at the hotel. But with the prospects of shopping for a new dress and a visit with Eliza and possibly her best friend and sister-in-law, Addie, if she wasn't busy helping her father see patients, Amanda couldn't help but look forward to the day. She might even reconsider that tutoring position.

～～

Seth Grover was growing weary of his double life. On the surface he presented himself as a man to be watched—a quiet, soft-spoken stranger who was good with a gun and who had no visible means of support other than being very good at playing poker. That combination made most folks believe he was probably operating on the shady side of the law, which suited his purposes most of the time. The truth was that he was an undercover agent for the Wells Fargo Company, hired to go wherever he was needed to foil outlaws targeting the company's wealth. Most recently, he'd been charged with doing whatever it took to stop the string of robberies that had cost the company close to half a million dollars over the last few years.

As a youth, he'd sown enough wild oats to earn his reputation as a rebel. In his first months undercover, he had quickly established himself as a man good at poker and handy with a six-shooter. The combination gave him the right to travel under his own name, for many outlaws had been brought up in good families with strong moral values before they turned to lives of crime.

For several weeks now, he'd been hanging around the small town of Whitman Falls—a place the railroad had bypassed, but a thriving town nevertheless. Fort Lowell was near enough that the stagecoach carrying the monthly payroll for the soldiers garrisoned there came right through town on its way. That delivery was one of the reasons Seth had decided to take a room above the local saloon and stay for a spell. The fact that the saloon's owner—Lilly Goodspeed—was a friend and one of the few people who knew his true profession helped make his stay in the small town more tolerable.

An outlaw gang run by the notorious Stock brothers and thought to be responsible for a couple of bank robberies and stage holdups in northern Arizona was rumored to be moving south. Seth had a hunch that they planned one more big strike—possibly the payroll—before they headed out for the border and Mexico. It was a pattern he'd seen before, and it was his job to make sure they didn't succeed—hopefully without revealing his true identity.

He also had a personal reason for foiling this particular robbery. He'd gotten word from his mother that his youngest brother had run away from the family's Chicago home around the time that the gang had been operating farther north. He knew his brother, knew he was reckless and always seeking adventure. The latest reports Seth had received from his supervisor had mentioned a kid—fair-skinned and blond, with a missing finger—who appeared to be working as a lookout for the gang. The description was broad, but it fit Sam—a boy who had spent years in the city and one who knew little about life on the frontier.

It was certainly possible that Sam could have joined the gang—a long shot to be sure, but if he was that kid, this might be Seth's last chance to save his brother from spending his life on the run, rotting in prison, or getting killed.

As he walked from the shadows of the livery stable where he'd left his horse, he squinted into the sunlight and watched a wagon creak its way around the plaza that anchored the town. He spotted two women, the younger woman driving the team. Seth stopped next to a hitching rail and watched as she pulled to a stop in front of the mercantile.

He kept watching, telling himself that it was out of boredom. The higher the sun rose, the quieter and more deserted the streets seemed. A few people had sought the shade of chestnut trees, but other than that there was little activity.

The older woman climbed down while the younger woman set the brake, wrapped the reins around it, and jumped down as well. She was talking the whole time, waving her hands to make her point, and when she pushed her sunbonnet off her head and allowed it to hang down her back, held by thin ties, he saw that she was a redhead—strawberry blond, his ma would say.

Either way, in Seth's experience, women with red hair, and the lively temperament that seemed to go along with it, could be trouble. It was as if something in their blood made them high-spirited. Still, there was no doubt she was the prettiest thing he'd seen in some time, and he was far from immune to the natural desires of a man in his prime.

He forced himself to look off to the opposite side of the plaza, toward the saloon. He mentally reviewed the information he'd picked up the night before while playing cards with a couple of strangers and a local by the name of Gus Abersole, who seemed to be a fixture in Lilly's saloon. One of the strangers had asked Gus about the garrison at Fort Lowell, how many men were stationed there and such. The man kept his tone casual, but Seth was practiced enough to know when somebody was fishing for information. Abersole's tongue had been loosened by the three shots of rye the man had bought him. He'd babbled on about troop numbers and routines until Seth had wanted to clobber him.

His thoughts were interrupted by a feminine squeal

of delight, and he looked back toward the mercantile in time to see the store's owner greeting the new arrivals, and then leading the women inside. As the younger woman held the door, Seth got a better look at her. She was a beauty all right, and there was something about the way she carried herself that made him want to move closer.

It wouldn't hurt to indulge himself. After all, he'd been working hard for weeks now. On the other hand, why tempt fate?

Against his better judgment, he pushed himself away from the hitching rail and headed for the store. He'd been meaning to buy some jerky to have with him on his nightly rides to survey the area as he looked for possible places where a gang just might choose to ambush a stagecoach or the wagon carrying the payload.

Once again, the change in light from the strong sun to the shadowy, cooler interior of the store took some getting used to. Seth was aware that the women had all been talking when he entered, and now, as he shut the door and the bell above it went silent, all conversation had stopped.

"May I help you, sir?" The proprietor stepped forward, but he heard the wariness in her tone that he'd grown used to over the last couple of years. He knew she had seen him around town, but this was the first time he'd come to her store. Whitman Falls was a small place, and his way of dressing all in black—from his hat to his boots to the sack coat he wore to cover the pistol he carried—was hard to miss. Further, it sent a message for folks to keep their distance.

"Yes, ma'am. I could use some jerky."

Eliza McNew led the way toward the back of the store past the two women. Seth tipped his hat and waited at the counter. "Ladies," he murmured.

The younger one let out a gasp that had the older woman looking at her with surprise. She stared at him, her hand fluttering around her mouth, her eyes wide with recognition. But Seth felt certain they'd never met—he would remember meeting a woman as beautiful as she was. Still, there was something about her.

The older woman stepped forward and extended her hand. "I don't believe we've been introduced. My name is Constance Porterfield, and this is my daughter, Amanda. And you are?"

"Name's Grover, ma'am." He accepted the handshake and was surprised at how firm and strong it was. Porterfield. The local marshal was a Porterfield—couldn't be a coincidence. "I met Marshal Porterfield when I first came to town—any relation?"

"My son. He's planning on running for district sheriff," she added with the obvious pride of a mother, and, perhaps, the need to impress Seth with the fact that this family had the law on their side.

Seth and Jess Porterfield had come to an understanding a couple of weeks earlier when the marshal had confronted Seth and suggested he move on. He had decided to take Porterfield into his confidence without revealing that his true concern was the fort's payroll. The marshal had agreed to give him the time he needed to foil the gang on one condition. *"Stay away from my sister."*

Seth had laughed and told him that wouldn't be a problem since he didn't know the man's sister. But now that they'd been introduced and he'd gotten a good look at those cactus-green eyes and plump, rosy lips that could stop a man in his tracks, Seth was pretty sure he might have trouble keeping the bargain he'd made.

"It's been some time since we've had anyone move to Whitman Falls, Mr. Grover. Are you thinking of settling here with your family?"

He ducked his head to hide the smile that curved his lips. Mrs. Porterfield was clearly good at gathering information. He was well aware that she was really inquiring about his marital status and intentions for making Whitman Falls his home. "No, ma'am. Just passing through."

The shopkeeper wrapped the jerky in brown paper and handed it to him. "On the house," she said. "My way of welcoming newcomers."

Seth doubted that. The way Eliza McNew's hand shook slightly as she presented him with the package, it was more likely that free jerky was her way of letting him know she would be obliged if he didn't cause her any trouble or rob her store.

"That's mighty kind of you, ma'am." It wasn't the first time a business owner had offered him free stuff hoping that he would leave them alone. It meant his cover was working.

But Mrs. Porterfield did not seem intimidated. "Exactly what is it that you do, Mr. Grover?" she asked. The daughter remained silent, but she looked directly at him—in fact, it was a little like she was looking him over, trying to come to some decision.

"At the moment, I need to check on my horse,

ma'am." Seth tucked the package of jerky in the patch pocket of his coat and saw the daughter's eyes widen with interest when his action revealed the gun he wore strapped on his hip. He tipped his hat. "You ladies enjoy your day," he said as he set his hat lower over his eyes and left.

It occurred to him that Amanda Porterfield had not exhibited the usual female reaction to seeing a gun. Her eyes had widened, to be sure, but with excitement, not alarm. She had been unable to look away.

"Another sign she's trouble," Seth muttered. If she had the sense God gave her, she'd surely be a little more wary. After all, she didn't know him, and he was totin' a six-shooter and refusing to answer simple questions.

Stay away from my sister, the marshal had warned.

"Good advice," Seth said as he crossed the street to the livery, where he could hear the clang of metal on metal as the blacksmith pounded a new shoe into place. Of course, from the way she was studying him back there in the store, he had a feeling that Amanda might have other ideas.

He'd have to make sure he avoided any further contact.

∽ଵ

Amanda barely heard the conversation running between her mother and Eliza as they ate lunch. She was still thinking about the stranger.

A few weeks earlier, when she'd visited Addie, she had seen him from her friend's bedroom window. He'd been standing across the street, not far from the jail. He'd looked dangerous, and at the same time, there had been something about him that made Amanda unable to look away.

That day she had observed him from a distance. Standing right next to him was a different experience entirely. It had, quite frankly, taken her breath away.

"Of course, taking the position to tutor these children would mean a move to Tucson, and Amanda knows no one there," Eliza was saying. "Wouldn't you be terribly lonely, Amanda?"

"Addie and Jess might make Tucson their home one day, if he gets himself elected and Addie can set up her practice," her mother interjected. "And with Addie all involved in that jail reform project of her hers, they go there at least once a month now."

"Maybe they know someone willing to rent a room," Eliza suggested. "Or it's possible that room and board are part of the salary."

"I haven't even applied yet," Amanda reminded them, but the way her mother barely glanced at her before continuing her conversation with Eliza told her that the decision had already been made well before now. "You tricked me," she said. "You and Doc Wilcox have already set this in motion."

Eliza grinned while Constance Porterfield pursed her lips and frowned. "I wouldn't say that I deceived you. I did have a conversation with Doc, and we did go over the pros and cons of your applying. He said he would speak to his friend—Mr. Baxter—in Tucson, and in the end…"

"In the end, don't I get some say?"

"Not really," her mother replied. "Not unless you

want to spend another season on the ranch where, with your younger brother off sketching canyons and waterfalls in Yellowstone, we are short-handed, and there is the distinct possibility that you might be called on to take his chores. That is more a probability now that Maria is expecting and unable to do her usual level of work, as if she were any man."

"I am not Maria," she reminded her mother through gritted teeth.

She was so weary of her perfect sister's ability to do pretty much anything she set her mind to. Amanda had long ago understood that, as far as neighbors and friends were concerned, her own role in the family was that of "the pretty one." But lately, instead of being flattered by this, the label had begun to irritate her. Recently, she'd been reading about some women in the East who had been active abolitionists during the war and then turned their attention to the fight for a woman's right to vote. The point was that women were beginning to stand up and speak out, which appealed to her. She saw a possibility to be more than just the pretty one.

"No," her mother replied, placing a gentle hand on Amanda's clenched fist. "You are not your sister, and more's the good in that. You have gifts of nurturing and inspiring others that she cannot equal, Amanda, and now you have the opportunity to share those unique talents with the Baxter children. Do you have any idea how very proud your father would be of you?"

Amanda knew when she was being hoodwinked. Her mother was a master at the craft. Everyone knew how devoted Amanda had been to her father—how much she had strived to please him. Invoking his memory—and the promise of his approval—always worked.

"You don't play fair," Amanda muttered.

"I know," her mother admitted. "But I always do what I think best for you—what I think your father would want for your happiness. The truth is that you are miserable these days, so why wouldn't you leap at the opportunity to change your surroundings?"

"But teaching? I mean, how does that differ from me taking care of Max?" They had adopted little Max when his mother deserted him after accusing Chet of being the father. Once that lie had been debunked, she'd run off with their foreman, leaving her child behind. To Amanda, Max had become another younger brother, and more often than not, watching over him had been her responsibility.

Eliza laughed. "The difference is that you will be helping the Baxter children learn, and believe me, from what Doc said, you will have your work cut out for you."

Amanda realized how little she knew of the proposed job. "How old are these children, and what does their father do? And why do the Baxters need a private tutor for their children in the first place?"

She saw her mother exchange a glance with Eliza. "The children are twins—a boy and a girl. I believe Doc said they were around fourteen. They…"

"Fourteen? That's practically grown," Amanda protested.

"Yes, well, Mrs. Baxter died several months ago," her mother explained. "Mr. Baxter owns a bank in

Tucson so he's away from home a good deal, and he needs help. They have a housekeeper, but she is not educated, and he wants the best for his children, especially the boy."

"And where will I live?"

"There's a boardinghouse. Doc has apparently proposed your room and board as part of your compensation."

"A boardinghouse?"

"You wanted a little independence," Eliza reminded her. "I should think the arrangement is far better than being offered a room in the Baxter house."

She had a point. "What if it doesn't work out with the Baxter children?"

Her mother cupped her cheek. "Oh, Amanda, how could they resist you? I know you'll find ways to win their loyalty. You'll be quite wonderful."

Eliza seemed less convinced. "Just remember that children—especially those who are truly bright—have been known to use their intelligence for testing authority rather than for learning."

"Not unlike you, Amanda," her mother said as she cleared away the dishes from their lunch and repacked the hamper.

Amanda had to admit that life in a town the size of Tucson was likely to offer far more opportunities for adventure than staying at the ranch. And there was a bonus. Maria wouldn't be there to boss her around. And with the territory on track for statehood sooner rather than later, it occurred to Amanda that there might be an organization of women there willing to fight for the right to vote. She could perhaps join forces with them. She could also help Addie with jail reforms. In short, she could reinvent herself in a community where no one knew her.

"Well, I suppose I could at least apply," she said, making sure she included an edge of grudging willingness in her tone. Of course, she didn't fool her mother for one minute.

"Excellent. However, let us be clear on one matter," Constance Porterfield said in that low, calm voice she reserved for laying down the law to her children. "If you do this, you are going there to teach these children. I saw how you set your eyes on that young man who just left, and if for one minute you think taking this job will give you the opportunity to find romance—especially with someone like that— think again."

"Oh, Mama, I don't know where you get these ideas, but—"

Her mother dismissed further discussion with a wave of her hand. "As soon as we have finished our shopping, we will pay a call on Addie. Hopefully, she will agree to keep an eye on you. And if Jess wins the election, and they move there, I have no doubt that your brother will make sure you behave appropriately." It was obvious to Amanda that her mother had looked at this matter from every possible angle.

"Addie is my friend and sister-in-law, not my keeper," she snapped.

"She is also mature beyond her years, and I know I can trust her to make sure you remain focused on your duties and not on some handsome but highly inappropriate suitor. I warn you now, Amanda, if I hear of one encounter with any wild young stranger, even by chance, I will come to Tucson myself and haul you back to the ranch."

"There are bound to be eligible men in Tucson, and they will all be strangers to me," Amanda protested. "I can hardly avoid them."

"You can avoid young men like that Grover fella, and you will."

"When Chet Hunter showed up at the ranch, and Maria started…"

"I was half out of my head with grief over your father when Chet came. You know that."

"I also know that things worked out just fine for Maria and *her* stranger, so why should there be so much fuss about me and…" She had gone too far and realized it the minute she saw her mother give Eliza an I-told-you-so look of triumph. "Not that I have a care what any man thinks or does," she hurried to add.

Both Eliza and her mother snorted with derision. "Your mouth to God's ears," her mother said. "Now let's see about buying you a dress that's proper for a schoolmarm. Something with deep pockets, I should think."

"I thought I was here to buy a party dress," Amanda said.

"Oh, all right, we'll buy one of each."

By the time they headed back to the ranch late that afternoon, Amanda's life had taken a complete turnabout. She was newly outfitted with not one but two dresses, Doc had assured her that an interview with Ezra Baxter was a mere formality, and Addie had solemnly agreed to be her jailer. Although, as soon

as Amanda's mother turned away, she had squeezed
Amanda's hand and grinned as she had when the two
of them had been girls playing together.

Her brother, on the other hand, had scowled at her.
"I can't have any trouble, Amanda. If I'm gonna be
running for sheriff and..."

"Your sister knows how important the election is
for you, Jess. It shouldn't be too much to ask that you
watch out for her once you gain the office and you
and Addie move to Tucson." Their mother had a way
of simply assuming that once any one of her children
set sights on something it would be achieved.

"I could campaign for you," Amanda suggested,
giving her brother a teasing smile.

"Don't do me any favors," he grumbled as he kissed
her cheek and then held the door open for them.

Once outside Doc's office, Amanda spotted Mr.
Grover. He was sitting outside the saloon, his boots
propped on the hitching rail and his hat covering most
of his face. She had the oddest feeling he was watching
her and only pretending to nap.

Her mother had deliberately steered her toward the
opposite side of the street that ran along the plaza—a
move she would have made under any condition
to avoid walking past the saloon. Once they had
returned to the mercantile to collect their packages
and bid Eliza farewell, she saw that the stranger had
moved on and was now standing outside the livery
around the corner from Eliza's store, talking to the
blacksmith about the horse he was examining. She
and her mother climbed onto the wagon, and she
picked up the reins.

"Eyes to the front, young lady," her mother muttered as they passed the livery, and the cowboy dressed all in black tipped his hat—proof that she had been right to think he was watching her.

On the ride back to the ranch, she couldn't stop thinking about the man. When they were shopping, she'd heard Eliza whisper to her mother that it was probably a good thing Amanda would be leaving Whitman Falls. Eliza had been sent a wanted poster that pictured a Sam Grover to post in her store that also served as the local postal station.

"He's suspected of being part of a gang of notorious outlaws," she had whispered. "Grover's not that common a name around these parts. There *has* to be some connection, and if they are related, the young outlaw most likely learned his ways from his brother, don't you think?"

Eliza also said that when she had repeated her suspicions to Jess, he promised to keep a close eye on the stranger. "The man has taken a room above the saloon, and word is that he's an accomplished card player, as well as a fast draw with that black-handled gun." All this information was exchanged while the two older women thought Amanda was trying on dresses and bonnets and too absorbed in her shopping to hear their conversation.

But she had heard it all, and she was well aware that with every new detail revealed about him, she should have been disgusted. The truth was that she was absolutely fascinated, and the idea that he—and whatever adventure might be following him—would be in Whitman Falls, while she was in Tucson, was the one detail that dampened her enthusiasm for her new circumstances.

∽

It didn't take Seth long to learn why the Porterfield women had been in town. He felt some sympathy for the folks in Tucson because the younger one was trouble that came packaged in a tall, slender body tied up with a mass of strawberry blond hair that reminded him of the heat at high noon. She had a pair of green eyes that seemed to see everything and like most of what she saw. Seth knew that look, having seen it often enough on his younger brother's face. He'd be willing to bet that Amanda Porterfield thrived on excitement.

She had also led a sheltered life, if he was any judge of her mother's influence. That combination, along with her breaking free of her mother's apron strings to live away from home, could make her reckless. And still, knowing all of that, he could not shake off the fact that she was the most beautiful woman he'd ever seen, with a fire in her eye, and a way of looking at a man that made him feel anywhere from a couple of inches to ten feet tall, depending on her mood.

The news that she was moving to Tucson to teach some rich man's kids troubled Seth. The fact that he had just that morning gotten word that had him looking at a move to Tucson as well could complicate matters.

"Best keep your distance, Grover," he muttered to himself as he stepped inside the saloon where the owner, Miss Lilly, was seated at a table studying the ledger her manager and bartender, Pete Townsend, kept for her.

"You know how to read, cowboy?" In spite of their long friendship, Lillian understood the need to treat Seth as if he were just another stranger.

"Yes, ma'am."

"Any good with figures?"

"Pretty good."

Miss Lillian kicked the chair opposite her away from the round table and motioned for him to sit. "Take a look at these. Tell me what you see."

Seth was aware of Pete wiping glasses with a dish towel and scowling at his boss. "Don't you trust me, Miss Lilly?" Pete asked.

"I make it my business not to trust anybody. Nothing personal, Pete." She shoved the ledger toward Seth. Pete threw down the towel and stalked out the back door.

"Now, Lilly, what's your problem with Pete? You've known the man for a decade or more, and in all that time, you've never found fault with his bookkeeping."

Lilly grinned, and after a glance toward the back door, whispered, "Had to have some excuse to talk to you, Seth." She leaned closer. "I heard talk earlier today that a couple of them robbers you been stalking may be headed this way herding a dozen horses or so. Sounds like they mean to hole up somewhere in the area and get ready to make a fresh strike before crossing the border. I figure that's the reason for rounding up spare horses—they'll need fresh mounts for the escape. And take a look at this," she added, pushing a crumpled bill across the table.

Seth studied the money, noting the serial number. He had a memory for numbers and knew instantly that the bill had come from a robbery committed a month earlier. "Who passed this?"

"One of those two playing cards with you and Gus last night."

Seth had no reason to question Lilly's information. The two had worked together on other cases before she'd bought the saloon in Arizona. On one such case, she had saved his life, throwing a heavy glass beer mug at a man about to stab Seth as he fought off two others in a brawl. The minute he'd walked into her saloon, the Dandy Doodle, one night when the place was filled with customers, she'd played her role to perfection. She'd made a point of acting like she'd never seen him before but sure didn't like what she was seeing now. She'd rented him a room, saying at the first sign of trouble she would evict him, and he might as well know right away she did not tolerate card sharks or cheaters in her place. All of it a well-rehearsed act for the benefit of her other customers.

"Did you hear anything they said after I left?"

"Not them, but another customer who stopped in earlier today was jawing about a gang having been seen north and east of here—Texas, maybe—and heading south."

"Why was he talking about it at all?"

"He'd come in on the stage and heard about the robberies. It's gossip, I know, Seth, but you can't discount it altogether."

Seth nodded. He was piecing together the information he'd been gathering ever since arriving in Whitman Falls. He still thought the next hit would be either the delivery of the payroll to Fort Lowell or the train that bypassed town on its way to Tucson. On the other hand, there was also the possibility they would go after the delivery of payment to miners in the hills closer to Tucson—a payroll that would come by train and then be transferred by mule to the mines. Trouble was, he couldn't be in two places at once. He'd have to gamble.

He picked up a deck of cards. "Pick one, Lilly," he said, fanning the cards in front of her. She slid one out, looked at it, and laid it face down on the table.

"One more," he instructed, and after she'd chosen, he shuffled the cards. "The card there on the left is Tucson. On the right is staying here." He dealt two cards, placing them face up on top of Lilly's—a four of spades on her Tucson card and the king of hearts on Whitman Falls. He let out a breath, certain that the decision had been made.

"Looks like I stay put," he said, reaching for the cards.

"Not so fast, cowboy," Lilly said with a grin. She flipped her card for staying in town over—it was the ace of diamonds, beating his king. Then she turned over the Tucson card to show the three of clubs. He'd won with a four.

"Pack your saddlebags, Seth. Looks like you're headed for Tucson."

Two

AMANDA COULD NOT RECALL A TIME WHEN SHE HAD been more excited. A week after her shopping trip in town, she was on her way to Tucson. On the ride there, their foreman, Bunker, prattled on and on about his memories of the town, but she was so focused on her own dreams of what adventures might lie ahead that she barely heard him. They arrived late in the afternoon, and he agreed to deliver her belongings to the boardinghouse, while she hurried to the bank to meet with Mr. Baxter.

Once inside and seated on an upholstered bench outside the banker's office, she was so nervous that she had trouble sitting still. His name and title were prominently displayed on the glass panel of the office door: *Ezra G. Baxter, President.* She could see her prospective employer hunched over paperwork whenever his secretary—a thin, nervous man—hurried in or out, always taking care to close the door with a soft click. After waiting nearly half an hour, she wondered if perhaps she had been forgotten.

The secretary, who had not introduced himself,

glanced her way every few minutes with an apologetic smile. Amanda stood on the pretense of taking a closer look at a painting that hung just across from the banker's office. Now she was standing near the door and could hear paper rattling, as if someone were wadding it into balls and tossing it aside.

"Fitzhugh!" the banker bellowed, and Amanda was so startled that she leaped back and nearly collided with the secretary, who begged her pardon and then scurried into the office, once again closing the door behind him. A second later, he opened the door, raced to his desk where he grabbed a stack of papers and folders, and then indicated that she should follow him into the office.

"Mr. Baxter, this is Miss Porterfield," he said, his voice cracking.

The banker stood. He had gray hair that was beginning to thin. He was short and stocky with eyes so small that Amanda could barely discern their color—only that they, like his hair, appeared to be gray. He wore a white shirt, a black string tie, and a charcoal-gray frock coat.

"Miss Porterfield." He indicated a chair across from his, waited for her to be seated, and then sat down so heavily that his chair cried out in protest. The secretary hovered nearby, still clutching the paperwork. "I believe we have some acquaintances in common—Dr. Wilcox?"

At first Amanda thought he meant Addie and wondered how they might have met. But then it dawned on her that he was speaking of Addie's father.

"Yes, sir," she said. She noticed that he had not

introduced his secretary, and she frowned. She did not like it when anyone was treated as anything less than equal. She and her siblings had been raised to show respect for every individual.

The banker studied her for a long moment. She focused on his bushy eyebrows and long sideburns to keep from meeting his gaze directly, and perhaps appearing impudent. "As you are no doubt aware, I find myself in something of a bind," he said. "The recent death of my wife—mother of my two children—has become a problem."

A problem? Who thought that way about someone he supposedly had loved? "My condolences, sir," Amanda murmured.

"The truth is that I had thought to hire a man to tutor my children, but others have convinced me that simply will not do, given my daughter's age. Therefore, you have been recommended as a substitute."

Amanda flinched. She did not like being relegated to the position of substitute. "I am applying for the position of tutoring your son and daughter, sir. I am not interested in a temporary position as a substitute while you seek a more suitable candidate."

Baxter frowned. She met his gaze and smiled. "Yes, of course. That is why we are here." He cleared his throat and continued. "You will receive a monthly stipend of fifty dollars in addition to room and board at Miss Dooley's boardinghouse. I will need your services only for the remaining weeks of the term. You will—"

"Why do you feel the children need tutoring? It is my understanding that they are quite bright and—"

Baxter pursed his lips and glared at her. He was a man clearly used to giving instruction and asking questions rather than answering them. He glanced over his shoulder at his assistant, who quickly sorted through the papers he carried and handed one to him. "I hold here the attendance record for my children for the months since their mother's passing," he said as he skimmed the paper, then passed it to her.

"According to this, your daughter has missed a good deal of class time, and your son has hardly been in school at all."

"Precisely."

"And of the days missed, how many were due to illness, or to the time surrounding the loss of their mother?"

"She was not lost, young lady. She died." He pointed to the stack of papers and folders. "It's all here, Miss Porterfield," he said testily. "May we perhaps not get the cart before the horse in the matter and complete the interview?"

"Of course. I apologize," Amanda said softly as she clasped her hands primly on her lap and tried to arrange her expression to one of respect and rapt attention. Inside, however, she was wondering what she might be getting into. Her instinct was to end the interview immediately, find Bunker before he left, and head back to the ranch.

"I see that you come highly recommended," the banker continued as he picked up a piece of stationery lying on the large blotter that covered his desk. "Your father was respected throughout the region as well, and I believe that your brother will be on the ballot to become our next district sheriff."

"Yes, sir."

He removed his spectacles and took his time folding the stems and pocketing them before he leaned forward and said softly, "Tell me, Miss Porterfield, why should I entrust my children to your care?"

Why indeed.

Not for the first time since leaving the ranch early that morning, Amanda felt uncertain of her decision to come to Tucson. After all, what did she really know about teaching? She was educated—her parents had insisted on that—but she had begun to understand that her ability to read and write, her knowledge of such topics as geography, history, and art, and her grasp of the basics of mathematics and science was only the beginning. Imparting that knowledge to young minds would take discipline and creativity and...

On the other hand, it could be an adventure. Amanda smothered a smile as Baxter once again cleared his throat and drummed his fingers on the desk impatiently.

"I love children," she began, and saw that this made the banker sigh with exasperation, so she changed tactics. "However, I also understand that they can be a challenge—especially once they reach their teen years. I am not so very far from that age myself, Mr. Baxter."

The flicker of interest that passed over the man's haggard face told her she was on the right track. "Go on."

Amanda scrambled for some credential she might offer. "Living on a ranch rather than in a town can expose one to many different personalities and circumstances," she said. "I assure you that I have faced, or at least been privy to, any number of difficult situations."

"Such as?"

She told him of her younger brother Trey's illness as a child, and then of her father's shocking death that the family first thought was an accident, but later turned out to be murder. She told him of her mother's debilitating grief that was lessened by the family taking in an abandoned toddler. And the more she talked, the more certain she was that instead of convincing him she was the right person for the job, she actually validated his opinion—and hers—that she was the last person he should trust to tutor his children.

"I know the examples I offer are…"

"And what of your plans, Miss Porterfield?"

"My plans?"

"Yes. To wed and have a family of your own."

She was so taken aback that she stammered out the first thing that came to mind. "I have no plans, sir. Only hopes."

To her surprise, he smiled and stood. He came around the desk and offered her a firm handshake. "Welcome, Miss Porterfield. It is my opinion that you will have your challenges, but the fact is that you are the sole applicant for the position, and I have no choice." He nodded to his associate, who finally set down his burden of papers and folders on the desk, then stepped away as if awaiting further instruction. "Please join my children and me for dinner tomorrow evening. Our home is just behind the boardinghouse. You will meet Ellie and Eli, see the library where you will conduct sessions, and make sure you have whatever supplies you may need for the task. We dine promptly at six." He shook her hand again, dismissing her, as his secretary collected the untouched papers once again before moving to open the door and ushering her out.

When the door had clicked shut, Mr. Fitzhugh pulled a leather satchel from under his desk, packed the papers and folders inside, and presented it to her. "You will want to go through these thoroughly before tomorrow's dinner," he said. "Mr. Baxter will expect you to know everything about his children before you are introduced." He glanced at the closed door leading to his boss's office and lowered his voice. "I'm afraid they can be something of a challenge—especially now that their mother is gone."

Amanda accepted the satchel. "I'll return this. Thank you."

"No need," he assured her. He blushed and then walked with her past the tellers—both of whom seemed more interested in her than in the customers they were serving.

It was when she reached the street that she realized it appeared she had the job and could begin her new life as an independent woman. She smiled all the way back to the boardinghouse.

Miss Dooley's was an imposing Queen Anne structure wrapped with a spacious porch, featuring twin garrets on the second floor with windows that overlooked the town. In the midst of a cluster of adobe dwellings and shops, the place was an oddity, to be sure. Bunker had told her the Dooley family had settled in Tucson from Ohio, and that Mr. Dooley—the current owner's father—had built the house in this style to pacify his wife's wish to return east as soon as possible. "It's not the usual kind of place you expect to see in these parts, but folks around here have gotten to like it. Miss Thelma Dooley is the last of the family—never married, took good care of her folks in their later years, then turned the place into a boardinghouse."

Amanda stood staring up at the house's gleaming windows and twin garrets. Oh, she did hope she would be assigned one of those garret rooms. She climbed the front steps and lifted a brass door knocker to announce her arrival. Before she could lower the knocker, the heavily carved solid wood door swung open, and a man filled the doorway.

Amanda gasped and nearly dropped the satchel. For this was not just any man. This was the man from Eliza's store. The stranger she'd been warned to avoid. This was none other than Mr. Grover.

Amanda stepped farther away from the door, teetering dangerously on the edge of the porch's top step. Mr. Grover reached out, catching her by the forearm before she stumbled. "Easy there, miss. Didn't mean to startle you." He released her arm and held the door open for her to enter.

Their eyes met, and she saw recognition cross his handsome face, followed by a scowl. "Miss Porterfield, I believe." She noticed he did not have the manners to remove his hat, and that irritated her enough to bring her to her senses.

"Do we know each other, sir?"

The scowl turned immediately to a grin—and not just any old grin, but the most charming one Amanda had ever seen. The man had dimples. "My mistake," he said.

Flustered beyond the ability to speak, Amanda swept past him and through the doorway with all the grandeur she could manage. Once inside, she heard his boots on the steps leading to the street, accompanied by his soft laughter.

And then it hit her—Mr. Grover could also be boarding with Miss Dooley. What other business could he possibly have on the premises? Or maybe he had come to ask about a room but been turned away.

"Oh, please let it be the former," she whispered, for living in close quarters with the handsome, mysterious cowboy practically guaranteed the adventure she longed for.

"Miss Porterfield?" The voice cracked with old age as a small, bent woman of indeterminate years emerged from the shadowy depths of a room just off the foyer. Amanda had remained standing in the doorway as she tried to regain her composure. The woman edged past her and closed the door, leaving them in near darkness with only a thin thread of sunlight highlighting a thick layer of dust on an ebony, mirrored coatrack that dominated the space. "You'll have to learn to shut the door behind you on coming and going. I can't take the dust." As if to prove her point, she launched into a prolonged coughing spell.

"I apologize," Amanda managed once the coughing eased.

"Since you are here, I am assuming that Ezra Baxter has hired you, although I knew he would—no choice, really. That will not be the case here, I assure you. There are rules to be followed," the woman continued. "The front door is locked promptly at eight in the evening. I have the only key. You will have a key for your room, of course. Meals in the dining room daily at six and five." She pointed one spindly finger toward a room on the opposite side of the hall. "Noonday is not served, except on Sundays after church. No supper is served on the Sabbath. If you plan to be absent for any meal, I need notice a day in advance."

"Yes, ma'am," Amanda said. "Mr. Baxter has asked that I come for supper at his home tomorrow evening."

"Very well." Miss Dooley said no more. In fact, she seemed to have momentarily forgotten that Amanda was still there.

"Is my room…"

"Top of the stairs, first door to your left. It's open, and your trunk is there. I told your friend Mr. Bunker there was no reason for him to wait. I knew Ezra would hire the first person who came through the door—he's that desperate. Your friend asked me to wish you luck and tell you good-bye. I'll get the key and be up directly."

Amanda was halfway up the stairs when the woman added, "I'll tolerate no male visitors except in the parlor with me present, unless they are family, and there will be no spirits on the premises at any time. Understood?"

"Yes, ma'am."

Amanda trudged on, pausing on the landing to look out a small arched window at the street below. She saw Mr. Grover standing outside a shop on the main street. He was talking to another man, and their conversation seemed quite serious. At the top of the stairs she faced a long, narrow hallway with doors to either side. One door was partially open and revealed a sink.

"Bath at the end of the hall is shared," Miss Dooley shouted from below. "Best fasten the latch when you are in there or risk being interrupted." Miss Dooley's voice faded as a door on the first floor near the back of the house opened and closed with a bang.

Amanda stood for a moment at the top of the stairs to get her bearings. She breathed in the scent of furniture polish, the leftover odor of fried bacon from what she assumed was breakfast served earlier that morning, and cigar smoke she identified as coming from a room at the rear of the hall. She heard a man clear his throat, as if trying to rid himself of some blockage in his lungs. He sounded as if he was choking, and she was tempted to go to his aid when she heard Miss Dooley mounting the stairs.

She leaned over the bannister and motioned toward the open door. "Is he all right?" she whispered.

"Ollie? He's fine. Don't pay him any mind." She opened the door to the room she'd indicated would be Amanda's. "Well, come in," she barked as she moved quickly to the windows and pushed back the heavy draperies to reveal one of the large rounded windows Amanda had admired from the street. And when she saw her trunk at the foot of the four-poster bed, she felt a swell of pleasure tighten her chest.

She had done it. She had left her childhood home and come to a place where she was in charge of her comings and goings, the people she would meet, the things she would do. For the first time in her life, Amanda felt truly grown-up.

"I'm full up," Miss Dooley was saying as she smoothed nonexistent wrinkles from the coverlet on the bed. "There are five of you. Oliver Taylor works at the saloon down the street. He sleeps during the day and is out much of the night. Across the hall from him is Mrs. Rosewood—she lost her husband some time ago, moved in here last fall, and keeps mostly to herself. Then there is Miss Lucinda Jenson, who opened a hat shop last month."

"And the fifth boarder?"

Miss Dooley frowned. "Just left. He's as new as you. Mr. Grover is the name he gave." She hesitated. "I am unsure of his occupation, but he paid in advance, and in these hard times one cannot afford to reject a lodger who does so." She spoke as if talking to herself rather than Amanda—as if trying to convince herself she had made the right move. But then she turned her sharp eyes on Amanda and added, "You would do well to stay clear of that one. He is too handsome for his own good, and men like that…" She handed Amanda the key and scowled, waiting for her to agree.

"I'm quite sure that I will be busy enough with the Baxter twins that I will have little time for socializing," Amanda assured her.

Miss Dooley let out a huff of disbelief. "You're quite a pretty thing, aren't you? I cannot imagine what Ezra must have been thinking, hiring a mere girl to take charge of those children. You have experience?"

Amanda was not about to allow herself to be interviewed by Miss Dooley now that she had secured the approval of Mr. Baxter. "I am prepared to meet the requirements of the position," she replied as she walked to the door and waited for her landlady to take her leave.

"Supper promptly at five," Miss Dooley repeated.

"Yes, ma'am."

Amanda closed the door and then, in a fit of pure joy, took a running leap onto the bed and nestled into the soft feather mattress.

∽

Seth's decision to move on to Tucson had come with some complications. For one thing, the hotel was expensive and full up, while the rooms over the three saloons in town were rent-by-the-hour accommodations.

His remaining choice was between camping outside of town or taking the last available room at the boardinghouse. In the end, he had opted for the boardinghouse.

He'd met briefly with his Wells Fargo contact when that man had come through town on the stagecoach. The agent had taken a certain amount of pride in providing Seth with what he called the perfect cover for his activities. "The groundwork's been laid for folks to think you are checking out land for potential investors from the East. Most folks won't believe it, but after a week no one will pay your comings and goings the slightest mind. As long as you stay out of trouble," he'd added.

But trouble was part of the job. The cover story would do for explaining why Seth often took forays into the countryside, checking out various locations. But to gather information Seth also needed to frequent local dens of pleasure, play cards, and down shots of rye whiskey with the locals. Sometimes those encounters could lead to fights. Sometimes his best source of information came from spending a night in jail with others.

Back in Whitman Falls, he'd had Lilly at the Dandy Doodle to act as an extra set of eyes and ears. Here in Tucson that would not be the case. He'd already had the opportunity to study his housemate and local bartender, Oliver Taylor, and found him to be a man with a drinking problem of his own, and far too much interest in gossiping to be of use. The landlady was the suspicious type and would be more so if he started asking questions. The current district sheriff was rumored to be in cahoots with some shady businessmen in the area and, unless Jess Porterfield could defeat him in the next election, was likely to hold his position as the local lawman. Seth was on his own. The last thing he needed was the distraction of Miss Amanda Porterfield.

The fact that the Porterfield woman would also be bunking at the boardinghouse had never occurred to him. The fact that she was in Tucson at all was bad enough. The fact that apparently she would be living close to him, taking meals with him, and generally, be aware of his comings and goings was most unsettling.

Of course, it wasn't that she was the problem—he was. From the minute he'd laid eyes on her back in Whitman Falls, he had been unable to get her out of his mind. He wondered if his fascination with her was really a sign that it was time for him to give up his undercover work and live a normal life—with a wife and family and people who knew and accepted him for who he really was. A wife that maybe looked a lot like…

"Drop it, Grover," he muttered, and tightened his resolve to ignore Miss Amanda Porterfield.

But sure enough, there she was, seated across from him at supper. He turned his attention to the other boarders, mentally recording their names and any possibility they might be a help or a hindrance in the work he had to do. To the Porterfield woman's right was Mrs. Rosewood, fifties, widowed, dowdy in appearance. Next to him was a shopkeeper, Miss Jensen, who could be trouble since she was already flirting with him. Miss Dooley presided from the head of the table while Ollie, the bartender from the saloon, took his place at the foot. The food had been placed in the center of the table for the boarders to help themselves family-style, but Seth couldn't help thinking they made a most unlikely family. Ollie had been the first to reach for the meat platter the minute Miss Dooley raised her head from the silent grace she informed them would begin every meal.

No one protested when the bartender took more than his share, and the only sounds in the room were the clink of flatware on plates, the muffled noise of street traffic from outside, and the necessity of having to chew and swallow without the cover of conversation. And through it all, Seth had the oddest feeling that Miss Porterfield was working very hard to keep a giggle at bay.

Her mouth twitched as she picked at her food and sipped her water. She kept her head down, focusing her attention on her plate, except for the couple of times she glanced at her dinner partners from under lowered lids framed in a lush fan of pale lashes. Then, as if a signal had sounded, the widow passed her plate to Ollie, who added the beef rib bones that he'd sucked clean to her leavings, then his cutlery, and passed the stack on to Miss Jensen, and so on around the table until Miss Dooley presented the stack of dishes to a hired girl who appeared from the swinging door that led to the kitchen.

A moment later, the girl returned balancing a stack of small plates and a steaming pie that she set in front of Miss Dooley. The landlady sliced the dessert expertly into six even pieces, dished a piece onto each plate, added a fork, and passed them down the line.

All this was done without uttering a single word.

The military precision with which this feat was accomplished was ridiculous, and Seth felt a bubble of laughter clog his throat at the same moment he made the mistake of glancing at Miss Porterfield. She had just taken a bite of her pie, and when she looked up, she actually winked, as if they shared a secret.

Seth frowned and concentrated on devouring his pie. This would not do. For her own safety, they could have no connection. At breakfast he would take a place at the far end of the table next to Ollie, so that looking at her would be less likely.

Seth washed down the pie with the rest of the water in his glass, wiped his mouth with the cloth napkin, and stood. "Thank you, ma'am," he said, addressing his landlady. "That was a mighty fine meal."

"For some of us, it is still in progress," Miss Dooley retorted, her fork in midair. "Do you have pressing business, Mr. Grover, that would prevent you from waiting until everyone has finished?"

Seth heard a soft snort and saw that Miss Porterfield had covered half her face with her napkin. The tremble of her shoulders told him she was laughing. He had to fight a smile as well because there was no denying the absurdity of the landlady's ridiculous rules that were more appropriate for toddlers than for grown men and women.

"You'll forgive me, ma'am, but my employer expects me to accomplish a good deal while I am here in Tucson. And while you made it quite clear that the start of the meal is sacrosanct, you said nothing about the length. Perhaps if you require your boarders to abide by your schedule, it would be best if I found other accommodations."

He had paid her a full month's rent in advance, although if things went well, he expected to be here less than a week. He had paid her with gold coins and had not missed the way her eyes had widened in surprise. Now she looked at him in horror.

"Not at all. You are quite within your rights to come and go as you please—within the confines of my curfews, of course."

"Then I'll say good night," he replied, including the others as he placed his napkin next to his plate, pushed his chair into place, and left.

He was barely down the front steps when he heard the bartender call out to him. "Hold on there, fella. I'll walk with you."

"On your way to work?" Seth asked, seeing no recourse but to wait for the short, pudgy man.

"I've got some time. Never saw anybody stand up to the old lady the way you did. Rocked her back on her heels, all right." He chuckled. "She's one tough old bird, that one, but she sets a fine table."

"You lived here long?"

"Going on five years now. Seen a number of boarders come and go—Mrs. Rosewood and me have been here the longest."

"The widow?"

"Yeah. Keeps to herself, that one. She don't go out much."

They walked along in silence past the closed shops. "Now those two young misses…" Ollie continued, chuckling under his wheezing breath. "That hatmaker sitting next to you was making eyes at you, all right, and the other one? You ask me, that little girl is headed for trouble, especially once she faces the Baxter twins." He let out a low whistle. "That whole Baxter family has got the idea they are something special. That boy is meaner than a cornered copperhead. Him and that girl will give her trouble she ain't never thought about," he predicted.

"Maybe you should warn her," Seth suggested.

"Naw. No chance of that. We keep different hours, her and me. You, on the other hand…"

"Why would I say anything? I don't know the family."

It was at least a partial lie. Seth had had the opportunity to check up on Ezra Baxter. Whenever he moved to a new location, Seth made it his business to find out what he could about locals—especially community leaders. He had discovered that in the months following the death of his wife, Baxter had struggled in both his business and his personal life. The boy was by all reports a wild one, always at the center of any trouble from boys his age in town, and the girl—well, he didn't know much about her. What he did know was that Baxter had taken up card playing, apparently as a way to ease his grief. He was bad at it, and he lost large sums on a regular basis. He also had a temper. Seth had not yet been at the table during one of the man's games, but if he could believe the local gossip, Baxter was a powder keg about to explode.

Not his business, of course, but Seth had long ago learned to be aware of any potential for trouble. He turned his attention back to Oliver. "Sounds like the family has seen some tough times."

"Haven't we all? No reason for them to go acting like they do. You just let the little lady know that I said she should watch herself around them—the boy especially." Ollie pulled a cigar from his shirt pocket and paused to light it, striking a match on a hitching post.

"What sort of trouble has the boy been in?"

"There's more than one respectable female in this town who's been accosted by that boy. Oh, nothing criminal, just takes a certain pleasure in scaring them. And that Porterfield woman being such a pretty little thing…" He drew on his cigar and shook his head.

"How old is this boy?"

"Fourteen going on twenty. I've had to run him off from the saloon more times than I can count. And just yesterday, the girl was caught shoplifting at the general store. Nothing came of it, of course. Folks feel sorry for them—being motherless and all—so they get away with mischief like that."

"Well, I expect Miss Porterfield knows how to deal with mischief," Seth said as the two men continued walking toward the saloon.

"There's mischief, and there's just plain meanness. These young'uns seem to enjoy hurting things—animals and people alike."

"Sounds like somebody ought to speak to the father."

"He's the cause of it all—takes a belt to those kids at the drop of a hat. Not your usual punishment, either. Folks say there's a cruelty to it—that he don't know when to stop. I'm telling you, it's her who needs warning. Their daddy has his own problems." They had reached the far end of the street where three saloons were open. Ollie headed for one of them. "You coming in?"

"Not tonight," Seth replied, and tipped his hat before moving on past the saloons to the livery stable where he'd boarded his horse.

He supposed he could slip a note under Amanda Porterfield's door—anonymous, just warning her to watch her back. He didn't need to get involved in her business. There certainly was no need for a conversation she might take as him being interested in developing a friendship. The way she had winked at suppertime already indicated that she was the sort who liked getting to know those around her. No doubt because they had met in the mercantile in Whitman Falls—even though she had denied remembering that—and having sized up the rest of the boarders, she had decided he was the most likely candidate to be her friend.

And the one thing Seth Grover had realized was that if a man needed to keep his true business a secret, he did not allow anyone to get too close. He'd made that mistake once, and it had ended in disaster.

❧

The first thing Amanda noticed when she woke on her first full day in Tucson was a small folded piece of white paper near her door. The second was the smell of coffee and fried meat wafting up from downstairs. The third was that she had just fifteen minutes to dress and get down to breakfast, or incur the wrath of Miss Dooley. She could already hear the high-pitched chatter of Miss Jensen as she talked to someone on her way downstairs.

Wanting to get off to a good start on her first day, Amanda ignored the note lying on the floor, scrubbed her face at the small basin in her room, cast off her nightgown, and hurriedly donned the clothes she'd laid out on the room's only chair. She twisted her hair into a topknot and anchored it as best she could while hopping on one foot as she thrust the other into a slipper. That would have to do until she could return to her room after breakfast and finish dressing. Tonight she would meet her pupils for the first time, and she intended to use this day to see what she could learn about them from others in town.

As she opened the door and stepped into the hallway, she heard the first of six chimes on the clock Miss Dooley kept on the mantel in the sitting room. Before closing and locking the door to her room, she picked up the note, thrust it into her pocket, and raced down the stairs, reaching her place at the table just as Miss Dooley bowed her head for the mandatory silent grace.

Under the guise of prayer, Amanda glanced around the table and immediately noticed that Mr. Grover had elected to sit elsewhere. She felt insulted. Did he think she'd flirted with him at supper the night before? She most definitely had not. If she had shared a glance with him, it was in the spirit of kindred souls who saw the humor in the landlady's regimen. If anyone was flirting with the man, it was Miss Jensen, who had batted her eyelashes so much that Amanda had been sure the woman had an uncontrollable twitch.

Well, she had far more important things to think about than to worry about why the man, once again dressed all in black—although he appeared to have left his gun in his room—had decided not to sit across from her. Even so, it did not escape her notice that he had selected a chair that would make eye contact between them nearly impossible, especially with the dour Mrs. Rosewood seated between them.

The hired girl, whose name Amanda had learned was Bessie, made the rounds pouring coffee for everyone except Mrs. Rosewood, who was served tea in a beautiful china cup. Mr. Taylor reached for the platter of sausages and eggs the minute Miss Dooley raised her head and placed her napkin on her lap. As seemed to be his habit, the bartender took more than a single portion of the food. He passed the platter to Mr. Grover, who offered it first to Mrs. Rosewood before serving himself. At least he had manners, Amanda admitted grudgingly as she accepted the bowl of fried potatoes Miss Dooley passed to her.

She took some and then turned to offer the bowl to Mrs. Rosewood. The widow ignored her, and at the same time, Mr. Grover held out the platter of eggs and sausages to Amanda, who saw no alternative but to trade serving dishes with him, her fingers brushing his in the process. Once the exchange had been made, she noticed how he silently offered to serve Mrs. Rosewood. The widow nodded and smiled slightly.

Amanda rolled her eyes. So not only was the milliner taken by the handsome Mr. Grover, but so was the grieving widow. Well, she would not be lured into whatever game he was playing. Clearly, he was a man so arrogant that he collected female hearts like trophies. He would just have to accept that her heart was not a collector's item.

They ate in silence again, ignoring as best they could the chomping, slurping sounds emanating from Mr. Taylor's end of the table. At supper the night before, she had found the scene amusing. This morning, with everything on her mind regarding the Baxter twins and her new job, she found it irritating.

Bessie came out to refill coffee cups and retreated again into the kitchen. Amanda could hear the ticking of the clock from across the hall. The beats seemed in perfect rhythm with the beating of her heart. Suddenly, she thought of her family back on the ranch, sharing breakfast and talking over one another as they shared news and plans for the day to come, and the vision of sitting at this table—day in and night out—with no conversation, no laughter, no interaction at all, was more than she could take.

"How was your evening at work, Mr. Taylor?" she ventured.

Everyone froze as Ollie glanced nervously at Miss Dooley. Everyone except Mr. Grover. "It certainly seemed as if that end of town was busy," he added, ignoring the way others glanced nervously at their landlady.

Well, she did not need—or want—his support. "Have you lived in Tucson long, Mr. Taylor?" she continued.

"Five years," Ollie finally managed.

"And what about you, Miss Dooley?" Amanda continued, even though Mr. Baxter had already offered details of her landlady's past. But she focused on Miss Dooley deliberately because she could practically feel Mr. Grover studying her with amusement.

Miss Dooley released a long, exasperated sigh. "Is it the will of all gathered that we partake in conversation during mealtimes?" she asked.

"All in favor?" Mr. Grover said as he raised his hand. Immediately, so did Mrs. Rosewood and Miss Jensen. "Looks like a majority, Miss Dooley," he said softly. "I mean, I assume since she spoke out that Miss Porterfield is in favor of the motion."

"I'll vote for talk at supper," Ollie announced. "But leave me out of it in the morning. All I want is to eat and get some sleep." He stood and left the room.

"Very well," Miss Dooley said. "However, there is to be no discussion of religion or politics—those topics can upset digestion. Agreed?"

The four remaining boarders nodded. Miss Dooley turned to Amanda. "I was born and raised here. I have watched this town develop from nothing to what it has become today."

Amanda smiled. "Then I wonder if you would be amenable to coming to speak to my students one day?"

"Why on earth would you want me to speak with your students?"

"I can't imagine that I will be able to maintain discipline if they have to listen to me lecture them for hours day after day. It would be wonderful to surprise them now and then by inviting local people to engage their minds and imaginations."

A rosy flush crept over the landlady's cheeks. She pursed her lips and fingered her coffee cup. "If you think I might have anything to contribute," she said softly.

"Oh, I do!" Amanda exclaimed. "In fact, I am quite sure that each of you here has something of value you could teach the children."

It did not escape her notice that the only person who did not looked pleased at her invitation was Seth Grover.

Three

THAT EVENING WHEN SHE ARRIVED AT THE BAXTER home at the appointed hour, she had second thoughts. Perhaps it would be best to get better acquainted with the children before extending invitations to others to interact with them.

Mr. Baxter opened the door before she had a chance to lift the knocker. "Come in," he said, almost too eagerly, and Amanda realized he was nearly as nervous as she was. He helped her off with her shawl and hung it on the hall tree while she removed her gloves and hat.

"It is so kind of you to—" she began, but was interrupted by her employer.

"Not at all. Come meet the children." He placed his hand lightly on her back—a gesture she found shockingly familiar and uncomfortable—and guided her toward the dining room, where a boy and girl were already seated at a table set for four, but with room enough for a dozen or more. The furnishings were heavily carved pieces, clearly meant to impress.

"Good evening," she said as she looked from one twin to the other and smiled.

They remained seated and sullen, barely glancing her way. From behind her, she heard Mr. Baxter clear his throat, and in unison the twins pushed back their chairs and stood. "Allow me to introduce you. My daughter, Eleanor—Ellie—and my son, Eli. Children, this is Miss Amanda Porterfield."

Before Amanda could say anything, Mr. Baxter pulled out the chair at the end of the table and waited for her to be seated. Once she was, he walked to the far end of the table and took his place. A woman of about fifty came through a swinging door as if she had been called. She carried a platter of sliced beef surrounded by vegetables and placed it in front of Mr. Baxter.

"This is Mrs. Caldwell, our housekeeper," Mr. Baxter said. While Mrs. Caldwell returned to the kitchen and brought out a basket of bread cut into thick slices, a dish of pickled peppers, and a pitcher of water, Mr. Baxter served a huge portion of food and passed it to Ellie, who passed it to Amanda.

She prepared to pass it to Eli, but noticed Mrs. Caldwell watching her. The housekeeper shook her head and used only her eyes to convey the message that this was Amanda's plate, so she set it down and waited. The plate Ellie passed to her brother had twice the portion she'd been served. Ellie's serving matched Amanda's.

Once Mrs. Caldwell took the empty platter and left, both Mr. Baxter and Eli attacked their food as if it might be their last meal. Ellie picked at hers, basically rearranging things on her plate, and only taking a bite when her father glanced her way. From the moment Amanda had arrived, it seemed as if everything about the evening was to be rushed.

"Where are you children in school now?" she asked as she cut into meat so tender she needed only her fork.

Both children looked at their father, who finished chewing, dabbed at his mouth with the pristine white napkin, and frowned. "My children are to be in school here with you," he said. "Did I not make that clear earlier, Miss Porterfield?"

"I had thought—that is, the word 'tutor' would imply someone to help them with studies underway at a regular school."

"Our home is their school. Are you having second thoughts?"

"Not at all." She tried smiling at the children, but they were not looking at her. Eli was tearing into a slice of bread and using it to sop up whatever food remained on his plate, and Ellie looked as if she might burst into tears at any moment. "May I ask where we will conduct our lessons?"

"The library serves adequately, does it not, children?"

Murmurs of assent with no real enthusiasm.

Mr. Baxter pushed his plate away, and Mrs. Caldwell magically appeared to remove it. In fact, she removed all the plates without any regard as to how much food still lay on Ellie's and Amanda's.

"My children are behind in their studies, Miss Porterfield. They were coddled by their mother, and that has left them well below the level at which they should be learning. Your job is to bring them up to that level before the end of the term."

"But that is only six weeks," Amanda blurted out. "Surely—"

"Miss Porterfield, in the autumn, my children will be attending a boarding school back east where their mother's family resides."

It was obvious to Amanda that this was news to the twins. Both heads shot up, and they exchanged a glance of pure horror before once again lowering their eyes as their father explained the plan. "It was always her wish that we return there, but clearly my business will not allow such a move. Therefore, in her memory, I am sending the children. However, they must be prepared to pass the entrance examination."

"My sympathies for your loss," Amanda said softly, and she directed her condolences as much to the children as to their father. "I was not much older than you are now, Ellie and Eli, when my father died suddenly." Both twins looked at her with something approaching interest for the first time since she'd arrived, so she continued, "He was a very special man. I miss him every day, as I am sure you must miss your mother. Perhaps, once we are better acquainted, you will share some memories you have of her."

She glanced at Mr. Baxter, fully expecting to see an expression of gratitude for her kindness, and instead saw something that approached fury. "It is not for you to speak of my wife with the children or anyone else, Miss Porterfield. If you have quite finished, I will show you the library, and then we can have coffee and pie while we discuss your role in my children's future."

"Of course. And perhaps the children and I could—"

"The children are going to their rooms," Mr. Baxter said. He stood, clearly expecting the twins and Amanda to do the same, and without the slightest word or gesture of affection, he waited for Eli and Ellie to mutter their good nights and leave the room. Once they had, he indicated that Amanda should proceed across the hall to a room where the thick adobe whitewashed walls were lined with bookshelves, and a fire blazed in the hearth that dominated the far corner.

"Please be seated, Miss Porterfield."

For the next half hour, Amanda endured the man's tour of the space, directed from his seated position. Here were maps she could have the children study. Over there was a selection of reference books, a dictionary and thesaurus and other tomes. On the far wall she would find a selection of the classics of literature. To either side of the fireplace were shelves filled with books on banking and finance and accounting. His collection certainly rivaled the one her parents had assembled back home on the ranch. She felt a twinge of excitement at the availability of so much fodder for her lessons.

"Is there a section for art and music and…"

Mr. Baxter frowned and then sighed heavily. "Miss Porterfield, you will have no time for frivolity. The children must learn the basics—the fundamentals. They will need drilling from morning to night."

She looked up at the dark ceiling beamed with rough-hewn cedar and overlaid with aspen saplings. "But surely some breaks for exercise and such are in order," she protested, and saw that by the look on his face, she was digging her way straight out of a job.

"Young lady, as I have already told you, I have had serious doubts about hiring you, but the fact remains that you are the only possibility, and time is short. Until you have delivered on your assurance that you are up to the job, you should know that other than providing you with room and board at Miss Dooley's, it is my intent to withhold your actual pay."

"You can't do that," she blurted.

He smiled. "Ah, but I can," he replied. "Do you wish to take this position or not? If not, then let us put an end to it right now."

She thought about her earlier joy at the idea of living in a town the size of Tucson on her own. She thought of how her parents had urged her never to back down from a challenge. She thought of those children upstairs being sent off without the dessert that Mrs. Caldwell had brought to the library.

"I will teach your children, sir," she said firmly. "But I insist on being paid at least a portion of my salary each week. I will have expenses—incidentals."

"You drive a hard bargain, Miss Porterfield." Once again he smiled and reached to pour her more coffee.

Amanda stood. "And now, sir, thank you for dinner. I look forward to getting better acquainted with your children when I begin our lessons tomorrow. For now, I will say good night."

He slowly set the coffeepot back on the heavy silver tray, and she could tell that he was not happy that she had taken control of their meeting. He followed her to the front door where he waited while she retrieved her wrap and gloves. This was a man used to being in charge. He was a man used to deciding when an evening had come to an end. But, Amanda realized, he was also a man who needed her, and that pushed the power to her side of the board—at least for now.

As his time in Tucson wore on, Seth was beginning to think the information he'd been given about the gang heading that way was wrong. In his canvass of the territory outside town, he'd seen no sign of anything unusual. He'd been looking for evidence that a herd of horses was being driven in from the north. The bank robbers would want fresh horses available for their robbery and getaway. He'd also been looking for places in the outlying areas where the train would have to slow to make a curve, allowing robbers to jump onboard, or where a wagon carrying the payload for the fort would come to a near stop to navigate a sharp bend in the trail.

Although he had identified at least three locations where the robbers might position themselves and make their strike, he'd seen no indication that anyone had rearranged boulders to create a cover, nor had he seen any recent tracks to prove activity in those areas. Unless he could uncover some clue that the Stock brothers and their gang were holed up somewhere outside town, biding their time as they prepared for their next big hit, he probably ought to move on.

But Lilly's information was rarely wrong, and the Stock gang had gotten a lot smarter about the jobs they pulled. Most of all, the wanted poster he'd seen confirmed his suspicion that his brother Sam had joined the outfit. Seth was determined to get the kid away from the outlaws.

The truth was that Sam ought to be in school. He was only fifteen—big for his age and smarter than most. But he had a wild streak that had shown itself almost before he could mount a pony. He had defied their parents, refusing to attend the local school and declaring he would educate himself. He had done just that, devouring the books that lined the shelves of the family's library back in Chicago, and finding local transplants from the frontier who were willing to teach him how to ride and handle a rope—and a gun. Their mother had dreamed of the day that her youngest son would become a lawyer or a doctor or start a successful business. But Sam had other ideas. One night he'd left home for good, leaving only a note that said he would write.

He never had. Their mother had begged Seth to track Sam down and bring him home. It was while trying to fulfill that promise that Seth had come to suspect the possibility of his brother having hooked up with the Stock brothers. Hopefully Sam's role in the gang's escapades had not gone beyond holding the horses or serving as lookout.

To a certain degree, Seth blamed himself for Sam's wild streak. He was six years older and so had not been around much to be the kind of influence he might have been. And there was no doubt that his choice of careers had set a poor example for his brother. Seth had gone down a road that his parents never would have imagined for their eldest child.

He had refused his father's offer to take him into the family's meatpacking business, choosing instead to join Wells Fargo. His mother had been mystified at the decision, even after he had tried to explain that down the road he would have opportunities to move into a well-paying and far less dangerous management position.

"But if you are concealing your identity, how will you ever meet a proper young lady—one you can marry and build a life with?"

In those days, marrying had not really been high on Seth's list of goals for his future. After over two decades of marriage, it seemed to him that his parents were both bored and boring. They were good people, but their love for each other had never seemed close to the kind of passionate devotion that Seth wanted should he ever marry. Oh, he'd had his share of romances, but in every case but one, the relationship had died from lack of fuel to keep the fire going in his long absences while on a case. The one he'd thought would work out had gone sour for entirely different reasons and had almost cost him his career. It still stung that he had so badly misjudged the woman and her true motives.

All of these thoughts kept Seth alert as he rode out after supper each night to look for campfire smoke, an abandoned miner's shack that showed signs of occupation, or any evidence of a gang holed up and waiting for their opportunity. This night—like every other night over the last week—had yielded nothing. He stabled his horse and then walked past the saloon, where he could hear raucous laughter and music from

a tinny piano. He walked up the deserted street toward
the boardinghouse, where a single lamp glowed in
the downstairs sitting room window. No doubt Miss
Dooley was counting down the seconds until she
would lock the front door promptly at eight.

Seth smiled and wondered how shocked she would
be to realize that he had figured out a way to come
and go any hour of the day or night and would
have no trouble gaining entrance to the house. He
removed his Stetson and hung it on the top hook of
the hall tree.

"Evenin', Miss Dooley," he said as he started for
the stairs. But he stopped, because Miss Dooley was
nowhere in sight. It was Amanda who sat at the
small desk, her back to him, her head resting on her
folded arms.

Every bone in his body told him to keep climbing
those stairs. Told him to go into his room—across the
hall from hers—and close the door. Told him not to
turn and enter the sitting room and place his hand on
her thin shoulder. Not to notice the way her full lips
were slightly parted in sleep. Not to look too closely
at the perfection of her skin or the way a tendril of
her hair fluttered with each breath she took. And definitely not to piggyback on his earlier thoughts about
love and romance, or for even one second consider
the possibility that a woman like Amanda Porterfield
might make a good match for him.

The second he touched her, she jerked awake,
her eyes opening wide with surprise. But not alarm.
Seth had noticed that not much seemed to alarm
Miss Porterfield.

"Sorry, just thought you might want to head to your room," he said.

She yawned and stretched and glanced at the clock on the mantel. "I have to lock the front door," she said. As she rose from the chair and searched her pockets for the key, she pulled out a crumpled piece of paper that he recognized as the note he had slipped under her door to warn her about the Baxter kid.

"Miss Dooley had a stomach ailment and wasn't feeling well, and I promised…" Having completely forgotten about the note slipped under her door earlier that morning, she unfolded the paper and scanned the message, then refolded it and returned it to her pocket. She pulled the key from a second pocket.

Seth held out his hand for the key. "Allow me."

She hesitated, then placed it in his hand but followed him to the door, as if to be certain he did as he said. He turned the key in the lock, tugged on the door to show that it was indeed secure, and handed back the key. "All safe and sound," he said as she folded her fingers over the metal.

They both stared at his larger rough hand covering hers before she pulled away and replaced the key in her pocket as she returned to the sitting room. To his surprise, she did not gather her books and papers or make any move to extinguish the lamp. Instead, she sat back down at the desk.

"You're not going up?" he asked.

"Not yet. I need to… I have some work to finish. Good night, Mr. Grover."

He had been dismissed, and it rankled him. "Good night, Miss Porterfield," he grumbled, and prepared to

leave the room. But he hesitated before climbing the
stairs and looked at her—the way she sat so straight
in that chair, with her upswept hair coming down in
places where her nap had unsettled it. The way she
made no movement to enter any notes in the note-
book or turn its pages bothered him.

"That note you just read—was it something to
upset you?" He knew exactly what the note said. It
was her dismissal that puzzled him.

She grimaced. "It might have helped to read it
earlier in the day. It has to do with the Baxter boy.
But then, since you were the author of the note, you
know what it says."

"I'm afraid I don't know…"

She smiled and pointed to the register on Miss
Dooley's writing desk where he had signed his name.
"You have distinctive handwriting, Mr. Grover."

He shrugged, caught. "Ollie said I should warn you."

"That was kind of him—and you."

Seth reminded himself that he had a job to do, and
getting tangled up in her business was at best a distraction, and at worst could be downright dangerous—for
her as well as him. The silence between them felt
heavy with unspoken possibilities. He was about to
leave the room when she asked, "Where do you go
at night?"

He saw it as the invitation he hadn't realized he'd
been looking for—an invitation to return to the room.
"Here and there," he replied as he relaxed into one of
the large overstuffed chairs. "What are you working
on?" He nodded toward the papers and books spread
over the surface of the desk.

She gave him a rueful smile. "I am trying to sort through the record of the children's work over the last few years. There is a marked difference in their performance since their mother's death."

"Isn't that to be expected?"

"Of course. After my father died, I was inconsolable, and once I learned his death had not been an accident, but rather he'd been murdered, I was so...angry."

"Have you told Baxter and his children about your father?"

"I mentioned it at dinner, but Mr. Baxter was not pleased, and I suppose he had a point. Perhaps he thought it would appear that I was attempting to compare their pain to my own. And I guess, unintentionally, I was. On the other hand, from what I learned talking to neighbors and shopkeepers today, Mrs. Baxter was ill and died peacefully in her sleep. My father was brutally murdered and..."

"I see what you mean."

"I do understand the importance of presenting myself in such a way that the children do not see weakness in me. Several people have already commented that I am far too young and..."

"Pretty?" She looked down at her hands, and he knew he'd made her blush. "That's a compliment, Miss Porterfield," he added.

"Thank you." A moment passed during which she pretended intense concentration on the records before her.

"Perhaps I might offer a suggestion or two. After all, I was once a boy that age, and trust me, I caused my teachers many a long night."

She glanced at him, and he held out his hand for the records she had been comparing. "This really isn't necessary," she protested. "In fact, I should…"

"Now, Miss Porterfield, you do not strike me as a person who lives her life based on 'should.' My guess is that you'll just go off to your room and spend a sleepless night trying to work this out, and as my mother used to say, 'Two heads are better than one.' It's important that you maintain the upper hand from the outset, right?"

She nodded.

"And you do wish to make them understand that— pretty or not—you are the one in authority?"

She sighed and then nodded again.

"Very well then." He eased the papers from her and held them closer to the lamp. "Eli shows an interest in and aptitude for arithmetic both before and after his mother's death," he noted. "And the girl…"

"Ellie."

"Ellie has made her best marks in reading and spelling." He handed the papers back. "In your shoes, I would play to their strengths—gain their trust by acknowledging their abilities."

She glanced toward the hallway that led to Miss Dooley's rooms. "Thank you, Mr. Grover. I'll give that some consideration." She picked up a piece of paper from the pile on the desk. Once again, he had been dismissed.

"Seth," he said softly, even as his mind warned him against getting too familiar. "Okay, Amanda?"

She nodded. "Thank you, Seth." It was a whisper, and he realized she was exhausted and very close to tears. Clearly, she was working hard to maintain her composure until he went upstairs. He stood, but did not immediately move toward the stairs.

"You are going to do just fine, Amanda Porterfield."

"You can't know that," she replied softly.

"Well, I know that now we're having normal conversation at meals. We boarders are digesting our food a lot better than we were when we sat there in silence. That was your idea. You were the one who taught us that, and if you can teach a bunch of grown-ups who already think they know everything, I have no doubt you can handle a couple of kids who know next to nothing."

In his zeal to make her feel better, Seth hadn't realized his voice had risen until he and Amanda turned at the sound of a door slamming, and then saw Miss Dooley glaring at them as she clutched her robe to her throat. "Miss Porterfield," she began ominously, ignoring Seth as she focused her wrath on Amanda.

Seth stepped between the two women. "Now, Miss Dooley," he began, holding up his hands as if to fend off actual blows, "I can explain everything."

The landlady stepped around him as though he weren't there and advanced on Amanda. "Young lady, I have entrusted you with the key to my house, and you repay that trust by breaking one of my house rules?"

"I…" Amanda swallowed as she clutched her books and papers to her chest.

"It is all my fault, Miss Dooley," Seth interrupted. "I was a couple minutes late getting back. Miss Porterfield was reluctant to allow me in—and rightly so. I persuaded her that you would understand. After all, Mr. Taylor is allowed special privileges because of his unusual work schedule and—"

Miss Dooley turned on him. "If you think you can persuade me to hand out keys to anyone who takes a notion to come and go at all hours… Mr. Taylor has employment that requires…"

He saw that he'd had the desired effect on the landlady. She did not think anyone knew she had provided Oliver Taylor with a key to the front door so he could gain entry after the saloon closed and he had finished his cleaning chores sometime before dawn. The fact that she had been caught breaking one of her own rules frustrated her to near speechlessness.

"I do not need a key, Miss Dooley," he said. "I assure you that tonight was a one-time event and should it occur again, I will spend the night at the livery with my horse. Agreed?"

Miss Dooley scowled, and he saw Amanda use the opportunity to edge her way toward the hallway and stairs. "I'll say good night then," she murmured.

"Not so fast, missy. There is still the matter of you having a gentleman caller without a chaperone present—and at this hour, to boot," Miss Dooley added as the clock struck eight thirty.

Seth laughed. "Now, Miss Dooley, Miss Porterfield and I both reside in your house, so who is calling on who?"

"Whom," he heard Amanda whisper.

He chose to ignore the correction. "Surely the residents of your house cannot be expected to avoid running into one another from time to time, and it would be impolite not to inquire after their health, or how their evening was going, now wouldn't it?"

Miss Dooley grimaced, and he noticed that her skin was paler than normal and there was a sheen of sweat on her brow.

"Miss Dooley, you clearly are not well, and I am so very sorry to have upset you. Please allow Miss Porterfield to escort you to your room while I go to mine." He nodded to Amanda, who immediately set her books and the records for the Baxter twins on the stairs and came to the landlady's aid.

"Let me make you some ginger tea," she said. "It will ease your stomach. My mother always…"

Seth watched the two women walk down the hall before extinguishing the light, waiting a moment for his eyes to adjust to the darkness, and then making his way up the stairs. He set Amanda's books and papers outside her door, and once inside his room, he lay on his bed listening for her.

He did not need Miss Dooley to reprimand him. No, once again he reminded himself that his fascination with the teacher—in spite of his determination to have nothing to do with her—would have to stop.

On her first day with Eli and Ellie Baxter, Amanda brought lessons and exercises to test their knowledge and took Seth's advice to appeal to their individual interests and strengths. She considered the need for outdoor activity as well, and planned a walk in the intricate desert garden their mother had created on the grounds of the large home.

She felt fully prepared to face the day as she approached the house. But she hesitated when she heard loud voices from within—an argument between Mr. Baxter and his son. Reluctant to have her employer think she had been eavesdropping, she went to the kitchen entrance where the housekeeper was hanging laundry on a line stretched between two saguaro cacti.

"Good morning, Mrs. Caldwell."

"Good morning, dear. Though since we are both working for the Baxters, perhaps we might be less formal when we are alone?" She wiped her palm on her apron and offered a handshake. "Name's Kitty."

Relieved to have found someone in this house who seemed to know how to smile, Amanda returned the handshake. "I'm Amanda."

She glanced toward the open door leading to the kitchen. The voices were muffled now, but the argument clearly had not been settled. "I thought maybe…"

"Oh, pay no mind to that. That sort of hollering is normal in this house, especially since Mrs. Baxter died—God rest her soul."

The idea that a child at any age would dare speak to a parent in such a tone was unthinkable to Amanda. Her confidence wavered. If Eli Baxter could shout at his father in such a manner, how on earth did she expect to win his respect?

"Where is Ellie?"

Kitty shrugged. "Lurking about, you can be sure of that. She's a sneaky one, all right. Last night, after you left, I heard her moving around down in the library where you'll be holding your sessions. I went out to see what she was doing, and she was breaking all the chalk for the chalkboard Mr. Baxter had installed last week. Crushing it, she was."

"I see."

"I was able to keep one piece before she destroyed that as well. I sent her back to bed, and she went. After that I locked the door to the library—opened it this morning when the family was at breakfast." She pulled a piece of chalk from her apron pocket and handed it to Amanda.

Amanda swallowed hard but realized her mouth had gone dry.

"Ah, Miss Porterfield, there you are." Mr. Baxter stood in the doorway, a scowl on his face as he squinted into the bright morning light. "Well, come along. The children are waiting, and you have already made me late for my first appointment of the day." He turned on his heel and marched inside the house.

Kitty gave Amanda a look of sympathy as she followed her employer through the kitchen and on to the library he had shown her the evening before. The sliding doors were closed, and she saw Mr. Baxter frown as he pushed them open.

Because the heavy draperies that covered the windows were drawn, and no lamps had been lit, the room was dark. Amanda was aware of the presence of her students—Eli lounging on top of the large, heavy table that dominated the center of the room, and his sister standing nearby.

To her surprise, Mr. Baxter stood aside to allow her to enter the room. "I will be home at five thirty, Miss Porterfield, and I will expect a full report of your first day."

Left standing in the doorway alone with the Baxter twins, Amanda set her satchel on the floor, took a deep breath, and strode to the first of three large windows. She pulled the drapes aside, moved to the other two windows and did the same, and suddenly, the room was flooded with light—and her students were shielding their eyes from the brightness.

"That's better," she said as she retrieved her satchel and set it on the table, then turned to Eli. "Mr. Baxter, our first lesson of the day will be the proper use of furniture for its intended purpose. This table is our workspace for our lessons. That chair is where you will sit. The one across from you is where your sister will sit."

"And where will Teacher sit?" Eli asked.

"Teacher will stand," Amanda replied. She walked to the chalkboard and pretended to look for a piece of chalk. Behind her she heard snickers, but they stopped when she dug into the pocket of her dress and pulled out the chalk Kitty had given her. "Each morning I will post the work to be accomplished for the day. Each afternoon I will post the assignments to be completed that evening." She listed the lessons she had planned down the left side of the board, then deliberately paused mid-list and looked around the room. She frowned and checked behind a door that led into a small closet.

As she had hoped, her actions, coupled with their curiosity, brought Eli to a standing position. "Looking for something, Teacher?" Eli smirked.

"My name is Miss Porterfield. Please address me properly or stay silent." She scanned the bookshelves for effect and then opened a cupboard and rummaged through the contents.

"Miss Porterfield," Ellie said, "Father does not like it when someone looks into closets or drawers without his permission."

Amanda turned and looked directly at the girl. "How do you know he didn't give me permission?"

Eli immediately came to his sister's defense. "Because he just wouldn't. What is it you need?"

"I was looking for a Bible, Mr. Baxter. I did not see one among the collection when I met with your father last evening. It is customary to begin the day with a reading from the Scriptures, as well as a prayer."

"We don't pray," Ellie murmured.

"And since we don't go to church, we ain't got no Bible." Eli glowered at her.

"That would be 'We do not have a Bible,' Mr. Baxter."

The girl glanced at her brother. "We learned the Lord's Prayer when we were at regular school," she said softly.

"Excellent suggestion. You have just earned an extra minute of recess, Miss Baxter. Well done."

The twins stared at her, and she hoped they could not see that her last statement had been an impulse—one that apparently had worked.

"I don't get it," Eli grumbled. "How come she gets…"

"Oh, did I not explain the reward and penalty aspect of our lessons? Well, we will get to that eventually—once I have located a Bible, and we have properly begun our day." She closed the closet door.

"I suppose we might make do with the prayer for today."

"Mama had a Bible," Ellie volunteered. "It's upstairs in the attic with her things. Want me to get it?"

"Not today. For today we will say the prayer and move on to our work. I'll make sure to bring my Bible tomorrow." Amanda straightened her posture, bowed her head, and waited for the twins to do the same. Neither moved. "Is there a problem?"

"Ellie offered to bring Mama's Bible. You forgot to give Ellie her extra time at recess—her reward," Eli said.

"I did not forget, Mr. Baxter. Not everything in life brings a reward. Some things are done simply to solve a problem. Other things are done out of kindness or a need to set something right."

Amanda folded her hands in prayer as a reminder and once again bowed her head, taking care to keep her eye on the children. She noticed Ellie followed her example, but Eli stared out the window. "Our Father…" She continued alone until she heard Ellie quietly join her for "…forever and ever. Amen."

When she looked up, Eli was glaring at her. "Where's the justice in not giving my sister her reward?" he demanded, his arms folded tightly across his chest.

Amanda was definitely making this up as she went along, but so far she had managed to engage both children, and she saw that as a minor victory. "If you and your sister would please be seated, Mr. Baxter, I believe you have identified a topic worthy of discussion." She waited while Eli flung himself into one of the leather-upholstered straight chairs at the table. Following his lead, Ellie took the place opposite him.

"Very well. Now let us consider the words of the prayer. What does the word 'hallowed' mean?"

"Holy?" Ellie guessed. Eli rolled his eyes.

"What else?" Amanda asked, focusing her attention on Eli.

"I don't know. In case you haven't figured it out, I'm the dumb twin."

"I refuse to believe that, Mr. Baxter. Any young man who would feel so passionately about his position that he would have the confidence to stand up for his beliefs as you did earlier is not dumb. Perhaps ill-advised, but not dumb."

His eyes widened. "You were listening?"

"I expect the entire neighborhood could listen. I did not hear the actual words exchanged, but the tone was there, and clearly, you were adamant on your position. However, we have digressed from the topic at hand. What is another possible meaning for the word, Mr. Baxter?"

"I give up. Maybe 'special' or…"

Amanda wrote both his and Ellie's answers on the board. "Now consider the phrase 'forgive us our trespasses'—what are trespasses?"

"I thought you were going to explain your rewards and penalties system," Eli complained.

"That will come, Mr. Baxter. Please use the dictionary to find a definition of the word 'trespass.'"

She pointed to a thick tome resting on a pedestal stand near the window.

To her amazement, he did. She wondered why

she had worried at all. These children were hungry for knowledge, hungry to show off what they already knew. She turned to the board and wrote other words from the prayer for them to define. For the first time, she felt hope that she might succeed in teaching them after all. If she could…

"Miss Porterfield?" Eli was standing next to the fireplace, pulling papers and books from her satchel and laying them carefully on top of the cold ashes left from the previous night's fire.

Amanda swallowed, and instinctively forced herself to remain calm. "What do you think you are doing, Eli?"

"Eli? What happened to Mr. Baxter? I mean, if you refuse to address me appropriately…"

From seemingly out of nowhere, Kitty came storming into the room. "You put those things back in that satchel, young man."

"Or what?" Eli sneered.

Kitty held up a baseball glove and a butcher knife. "Funny how accidents can happen," she said calmly. "As for you, little miss," she continued, turning on Ellie, "don't think I'm not prepared to tell your father why he'll be needing to buy more chalk."

To Amanda's amazement, neither child protested. Eli stacked the papers and books and dropped them on the table. Ellie looked as if she might actually burst into tears.

Kitty glanced at Amanda and smiled. "Please continue, Miss Porterfield," she said as she left the room.

With her confidence now shaken, Amanda pointed to the words she'd written on the board. "Please copy

these words, and be prepared to give me clear defini-
tions of each when we meet tomorrow. For now, we
will explore your skills with numbers." She wrote four
arithmetic problems on the board.

"Mr. Baxter, come forward and solve the first
problem," she said, having decided to make no further
reference to the previous incident.

He glared at her again, then pushed himself away
from the table, strode toward her, snatched the chalk,
and within less than a minute had correctly solved
not just the first, but all four problems. He worked so
quickly that the chalk broke into halves. He dropped
the pieces in the tray, dusted his hands on his trousers,
and sat back down. "Do I get my reward? Oh, wait, I
didn't really do anything but solve a problem, did I?"

Things continued to go downhill from there. By
the time noon came, Amanda was exhausted and
nearly out of ideas for how she might connect with the
children so she could actually teach them something.
Her thought had been to use this first day to establish
how well each of them could read, spell, and solve
simple problems in arithmetic. That way she could
plan lessons suited to their level. But she had allowed
them to distract her from her purpose, and now she
felt totally adrift.

Eli Baxter did not return after she accepted the
children's insistence that they be permitted to eat their
lunches outside when the weather was nice. Once
they were settled on the front porch, Eli asked permission to use the privy, and that was the last Amanda
saw of him. Ellie trudged back into the library, but
spent the entire afternoon staring out the window, and

there seemed to be nothing that Amanda could do to engage her.

Late in the afternoon, Amanda wrote two additional homework assignments on the board. She completed a brief report of the day for Mr. Baxter—omitting the fact that Eli had not returned after lunch—and left the appropriate books and papers the twins would need to complete their homework. She said good-bye to Ellie, who did not respond, and then slipped out the front door.

What had she been thinking to take this job? She was not qualified. She was intelligent and educated, but she clearly had no skills for teaching. Her only possible connection with the children was that she, like them, had suffered the unexpected death of a parent. She understood grief, but was that enough to form a bond? And what if she admitted defeat? That meant going back to the ranch and surrendering her newfound independence.

She squared her shoulders and greeted those she passed on her way back to the boardinghouse. She would make this work. There was too much at stake for her—and the Baxter children—to give up so easily.

Four

SETH WAS BONE-TIRED AND FRUSTRATED. AFTER NEARLY a week in Tucson, he was no closer to finding the Stock brothers or their gang.

"You got a letter," Miss Dooley announced as he started up the stairs to wash before supper. "Hand-delivered it was, although Bessie says she never saw who brought it. Just found it lying on the floor near the front door."

"Thank you." Seth took the envelope and put it in his pocket. He could see disappointment in Miss Dooley's eyes. Clearly she had hoped he would open the letter, and perhaps even say who had written it. For his part, he wondered who would write him here—who knew he was staying at the boardinghouse beyond his superiors at Wells Fargo?

"You'll be in for supper?" Miss Dooley asked.

"Yes, ma'am." He sniffed the air. "Smells like Bessie's got something going already."

"Stew takes time if you don't want the beef to be tougher than shoe leather."

"Well, I'll look forward to it," he said as he once again started up the stairs.

"Miss Porterfield's not in," Miss Dooley said, and he realized she was watching him carefully.

"Should she be?" he asked. "Are you worried?"

"No. I thought maybe…"

"Miss Dooley, there is nothing between Miss Porterfield and me other than a normal friendly relationship—the same that I share with you and everyone else in the house."

"She's awfully pretty."

"That she is. But then, so is Miss Jensen. And for that matter, you aren't bad-looking yourself," he added with a rakish grin that had the desired effect. Miss Dooley blushed scarlet, giggled, and waved a dismissive hand as she walked down the hall and into the kitchen.

Relieved that he had put her worries to rest, Seth closed the door to his room and took out the letter. Other than his name and the address of the boarding-house, there was nothing else on the envelope. The information was printed in the kind of block letters he had learned in school, and that made him wonder if the sender might be someone young.

He slid his thumbnail under the flap of the envelope and pulled out a single sheet of cheap notepaper. The words were written in pencil, and he moved closer to the window for better light. The entire message was three words.

Old Frost Ranch

Other than a smudged, dirty fingerprint on a corner of the paper, there was nothing else.

He'd ridden out to that abandoned property just a day earlier and seen nothing. He'd poked around the dilapidated outbuildings, even gone inside the shack that had once served as housing for the rancher and his family. The area was studded with small ranches like the Frost place. In most cases, the families had given up and moved on—either back to where they came from or farther west. The buildings they'd put up were left to the harsh sun and bitter winters. Seth had seen not one piece of evidence that anyone had visited the property in months, if not years.

It could be a trap—somebody trying to lure him out there. It would be the perfect place for an ambush. But that would mean someone had discovered his true identity. On the other hand, it could also be Sam—reaching out for help because he'd gotten in over his head.

He struck a match on the hearth in his room and set fire to the letter, watching it burn down until it nearly reached his fingertips before dropping it in the fireplace, the three words turning to ash.

He heard the soft click of the lock across the hall and knew that Amanda had returned. He wondered how her time with the Baxter twins was progressing. He'd had little chance to speak with her, and she seemed surprisingly reticent to talk about her work when the boarders gathered for meals. He wondered if the warning he'd given her about the boy had been necessary. He wondered how he might have a chance to talk to her without incurring the wrath of

Miss Dooley or the curiosity of the other boarders. He wondered if he was losing his mind even thinking of furthering a relationship with this woman—a relationship he already imagined going far beyond simple friendship.

&

All in all, Amanda's first few days with Eli and Ellie had been a disaster. Eli had continued to test her, mumbling answers, deliberately erasing work she had posted on the chalkboard and pretending to be sorry. Ellie had smothered her giggles at her brother's antics and retreated into sullen silence when Amanda called on her to read aloud or solve a problem.

Today, when Amanda reached her room at the top of the stairs, she had set her satchel on the floor and kicked off her shoes. As she sat on the side of the bed rubbing her tired feet, something long and black slithered from her bag. She let out a yelp and drew herself fully onto the bed.

"You okay, Miss Porterfield?" Ollie knocked at her door and pushed it open.

Amanda pointed, and Ollie chuckled. "The Baxter boy up to his old tricks again, is he?" He used a coat hanger to scoop up the snake, walked to the open window, and hurled it out. "Harmless," he said.

"Thank you," Amanda managed. "Harmless or not, I am not interested in sharing my room with the thing."

Ollie headed for the door. "Don't let that boy know he's gotten to you, Miss."

"Good advice. Thank you again."

At supper she ate in silence and excused herself

before dessert was served, citing the need to prepare lessons. She was well aware of the worried look Seth gave her as she passed his chair on her way out of the dining room. Briefly, she considered working in the parlor in the hopes he might come in, and they could talk. But in the end, she recognized the need to focus on making a success of her job and was relieved when she heard Seth leave the house shortly after dinner. She heard him talking and laughing with Ollie as the two men walked down the street and knew it was unlikely he would be back soon.

She wished she could find a moment to tell him of her thoughts for engaging the twins, especially Eli. Would Seth agree with her ideas or declare them as silly as she feared they were? And what suggestions might he make? It was frustrating not to be able to hold an innocent conversation with the man simply because Miss Dooley did not approve. Well, there had to be a time when she might encounter him outside the boardinghouse and ask his advice. She would watch for that opportunity—one Miss Dooley could do nothing about. In the meantime, she had work to do.

After staying up half the night and falling asleep fully clothed at the small writing table in her room, Amanda was nearly late for breakfast the following morning. Seth was not there, and while curious, she felt it best to leave it to Miss Jensen to solve the mystery of his absence.

"Mr. Grover is not joining us?" The milliner looked longingly at Seth's empty chair.

"He stayed at the saloon most of the night—came

back with me this morning, but then said something about looking at some land east of here, and rode off," Ollie reported.

Amanda tried to banish from her mind the picture of Seth drinking and gambling the night away. She thought about the way he vacillated between charm and sullen distance at mealtime. She could practically hear her mother saying, "I told you so."

And yet she felt that she knew another side of him—that night in the parlor he had been different, more like her brother Jess, or Maria's husband, Chet. He certainly had given her no cause for alarm.

The clock chimed the half hour, reminding Amanda that she wanted to arrive for work early so she could set up lessons for the day before Eli and Ellie came to the library—*if* they came at all. By the time she reached the Baxter home, she had strengthened her resolve to make this work out for everyone involved. After all, she was the adult, and they were children. She used the back gate that led to the kitchen entrance, having decided that would be easier than knocking on the impressive front door each day.

Kitty was kneading dough for bread. "Ready for the front lines?" she asked.

"Quite ready," Amanda replied, squaring her shoulders and tightening her grip on the satchel that Mr. Baxter's secretary had insisted she keep.

"That's the spirit. Call out if you need me," she added as Amanda continued down the hall that led to the front of the house and the library.

"Good morning, Miss Baxter, Mr. Baxter," Amanda said as she entered the room and slid the double doors

closed. She was surprised to see them seated across
from each other, their heads bent over the books she
had left the day before. They exchanged a look of
curiosity when she closed the doors, and then another
when she set down her satchel and took out her worn
Bible. She opened it and read one of the Psalms aloud
before placing it in the center of the table.

"On your feet, please," she instructed. She folded
her hands in prayer and waited.

The twins hesitated, then stumbled to their feet.
Amanda was shocked to see that Eli had a black eye
and Ellie's forearm showed a bruise as well.

She spoke the first words of the prayer and waited
for the twins to join in. She saw Ellie's lips move but
heard no sound. Eli did not bow his head or make
any attempt to say the words, but at least he was not
mocking her or his sister. *One step at a time*, Amanda
thought. This was progress.

Once the prayer ended, Amanda waited a few
seconds, then cleared her throat to gain their attention.
Ellie watched her warily while Eli glanced her way
and then returned to staring out the window.

"Before we begin the day's lessons," she said, "I
want to say something about how things have gone
up to now. I feel we got off to a poor start, and your
father expects me to teach as he expects you to learn.
He has not seen fit to explain why you are taught at
home rather than enrolled in the public school or the
one run by the monks. I can see that while some of
your choices may not be the best, you are both incredibly bright—certainly, Eli, you are creative, given your
antics. The snake was perhaps out of line, but it does

show evidence of a clever mind. And you, Ellie, have shown real promise in the way you consider all sides of a question. For either of you not to continue your education would be criminal."

Ellie's eyes sparked with interest. "You called us by our given names," she said.

"Yes, I did."

Eli remained stoic, although when she mentioned the snake, she noticed he stared directly at her. He squinted. "What are we supposed to call you?"

"I really think in my case you should continue with 'Miss Porterfield.' I'm not sure your father would approve of more familiarity." To her surprise, Eli nodded, and when he spoke, she thought she detected a bit of respect.

"I got kicked out," he announced.

"And you, Ellie?"

"Father was upset with those in charge, and he decided we should learn at home. Mother taught us until…" Her eyes brimmed with tears.

"I see. Very well; we have the foundation for why we are all here, and now we need to build upon that." Amanda realized she sounded more and more like her mother. "I have an idea that might interest you," she added, and—heaven help her—was pretty sure she gave the twins the same knowing smile her mother offered whenever she knew she had gained her children's attention.

She removed papers and supplies from her satchel. As she had hoped, dropping the conversation and leaving the twins hanging had worked. Eli turned his chair around, leaned his folded arms on the table, and glared at her. "So what's this big idea?"

She looked up as if surprised. "Oh, was that a question for me, Eli? When there are multiple people involved in a discussion, it is always helpful—and respectful—to address that person by name."

Eli rolled his eyes and unfolded his lanky body from the chair. "Miss Porterfield," he bellowed, "what, pray tell, is your big idea?" He sat down again and waited.

Ellie could not stifle a giggle, and Amanda had to admit that his antics could be amusing. She grinned at both children.

"We will come to that in due time, Eli, but I do thank you for your interest, and I look forward to our discussion over lunch today—that is, if you plan to join your sister and me." She actually winked at Ellie, who ducked her head to hide her smile. "For now, please take out your notebooks and write two pages on this topic." She turned to the board, took a fresh stick of chalk from her pocket, and wrote: *If I could do anything in the world, I would…*

Ellie studied the words for a moment and then bent close to her paper, her pencil flying as she filled line after line. Amanda noticed that Ellie had already completed one whole page before Eli began writing. When he did, he made exaggerated, large, childish letters that took up three lines on the page. Amanda used the time to write a list of words on the board.

The morning passed. She collected their essays and resisted the temptation to read them then and there. She would save that for tonight. She told them to study the words on the board, then she erased those words and had the twins write them in a spelling exercise, and finally, write a sentence using each word. To her amazement, Eli performed each task—grudgingly, to be sure, but he did what she asked. By the time the clock chimed noon, Amanda felt as if much had been accomplished.

"Go wash up, students," she said. "I'll tell Mrs. Caldwell that we will take our lunch in here today. The wind is strong, and I fear we would consume as much grit and dirt as we would nutrition."

As soon as the twins had left the room, Amanda hurried to the kitchen where Kitty was placing sandwiches and fruit on plates. "What happened to Eli's eye?" she asked. "And Ellie has a nasty bruise on her forearm."

Kitty did not look up, but continued preparing the lunch tray. "Mr. Baxter is a strict disciplinarian—always has been. When their mother was alive, the children could get away with more. But these days…" She shook her head and then wiped the corner of her eye with the hem of her apron.

"He beats them?"

"He loses his temper and, to be fair, Eli can be difficult. His size makes him think he can talk back to others and not be challenged. Their father is grieving, and I suspect all is not well at the bank. He has a good deal on his mind these days and…"

"But to strike your child in such a way…"

"As I said, Mr. Baxter is a strict man, and lately, he has been at a loss as to how best to deal with the children."

It was evident to Amanda that Kitty would defend her employer in all cases. To inspire such loyalty certainly spoke well of him, but still, striking his own children with such force seemed extreme. Should Amanda speak to him about her concern?

She heard the twins whispering in the hall. "I'll take the tray into the library," she said. "The winds are strong today, so eating on the porch might be uncomfortable."

Kitty nodded. "I'll bring glasses and water," she said. "He's a good man, Amanda," she added softly.

"Of course."

Eli and Ellie stopped whispering the minute they saw her.

"Eli, if you would be so kind as to take the tray, your sister and I can make room on the table for our lunch."

He did as she asked without comment or even so much as a hint of eye-rolling. Once they were seated and Kitty had brought the pitcher of water and glasses, Amanda took a deep breath and plunged into what she hoped might be the idea that would get them through this day and all the days to come.

"It occurs to me that learning is your occupation for the foreseeable future. Much as your father goes off to work each morning, the two of you come here. Much as your father has tasks and problems he must attend throughout his day, so do you have lessons and exercises you must solve."

"You're going to pay Ellie and me to show up here every day?" Eli's mouth was stuffed with food.

"Please finish chewing, and swallow before you comment, Eli. And the answer to your question is yes—in a manner of speaking."

"But Father is paying you," Ellie noted. "Are you going to give us his money? Because he will not like that at all."

"Your wages will not come in monetary rewards, Ellie."

"Then what?"

Amanda could not allow them to realize that she was making this up one step at a time. "We will use a system of rewards and penalties."

Eli slumped back in his chair, disappointment evident in every bone of his body. "So we're back to the way things started that first day."

"Not exactly." Oh, why had she not thought this out more thoroughly?

"Eli is very good with numbers and even percentages," Ellie said. "Father has a bookkeeper at the bank to keep an account of things. Eli could keep an account of what we are assigned, and what we complete, and…"

"Let her finish, Ellie," Eli said, his eyes on Amanda. It was as if he realized she hadn't thought this through, and once again, Amanda felt as if Eli were the one in control. So she decided to use that.

"How would you suggest we do this, Eli? I mean, assuming we can agree that you and your sister will approach your studies as a job, as daily work that must be accomplished to some end. How would you make that more palatable?"

His lips turned slightly up and into a hint of a smile as he sat back and folded his arms. He glanced at the list of homework assignments she'd posted the day before and then back at her. "How about if Ellie and me finish the homework and whatever lessons you set for us each day *before* the end of the day, we get to leave—go our own way?"

"First of all, it would be Ellie and I, not Ellie and me—and you present an interesting idea."

He blinked. Clearly, he had expected her to laugh at the suggestion and label it preposterous. "So you'll do it?"

She could not help but glance at Ellie's bruised arm, a glance that had the girl tugging at her dress sleeve to cover the injury. "I do not think your father would agree to such a plan. However, we might agree that if you complete your homework assignments and class work with marks of at least ninety percent accuracy, then we could use any time we have remaining to leave the house and explore other places."

She saw Eli's eyes light up and suspected he was thinking that once they were away from the house, he could go off on his own. "Of course," she added, "there would need to be penalties for abusing the privilege of such field trips."

"We could go hiking," Ellie volunteered. "We could ask Father to give us a tour of the bank. We could..."

"He'll never agree to the idea of us being anyplace but right here, so why talk about it?" Eli grumbled.

"You leave that to me, Eli," Amanda said. "What I need from you and Ellie is your very best effort so that I can present the idea to your father with evidence that you are both engaged in your studies and wish to excel."

By the time she walked back to the boarding-house later that afternoon, Amanda felt completely drained—but elated beyond anything she might have imagined possible.

Seth did not appear at supper, and when Ollie asked about his absence, Miss Dooley replied that he had not yet returned from the excursion he'd set out on earlier that morning. "He indicated that he would return in time for breakfast tomorrow morning."

"What is it that Mr. Grover does?" Miss Jensen asked.

Miss Dooley paused mid-bite and focused her attention on the milliner. She finished chewing her food and then tapped each corner of her mouth with her napkin. "We do not discuss other boarders in their absence. If you wish to know details of Mr. Grover's life, then you should ask him."

"He plays cards—I can tell you that," Ollie Taylor said, ignoring Miss Dooley. "Pretty good at it, too. He's made a goodly sum of money in the time he's been coming into the Blue Parrot." He reached for the meat and potatoes and helped himself to a second serving of each. "There's some that think he has to be cheating, but nobody's been able to catch him at it. On the other hand, he called out a man the other night for just that and proved to be right."

Amanda noticed the other women at the table, including their landlady, hung on Ollie's every word. She, on the other hand, realized she did not want Seth to be someone of questionable character—or career. She preferred to think of him as someone who had helped her find ways to approach her teaching, someone she might confide in. The truth was that she was far lonelier than she had thought she might be. She missed the ranch and her family and the cowboys who worked there and their housekeeper Juanita. She missed having anyone she might talk to about her day and how she might make tomorrow a little better.

Of course, Seth had been kind, but here was irrefutable evidence that he was indeed a gambler. Her mother would haul Amanda back to the ranch before she could blink if she showed the slightest interest in such a man. The fact that her mother had met him back in Whitman Falls and already formed the opinion that he was a man of questionable character only added to Amanda's certainty. If she wanted to stay in Tucson, she needed to keep her distance from Seth Grover.

And yet, later that night, after the front door had been locked and everyone else had gone to bed, Amanda sat at the writing table in her room, reading the essays, when she heard the clop of a lone horse passing below. She looked out and saw a dark-clothed figure riding a gray horse and recognized the horse—a distinctive dappled gray—as one she had seen Seth riding back in Whitman Falls. Both rider and horse moved with the exhaustion of having traveled some distance, piquing Amanda's curiosity—and her natural instinct to offer comfort. How many times back on the ranch had she seen her father come home after a long day on the range, and more recently, her younger brother Trey?

She watched until horse and rider had rounded the corner that led to the livery and recalled what Seth had promised Miss Dooley about staying in the livery should he not make it back to the boardinghouse before curfew. Well, the man had to eat, didn't he? And given the heat of the day had turned to a chilly night, would he not need a blanket?

Besides, Eli's large scrawl had revealed a desire to play baseball, and after seeing the glove and ball the boy clearly prized, Amanda thought perhaps she should take that to heart. Might someone—someone like Seth—offer suggestions for how best to use Eli's passion for the game to encourage him?

Moments later she had gathered a spare blanket and tiptoed down the stairs and into the kitchen, where she managed to find three stale biscuits left over from breakfast and destined to be crumbled up and fed to the chickens Miss Dooley kept at the back of the house. She took two and slipped out the back door, careful to leave it unlocked for her return. She stopped at a community pump near the fire bell tower Miss Dooley's father had built for the town and filled a tin cup she'd taken from a hook in the kitchen before hurrying through the dark night to the livery.

"Mr. Grover," she whispered when she got close enough to see that he had settled his horse and was raking fresh hay. He started, and an instant later, Amanda found herself facing the barrel of his six-shooter.

She dropped the cup of water. "It's me—Amanda. Miss Porterfield," she added. "The teacher."

He slowly lowered the gun. "You could get your-self killed, lady, sneaking up on a guy like that." He glanced outside as if looking to see who had come with her. "What do you want? Has something happened back at Miss Dooley's place?"

His voice was low and gruff—and dangerous. His clothes were covered in dust, and he had not shaved in at least a couple of days, which only added to his rough appearance.

Amanda began to regret her impulsiveness. After all, what did she really know of this man? And now, here she was alone with him. If she cried out, who would hear?

She was aware of loud voices and music coming from down the street at the Blue Parrot and the other two saloons. Other than that, all she heard was the snort of Seth's horse and her own rapid breathing. "I heard you pass, and I remembered what you promised about sleeping here with your horse if you were late again, and I thought…"

"You're shaking," he said as he holstered the gun and took the blanket from her. He opened it and placed it around her shoulders. "Come inside before somebody sees you." He led the way to an empty stall where she saw he'd already set up his bedroll and a small lantern. She felt foolish and was glad her mother would never know of this midnight escapade.

"I should go," she murmured, and turned back toward the door just as they heard a burst of angry voices coming from down the street. Amanda hesitated, pulling the blanket securely around her shoulders, not so much for warmth as for protection.

Seth went to the open door of the livery and checked the street. "Best just sit here until they've gone home," he said, indicating a hay bale inside the empty stall.

Once she had followed his advice, he didn't know what to do with himself. He finally settled on brushing his horse, although it was pretty obvious to Amanda that he had already taken care of that, along with providing the animal with fresh hay, oats, and water. Still, she was glad to have the horse between them.

"Where is it that you go so late at night?" she asked when the silence became uncomfortable.

"Here and there," he replied, pausing as if needing to consider his answer.

"That was the same answer you offered the other night. Is that your polite way of saying it is none of my business?" Amanda smiled, hoping he could see her well enough in the dim light to know she realized she had no business inquiring about his comings and goings.

"Yes, ma'am. It is."

With nothing else to do, Amanda let the blanket fall from her shoulders as she picked up the tin cup she'd dropped. "I passed a pump. I'll just go…"

"I have water," he said, and pointed to a canteen hanging on a nail. "You should leave that, though. I'll wash it out and make sure it's back in the kitchen before breakfast." He smiled. "I'm pretty sure Miss Dooley has every single cup and spoon counted."

Amanda felt herself relaxing. He was more like the man she'd been with that night in the sitting room.

"How will you get back inside the house?" he asked after a moment.

"I left the back door unlocked."

"Clever girl," he replied with a slight chuckle.

Amanda bristled at his calling her a girl. Was that how he saw her? It was most definitely how her family and friends back in Whitman Falls viewed her.

"I overheard Miss Jensen and Mrs. Rosewood talking the other day. Mrs. Rosewood thinks you are quite dangerous—she suspects you are on the run from something, and having noticed Miss Jensen's not-so-subtle attempts to garner your attentions, she felt compelled to warn her."

"The widow thinks I'm an outlaw?"

"Yes, and she's not alone. I'm pretty sure that Eliza McNew—the storekeeper who gave you the jerky back in Whitman Falls—does as well." She could have included her mother in the list but decided against it.

"And what do you think?"

"I think you are a man with a secret. I think you are involved in something you do not wish others to see. If I put those pieces together, I would have to agree that while there is no real proof, whatever your business, it is most likely not something within the confines of the law. And yet, the fact that Miss Dooley has agreed to take you in would belie that theory."

He let out a long low whistle. "Now you're talking like a professor."

"I *am* a teacher," she reminded him.

He set the curry brush on a shelf and came into the stall with her, perching on his saddle that rested against the wall. "How's that going?"

She knew what he was doing—deliberately switching the focus of the conversation. She could choose to bring the topic back to him and his mysterious midnight forays, or she could allow the matter to drop. She could talk about her teaching and let the man think he was in control. Over time she'd learned that the males of the species tended to relax when they thought that was the case.

"These first weeks have been challenging to say the least, not to mention exhausting," she said as she stood and brushed straw from her dress before folding the blanket. "And since it would appear that my interest in your profession is not quite as welcomed, I won't trouble you further." She walked to the door and turned back. "You should remember that my brother is currently running for the office of district sheriff, and once he is elected, I cannot speak for his interest in your affairs. Good night, Mr. Grover."

He was on his feet in an instant, following her to the door of the livery. "Amanda, let me walk with you."

"No, thank you. I made it here without incident, and I can certainly make it back as well." She glanced up and down the street and then started toward the boardinghouse. After a few steps, she turned to remind him to return the cup, but he was gone.

"So much for your concern for my safety," she grumbled.

Five

As soon as Amanda left the livery and started back to the boardinghouse, Seth darted to the other side of the street, where he stayed in the shadows provided by the closed shops. His intention was to follow her without her knowledge. The woman seemed to have no idea of the risk she had taken coming to this part of town at this hour. She was clearly determined to find trouble before it could find her, this strawberry blond with the quick mind and dangerous curiosity. A woman like that saw adventure, not jeopardy. No doubt she was an excellent teacher, one who could instill in her students the same inquisitiveness and enthusiasm for learning she seemed to possess. The problem for him would be to prohibit her passion for gathering information to dwell on him—or his business.

Once he had watched her tiptoe onto the back porch of Miss Dooley's place and slip inside, he returned to the livery, where he placed his pistol next to his bedroll, extinguished the lamp, and hoped for at least a couple of hours of sleep. He lay on his back, his hands folded behind his head, as he stared at the blackness of the hayloft above him. But he did not see darkness. He saw Miss Amanda Porterfield, with her wide emerald eyes and ready smile. He saw a woman in the fullness of her beauty, her skin tanned to a soft gold in spite of the bonnets she wore to protect herself from the harsh sun. He picked up the blanket she'd left and sniffed it, savoring the faint fragrance of her cologne—something that smelled like a field of wildflowers or fresh air or both.

When he fantasized about what she might look like as she undressed and prepared for bed, her hair loose and flowing over her shoulders, he groaned, swore, and silently vowed for the hundredth time to avoid further contact with the teacher. He would move to the hotel. He would camp outside of town. He would…

But when he approached Miss Dooley the following day about the possibility of moving to new quarters, she reminded him that his payment had been in full and—by his own terms—nonrefundable. However, if he preferred the hotel at twice the price with no meals included, that was his business. On the other hand, given that his work seemed to take him away at night, she might be persuaded to offer him the same arrangement she had with the bartender—a key of his own to come and go as necessary.

"In exchange for…?" Seth asked, admiring the older woman's shrewdness when it came to business.

"Another month's rent and board in advance—also nonrefundable." She squinted at him. "I will not question your business, Mr. Grover, but if you bring trouble or strife to my establishment, I promise you I will have Sheriff Richter here before you know it, and your new accommodations will be in the jail under the courthouse—a place I have it on good authority is not nearly as welcoming as my home."

Seth smiled. He had to give the landlady her due—she was a savvy negotiator. He offered her a firm handshake to seal their new arrangement. Of course, there was still the problem of Amanda, and that was going to take some work.

Certainly, while Amanda had given some evidence that she enjoyed talking to him and even wanted to know him better, she had not flirted. It was apparent that if she thought of him at all, it was as a potential friend and confidante, or as someone whose life was far more interesting than her own. Unlike the milliner, who flirted shamelessly through almost every meal, Amanda seemed quite immune to Seth's charms. The truth was that her interactions with him were no different than her conversations with Ollie Taylor. Not that Seth needed the complications of a romantic entanglement at this time, but still, it stung that this woman seemed completely oblivious to his appeal.

Having gotten little sleep the night before and having been challenged by Miss Dooley to leave or stay, but not expect a refund on his room and board, Seth stood at the open window of his room and tried to figure out his next move—his next move that had to do with the Stock boys and their gang. What he would do about Amanda was another matter altogether.

❧

After yet another full day—a Friday that gave her two days' reprieve—Amanda said good-bye to Kitty and trudged back to the boardinghouse. She could not recall a time when she felt so weary or so drained of interest in doing more than making her way upstairs, washing her face and hands, and then lying on her bed until it was time for supper. She had just finished washing up when she heard a light knock at her door. She groaned and forced herself to her feet.

"Come in," she called, and hoped she sounded more welcoming than she felt.

The door opened slowly and in walked Dr. Addie Porterfield. Amanda squealed with delight as she ran to embrace her dear friend and sister-in-law. "You are exactly the medicine I needed," she gushed. "Why didn't you let me know you would be in town today?"

Addie returned her hug before pulling off her gloves one finger at a time as she surveyed her surroundings. "I hadn't really planned on it, but Jess had some business here, and I thought of you and, well, here I am. How is the tutoring going?"

"It certainly makes me have a new respect for the teachers we tormented."

Addie smiled. "Remember when they built the schoolhouse in Whitman Falls?"

They had been fourteen at the time—the same age as the Baxter twins were now—and up to then Amanda and Addie had pursued their studies at home. But when the town council decided it was time the community had its own school, their parents made sure their daughters were among the first to register. "Remember the teacher the town hired that first year?"

"Mrs. Goodykuntz?" Amanda said, barely able to conceal a giggle.

"She was so ill-prepared. Thank heavens for our parents and the lessons they had insisted on teaching us at home."

"And now you're a doctor."

"And you, my friend, are a teacher. I'll bet the Baxter boy is already half in love with you, and the girl wants to be just like you."

Amanda sobered immediately. "I wouldn't say that. The truth is it has been…a little…disappointing."

Addie took hold of her hand. "Tell me."

And Amanda realized that this was exactly what she had needed—someone she trusted that she could confide in, admit her insecurities, and flush out her frustrations.

"For a few days, I thought it was going to work out, but then Eli lost interest and reverted to his old ways, slipping away when he could. And Ellie became increasingly sullen and withdrawn. I can't think what I might do to inspire the zeal for learning that you and I had. Oh, I have made some progress, but at times it's like walking on thin ice. The children are easily bored, and that makes them uncooperative. Their father owns the local bank so he's away at work from morning to night, and I fear that he will blame me for their failure."

"And the mother died, right?"

Amanda nodded. "She died last fall. I think the daughter—Ellie—is having the most difficult time adjusting to her loss. The boy is just angry. They have a housekeeper, but…"

"Are these children intelligent?"

"Oh yes. The boy—Eli—is truly gifted, especially when it comes to subjects like math and logic."

Addie smiled. "Well, his father *is* a banker." She

perched on the edge of Amanda's bed. "Perhaps you need to take some risks."

The suggestion was hardly surprising coming from her friend, who had never shied away from going against the grain, as Amanda's mother used to say. "I am trying new ideas," Amanda said, "but Mr. Baxter is—well, he is strict with the children and seems determined to prove something. Eli was dismissed from the public school, so Mr. Baxter removed Ellie as well. They aren't Catholic, and according to Kitty, their housekeeper, Mr. Baxter will not consider sending them to the school run by the monks. I mean, if only he were reasonable, like my father or yours."

Addie frowned and then bit her lip. To Amanda's shock, her friend's eyes glistened with tears. "Addie, what is it?"

"I did not come here to talk about teaching," she admitted. "The truth is I need your help."

"I can't imagine what I could possibly do to—"

Addie's expression transformed into a mask of sadness and heartache, as if someone had suddenly dropped a curtain over her. "My father is very ill, Amanda. He's unlikely to…" Her voice caught, and a single tear escaped.

Amanda put her arms around Addie and held her. "Oh, Addie, surely there is something…"

"No. He has kept it from us for months now. I should have known. I should have seen the signs. They were all there, but I accepted his explanations—a cold he couldn't shake, a lingering cough, weight loss, even the tone of his skin. And I call myself a doctor." She let out a bitter grunt filled with disgust.

"You *are* a doctor," Amanda insisted as she handed her friend a handkerchief and fetched a glass of water from the pitcher she kept near her bed. "You are probably the best doctor this area has ever seen." But all the while she tried to console Addie, she couldn't help thinking of the changes Doc Wilcox's illness would bring. Addie would no doubt take over the practice in Whitman Falls, meaning Jess would no longer seek election as district sheriff, meaning they would not be moving to Tucson, meaning...

What on earth is the matter with you? She forced herself to focus on Addie. She felt selfish thinking of her needs and wants at a time like this. "How can I help?"

"I wanted to ask if you might have some time to help me with the project I started to improve conditions for the prisoners at the jail. We've made some progress, but my fear is that if I can't keep up regular visits, things will go back to the way they were. But now, I see you have enough to worry about without taking on my—"

"Of course I'll do it."

"But you're already feeling a bit overwhelmed and—"

"Nonsense. You know me. I've always been overly dramatic. This will all work out. And besides, the term is almost over, and then I'll have plenty of time."

"I don't know, Amanda. Perhaps..."

"You just need to tell me what to do. We can start now. Maybe I can even persuade Miss Dooley to invite you to stay for supper, and then afterward, we can walk over to the courthouse."

As it turned out Miss Dooley did not need per-suading. When Amanda introduced Addie, the land-lady actually smiled. "Your husband is going to run for sheriff," she announced, as if this were somehow her idea.

"He would like to. However, I'm afraid we've had some bad news—news that will likely keep us both in Whitman Falls."

Once she heard of Doc Wilcox's illness, Miss Dooley not only declared that Addie must stay for supper, but she also sent Bessie scurrying to prepare a pot of tea that she was to take to Amanda's room, where she insisted Addie go to rest a bit. Once the tea had been delivered, and Miss Dooley had shut the door with a reminder that supper was at five, Amanda and Addie listened for the landlady's footsteps descending the stairs, and then burst into laughter every bit as therapeutic as Addie's tears had been earlier.

"She's straight out of one of Mr. Dickens's novels," Addie whispered as she poured each of them a cup of tea and then curled onto the bed the way they used to do when they were girls spending nights together.

"She is certainly full of surprises," Amanda agreed. "I think you just put me in good stead with her for the foreseeable future. Thank you."

"Does she not like you?" Addie was clearly sur-prised at the very idea.

"I have perhaps tested her patience," Amanda admitted, and then giggled as she relayed the story of her first dinner, followed by the breakfast, where she had decided she would go mad if they had to eat meals in total silence.

"Now that is exactly what I was talking about earlier. It's that kind of spirit that will win the hearts and minds of the Baxter children."

As always, Addie had brought Amanda out of her doldrums. Now it was her turn to cheer up her dear friend. "Tell me how I can help you with the jailhouse project."

They were still talking an hour later when Amanda became aware of footsteps on the stairway. "Oops! Time for supper." The two women paused at the mirror to check their hair and straighten their clothing before hurrying to the dining room.

Addie stopped at the door and grasped Amanda's forearm. "That's the stranger we saw in town before my wedding," she whispered as she nodded toward Seth Grover.

How to explain the man to her friend when Amanda knew so little of him herself?

"I know. He's here on business. Just another boarder," she whispered back, and hoped Addie's hand was far enough away from her wrist so she would not feel the staccato beating of her pulse that occurred whenever she saw Seth.

⁓

As Miss Dooley introduced the other boarders to Amanda's guest, Seth had an uneasy feeling about the lively young doctor. He could not have said why, but he had learned to have faith in his instincts, and as the meal progressed and news of her father's poor health became part of the conversation, he understood that he'd been right to trust his gut.

Addie Porterfield's husband was supposed to become the new sheriff. He was someone Seth was pretty sure he could rely upon, unlike the man who currently held the position. Now it appeared that due to the poor health of Doc Wilcox, all plans had changed. Amanda's friend—and sister-in-law—would take over her father's practice, meaning her husband would not be moving to Tucson. This was not good news for Seth.

"And what is it that you do, Mr. Grover?"

All eyes turned to him. The question was one he'd been asked by the others, but had managed to dodge with a joke or a noncommittal reply. Addie Porterfield did not seem to be the type who would be placated.

To his surprise, Miss Jensen came to his rescue. "Oh, it has something to do with investments and buying properties and such. Whatever it is," the milliner said with a smile, "it takes him away from us far too often, and sometimes for days at a time." The smile she gave him was possessive and knowing, as if the two of them shared a secret.

"Actually, my job is quite ordinary—and boring, I'm afraid. Not nearly as interesting as yours, Dr. Porterfield."

"You do not enjoy your work, Mr. Grover?" To his surprise, this came from Amanda.

"Like most jobs, it has its challenges," he replied. He turned his attention back to the doctor. "I look for properties my clients might be interested in for various reasons. There's really nothing complicated about it." He hadn't really lied. He did look at properties like the abandoned Frost ranch for his client, which just happened to be Wells Fargo.

Thankfully, his response led to a discussion of a large parcel of land not far from Whitman Falls that had recently been posted as available for sale. Seth knew the story of the Tipton Land and Cattle Company and the brothers who had owned it. One brother had shot the other in a fit of passionate rage and had gone to prison. Now the business had no one to manage it. It seemed both Miss Dooley and Ollie Taylor were also eager to fill the widow and milliner in on the scandal.

Blessedly off the hook as far as having the conversation focused on him, Seth took the opportunity to study Amanda. There was something different about her, something he thought must have to do with the arrival of her sister-in-law. He had a moment's concern that perhaps she might decide to return to Whitman Falls as well. Of course, that would be the best possible news for him, because then she would be out of sight, eventually out of mind, and she certainly wouldn't be making post-midnight visits to the stable to bring him a blanket. At any rate, with the school term coming to a close, and the examinations for entrance to the fancy boarding school scheduled for June, she would undoubtedly be gone by the end of the month.

He began to relax and enjoy his supper.

"Because of my need to spend as much time as possible with my father and manage his practice back in Whitman Falls, I have asked my sister-in-law to take on the work I began several months ago for the improvement of conditions in the district jail," the doctor announced, dispelling a lull in conversation that had fallen over the table. "It is a worthy endeavor that has received strong support from Judge Ellis, among others."

Seth shot a quick look around the table, assessing the reaction of the other boarders to this announcement. The widow looked alarmed, while Miss Jensen looked disgusted at the very idea anyone would willingly interact with criminals. Miss Dooley smiled approvingly, but Ollie Taylor scowled and paused in the act of devouring his meal to focus on both Porterfield women. "I'm not sure that's something you ladies ought to be getting mixed up in, especially not now that…"

He paused, and his jowly face went red with embarrassment. Seth guessed he'd been about to warn them about having to deal with the current sheriff now that it appeared Jess Porterfield had withdrawn from the race. Clyde Richter had held his position for a couple of decades and, if local gossip was to be believed, profited handsomely from the job.

"Any cause where people are suffering is one that must be pursued, Mr. Taylor, regardless of the risks," Amanda said. "From the little Dr. Porterfield has told me of the current conditions, even with the simple improvements she and others have been able to make, conditions in the jail are still deplorable. Dr. Porterfield and I plan a visit this evening, so she can show me the work she is doing there."

Miss Dooley cleared her throat as the ritual of clearing the table began. "Well, it is a noble and needed effort, but hardly the kind of discussion suited to polite mealtime conversation. Now, who would like some cinnamon tapioca?"

She nodded to Bessie, who removed the plates and returned with a tray loaded with small glass dishes and a large bowl of the pudding. As usual Miss Dooley served the dessert, and as usual the conversation turned to compliments for the fine meal.

Seth said nothing as he spooned the pudding into his mouth, but his mind raced with ways he might steer Amanda Porterfield in a direction other than one that would have her visiting the jail, especially this evening.

Earlier in the afternoon he had learned of the arrest of a young man matching the description of his brother. His intention was to go to the saloon, get into a card game, start an argument that ended in threats of bloodshed, and get arrested. It was the only way he could think of to get inside the jail without raising suspicion. After all, he was an outsider in Tucson, and to stop by the jail saying he was visiting someone would surely raise eyebrows—and a lot of questions he wasn't prepared to answer.

But then he had an idea. "Dr. Porterfield, I agree with Mr. Taylor's concerns. I wonder if you and Miss Porterfield would mind if I accompanied you this evening. One of the services I provide for my clients is making sure the community is one they would be pleased to dwell in—safe and well-managed."

It was a long shot, but he was pleased to see that no one at the table seemed to think his request strange.

"Delighted to have you join us, Mr. Grover," the doctor replied with a sidelong glance at Amanda, whose cheeks had turned the most charming shade of pink.

❧

"Why would you agree to such a thing?" Amanda whispered as she and Addie climbed the stairs to retrieve their bonnets and gloves. As soon as they had closed the door, she spoke in a normal tone. "What possible reason could Mr. Grover have for asking to accompany us?"

"My question exactly," Addie said. "One I believe I have an answer to."

"I'm listening."

"The man could not keep from looking at you throughout the meal. At one point, I seriously think he was debating which would be more delightful— eating his dessert or perhaps having you for dessert."

"Addie!"

Addie laughed. "You know it's true. Look at yourself in the mirror. Has there ever been a male who has come within ten feet of you and not fallen in love?"

"Now you're saying Seth Grover is in love with me?"

"Not yet, perhaps, but well on his way. Listen to the doctor, Amanda. This man has no reason to come with us to the jail. He was alarmed when I brought it up and said you were coming with me. He is coming with us to protect you."

"When did you become such a romantic?"

Addie smiled, and it was a smile Amanda could not remember seeing on her friend's face before. "I fell in love," Addie said softly. Then she rearranged her features to reflect what Amanda thought of as her friend's "doctor" face. "I recommend you do the same."

Amanda straightened the covers on the bed and handed Addie her hat and gloves before retrieving her own from the dresser in the corner. "You do realize that this is a ridiculous discussion we're having?"

"Ah, methinks the woman doth protest too much," Addie replied as she stabbed the hatpin into the hat and her upswept hair and walked to the door. "Romeo awaits," she added with a wink as she opened the door and motioned for Amanda to precede her down the stairs.

On one hand, Amanda was relieved to have Seth's attention focused on Addie as the three of them walked through town. He asked several questions about the project and seemed genuinely intrigued with the work Addie had already accomplished. On the other, she felt a bit like she had as a girl tagging along with her older brother and sister, listening to them debate some aspect of how best to break a horse or throw a proper lasso.

She tried to think of something she might ask Addie that would sound intelligent and knowledgeable, but once Addie got started talking about something she was passionate about, there was little need for anyone to say anything else—especially in the short time it took them to reach the courthouse, where the jail was housed in the basement.

Just as they prepared to mount the courthouse steps, Addie stopped talking mid-sentence and looked at a man standing just outside the door. "Well now, what have we here?" the man sneered. He was barrel-chested, chewing on a cigar, and wearing a tin star pinned to his vest. "If it ain't the little troublemaker."

"Good evening, Sheriff Richter," Addie said through tight lips. "As you are well aware, by order of Judge Ellis, I have a standing appointment to visit the prisoners."

"Not after courthouse hours, you don't. And there's nothing in whatever agreement you've struck with Judge Ellis that says you can come waltzing in here with anybody you like." He fixed his gaze on Seth for a long moment. His eyes were cold and challenging. Amanda had spent enough time around cowboys and ranch hands to know this was a man looking for a fight.

Seth took a step forward. "Now Sheriff, no need to deny Dr. Porterfield the right to see her patients. I just came along to accompany her and her sister-in-law here and back. If you prefer, you and I can wait outside while the ladies—"

"I can't stop the doctor, but this girlie is not coming into my jail. And neither are you, stranger."

Amanda's heart lurched when Addie clenched her fists and climbed the rest of the steps so she stood toe to toe with the sheriff. She could not believe her friend's courage. After all, it was Sheriff Richter who had once arrested Addie and taken her to this very jail. Addie's refusal to be cowed by this man made Amanda want to stand up for something—to stand up for something she believed in passionately.

Without hesitating, she took her place next to Addie and said, "We haven't met, sir. I am the tutor Mr. Baxter hired. Dr. Porterfield is my sister-in-law, and because she has duties she must attend to in Whitman Falls, she has asked me to visit the prisoners on a regular basis and see to their needs until she can return."

"Their *needs* are to make sure they obey the law and don't end up in jail," the sheriff snarled.

"Just let the ladies do their good work," Seth said. Amanda noticed he had remained on the sidewalk, his hands at his sides, and yet there was something in his calm demeanor—punctuated by the glint of the polished butt of his pistol—that made her glad he had come with them. "Seems to me I read an article in the newspaper about how Dr. Porterfield's efforts have received a good deal of support, not just from the council, but from regular voting citizens."

His reminder that the sheriff was facing an election was so casually inserted that others might have missed it. But it was evident Richter had not. "Are you threatening me?"

"Oh, for heaven's sake, Sheriff, step aside and let us pass." Addie started for the door. Amanda stayed close behind, and when the sheriff made a move to block their entrance, it was Amanda who pushed past him, begging his pardon as she opened the door just enough for Addie and her to slip through. To her relief, the sheriff apparently decided not to follow.

Their leather heels echoed on the marble floors of the deserted courthouse. It was an impressive building, and Amanda thought it might be a good place to bring the Baxter twins one day for a lesson in civics. She wondered if the judge Addie had mentioned would agree to meet with them, and she began to plan a lesson focused on government and the law as she followed Addie through a series of doors to one where an older man sat reared back on a straight chair, snoring loudly.

"Good evening, Josiah," Addie bellowed.

The man rocked the chair to all fours and stood, fumbling with a ring of keys as he did. "Evening, Doc," he replied, giving her a shy, snaggletoothed grin as he unlocked the door, and then picked up a lantern at the top of a narrow stairway with worn wooden treads that led into darkness.

Addie and the man she'd called Josiah chatted all the way down to the row of cells as if they were out for a stroll in the park. Amanda was so focused on the dirt and cobwebs and disgusting smells rising from below that she barely heard Addie explain about her need to be away and how Amanda would take over. Josiah looked back at her, raised the lantern, and gave her that same shy smile. Amanda sorely wished that Seth had not agreed to remain outside with the sheriff.

"Doc!" A woman shouted at Addie as she pressed against the bars of the last cell.

To Amanda's shock, Addie hurried past the other cells and grasped the woman's hands. "Minnie! What are you doing here?"

The woman ducked her head. "Now, Doc, you know exactly why I'm here. Good to see you, though. How's everything back home? Is that good-looking cowboy you married taking proper care of you?" She winked at Addie, and both women laughed.

Amanda cleared her throat, a reminder that she was standing not two feet away.

"Oh, Minnie, where are my manners? This is my sister-in-law and dear friend, Amanda Porterfield. My father is ill, and I'm going to be busy seeing his patients, so Amanda will take over here."

"But you'll be coming back," a man in a neighboring cell stated.

"I hope I will, Johnny, but we'll see how things work out."

"Your pa's pretty sick, is he?" This from another man sharing the cell with the first.

"He is."

"Then we'll say a prayer for him."

"How's that cough, Gabby?" Addie nodded to Josiah, who opened the cell so she could step inside. "And what happened to the extra lanterns we ordered?"

Josiah shifted nervously from one foot to the other. "Sheriff took them away—said they were a fire hazard."

Addie snorted. She had not brought her bag with her, but she removed her gloves and examined the man and his cell mate. She felt for fever, tapped their backs as Amanda had seen her do when she wanted to see if a person's lungs were blocked, and had Josiah hold the lantern closer so she could look into the prisoners' eyes.

Surely Addie didn't expect that Amanda would carry on any such examination. She questioned what her duties would be as Addie moved to another cell. It was evident that Addie had had contact with many of these prisoners before. She knew them by name, and they obviously had come to view her with respect. The one or two she did not know—a woman sharing the cell with Minnie, and one other man—were introduced by their cell mates, and Addie was always identified as "our little angel of mercy."

Amanda began to regret agreeing to take on this responsibility.

"The doc was in jail with me." Amanda turned her attention back to the cell occupied by the women. "Name is Minnie Price. I work over at the Blue Parrot." She thrust her hand through the bars, offering a handshake.

"There's surely nothing illegal about that," Amanda said as she took the woman's hand.

Minnie smiled. "No, miss. But forgetting to pay for a small piece of lace and a couple of feathers from that new milliner in town—well now, that can get a girl arrested faster than you can blink."

"Miss Jensen? That milliner?"

"Don't rightly know the woman's name, but it's the only hat shop I know of in town. That woman has a suspicious nature. Oh, she watched me close the minute I walked into her store, and she just made me so durn nervous that before I knew what I was doing, I had backed my way out and not even paid attention to the fact that I was still holding that lace and them feathers I'd only been admiring, I swear."

Minnie smelled of cheap perfume and wore a dress that exposed far too much bosom. She was hardly the sort of woman Amanda would normally associate with, and yet it struck her that a woman like Minnie might have a lot fewer choices in this life than she or Addie had. Not for the first time, she understood how truly blessed she was. After all, she had been able to leave home and come to Tucson and take a respectable position, and if none of it had worked out, she still had her family and the ranch. She had a home—a place she could go. What about Minnie? Who did she have to offer comfort and support?

Down the way, Addie continued to visit the prisoners, so Amanda pulled a small wooden stool closer to Minnie's cell and sat down. "Tell me what the doctor has done to make life more bearable for those of you held here, Miss Price."

"No need to stand on ceremony, honey. Minnie does fine." The woman's voice was filled with emotion, and she brushed away tears with the back of one hand. "Doc has made all the difference—in the food and the light, even if Sheriff Richter took it all away, and…"

"The food as well?"

Minnie nodded and leaned closer to Amanda, lowering her voice to a whisper. "It's fine whenever Sheriff Richter knows Doc Addie is coming for a visit, but between times…"

Amanda mentally ran through her schedule and decided she would make it her business to visit the prisoners more often than Addie had—unannounced. Perhaps Addie could speak with Judge Ellis about the change in protocol. That should at least solve the issue of the food.

She shuddered as Minnie filled her in on how Addie and James Matthews, the local pharmacist, and his daughter Ginny had set up a schedule of regularly seeing the prisoners. "If somebody new comes in," the woman continued, "Sheriff Richter is *supposed* to let the druggist know so he can come by. If Matthews thinks that prisoner needs medical attention, he gets word to Doc there."

"You say the sheriff is *supposed* to."

"Half the time he claims he was getting around to

it, but there's those like that boy down there at the end who could die a slow death before that lowdown, no-good varmint got them any help."

Amanda became aware of a low moan coming from the opposite end of the row of cells. She could hear Addie speaking in soft, calm tones as she instructed Josiah to bring her fresh water and clean rags. "And then please go outside and tell our friend, Mr. Grover, to go to the home of the district attorney. My husband is meeting with him. Both men should come here at once and bring my medical bag."

Josiah scratched his thin, lank hair. "Well now, Doc, that's not something I can do. If I leave my post, Sheriff Richter will fire me for certain and—"

"I'll go," Amanda said, and she was halfway up the dark stairway before anyone could object.

She began to realize that taking on this project for Addie was exactly what she had been seeking— something bigger than tutoring the Baxter twins— something that would make a real difference for people far less fortunate than the twins. She could help her dearest friend in the bargain.

Six

SETH'S TIME WITH SHERIFF RICHTER HAD BEEN PRETTY
much a standoff, the two of them keeping their distance, with neither abandoning his post outside the
courthouse door. The clock had chimed the half hour,
and dusk was settling in. Seth saw two men coming his
way and recognized one as Amanda's brother. Jess was
dressed in clothes suited to riding the range while the
other man was dressed formally, like a businessman, or
perhaps a lawyer.

"Tarnation," the sheriff muttered, and he stabbed
out the cigar he'd lit shortly after Addie and Amanda
went inside.

"Trouble?"

"Mind your own business," Richter growled even
as he pasted a fake smile on his face and descended
the steps to greet the two men. "Well, if it ain't our
district attorney and Marshal Porterfield. A little out of
your territory, aren't you, son?"

Seth saw the flash of anger that passed over Jess's
face, but the man held his temper. "Good evening,
Sheriff. Is my wife inside?"

"Looks like before long the whole family will be down there—your wife, your sister, you... You ain't by chance checking up on me, are you, son?"

Richter's constant insistence on pointing out the difference in their ages—and probably their experience— would have rattled most men. The sheriff was clearly trying to get a rise out of his opponent. But Jess stood his ground. "How's my prisoner doing?"

"Now, Marshal, let's understand each other— anybody locked up in this here jail is *my* prisoner."

The other man placed his foot on the bottom step leading to the courthouse. "I've come to question the man, Sheriff. I assume that would be all right with you?"

Seth remained standing near the courthouse door, observing the scene playing out on the steps below. He had thought it the safest place to be, until Amanda came barreling through the door and nearly slammed into him. She was about to say something to him when she evidently spotted her brother.

"Jess, Addie needs her medical bag. One of the prisoners is hurt, bleeding."

Jess Porterfield took a step closer to the sheriff. "I don't suppose this might be the young man I delivered to your care not two hours ago?"

Seth's attention was riveted on the two men. After all, there was every possibility the kid they were discussing was Sam.

He walked down the steps until he had joined the gathering. "I could go with Miss Porterfield to get Dr. Porterfield's medical bag, Marshal," he said quietly, giving no indication that he and Jess had ever met.

Jess glanced at him, then at Amanda. "You know this man?"

"He lives in the boardinghouse. Please, Jess, Addie needs her bag."

Jess hesitated, then nodded. "It's in the buggy by that small house on the corner." Jess pointed out the house and then headed inside the courthouse with the lawyer and Richter close on his heels.

"Stay here," Seth told Amanda. "It'll be quicker if I go alone." He took off at a run, found the bag, and was back in minutes. "Let's go," he said as he ran up the steps and held the door for her. "Which way?"

"Down here." She led him through a series of hallways and impressive solid wood doors with carved trim until they came to what looked like the door to a closet. It stood open, and he could see the darkness below and smell the odors of human sweat and waste.

"Stay here," he ordered, unwilling to have her experience such filth.

"No," she replied, and went ahead down the narrow stairway, as if it were a trip she had made a dozen times.

There was no need to seek further directions, for now the doctor, her husband, the lawyer, and the sheriff were all squeezed into a small cell where a man lay on a cot, his shirt ripped and covered in blood. Seth pushed through to reach the doctor and get a better look. If it was Sam and he was conscious, he was sure to recognize his own brother, though Seth hoped the kid would have sense enough not to reveal Seth's true identity by crying out for help. His heart hammered with a mix of fear and rage. If Sheriff Richter had hurt Sam…

"Here," he said, thrusting the bag at Addie. Then he steeled himself to look down at the cot.

It wasn't Sam.

A wave of disappointment mixed with relief left him light-headed. He leaned against the cold wall of the cell.

"Steady there," the doctor said, and he realized she was talking to him.

"I'm fine," he muttered.

"Well, you wouldn't be the first man to go weak in the knees at the sight of blood. Jess, I need some room here." She positioned herself between the injured man and the three lawmen, a clear message to get out of the cell.

"Here's the water and rags you wanted, Doc," a scrawny old man said as he set a pan of water on a small wooden stool.

"Where did you go for it? China?" she barked. "Sorry, Josiah," she added as she dipped a rag in the water and squeezed out the excess.

"How did this man get injured?" Richter demanded.

The deputy looked confused, but then he glanced at Richter and mumbled, "He musta fell. Musta happened right after you left him here. He was sure fine then." His voice shook, and there was little doubt that he was lying.

Richter turned to the man wearing the suit. "As I told you, Mr. Collins, the man put up a fight when he was brought down here. The deputy and me could hardly hold him, ain't that right, Josiah?"

Seth saw the deputy nod and then look away.

"This man did not fall," Amanda announced. "He has been beaten. Am I correct, Addie?"

The man moaned as Addie applied iodine to his cuts. "I would have to agree," she said, looking at her husband, who stepped back inside the cell. "He'll be all right," she said in a tone meant to reassure Jess.

"Can he be moved to Whitman Falls?" Jess asked.

"Now, why would you go moving him all the way there, knowing he has to come back here to face trial?" Richter asked. He snickered and shook his head as if Jess were about the dumbest man he'd ever met.

"You make a good point, Sheriff," Jess said as he studied Seth. "Sir, I didn't get your name."

"Grover," Seth replied.

"You from Tucson?"

"Just passing through."

Seth heard Amanda release an exasperated sigh. "He's looking at properties for investors who are his clients, Jess. He's perfectly…"

Jess ignored her. "Interested in making a little money on the side?"

"What do you have in mind, Marshal Porterfield?"

"Well, I'm thinking the sheriff's deputy has about all he can handle, seeing as how all the cells down here are fully occupied. I'm wondering if maybe you'd agree to watch over my prisoner here through the night—just to be sure he doesn't *injure* himself again before morning."

It was a gift—a chance for Seth to see if he could gain more information about the Stock brothers and their plans. It was a long shot, but he was pretty sure the marshal knew exactly what he was offering. "How much?"

"Does two bits an hour suit?"

"Now just a doggone minute," Sheriff Richter protested, but the lawyer interrupted.

"I think that's a fine idea. From what the marshal has told me, the man lying there could very well be mixed up with the gang that's been pulling off those robberies north of here. And if he's not part of the gang, then maybe he's got some idea where they could be hiding out. Seems to me this gentleman here might be able to gather some information the prisoner would be reluctant to give someone wearing a badge."

"You're the boss," Richter grumbled. "But this so-called businessman here has earned himself quite a reputation at the poker table over at the Blue Parrot. From what I hear, most folks wouldn't trust him to play a fair game of five-card stud, much less watch over a dangerous criminal. How do we know these two aren't in cahoots?"

"Sometimes you just need to have a little faith," Jess said, and then looked at Seth. "Deal?"

"Yes sir." This could be the break he'd been waiting for. He only hoped the doctor was good at her work, and the man would come around before daybreak so Seth would have time to gather what information he could before Richter showed up again.

"He should sleep for a while," Addie said, wiping her hands on one of the wet rags before dropping it back into the bloody water.

Josiah carried the pan away, and Seth took that opportunity to settle himself on the stool outside the cell. He was aware that Amanda was staring at him. She seemed undecided about what her next move should be.

"If you'd be so kind, Miss Porterfield, as to let Miss Dooley know I'm unlikely to be at breakfast tomorrow."

"Of course."

The doctor had packed her bag and was waiting with her husband to leave, and still Amanda lingered.

"Do you...will you be all right?" she asked, her voice a near whisper.

"Come on, Sis," Jess ordered. He waited for her at the foot of the steps while the others went ahead. "Grover is not someone you need to be concerned with," Seth heard him say as Amanda followed him up the steps. "He's..."

The rest was lost as the door closed, and other than the lantern at one end of the row of cells, the space was cast into darkness. The man on the cot moaned, the other prisoners settled back onto cots of their own, and Seth leaned back against the cold wall and planned his next move.

❧

After she'd endured a lecture from her brother about the dangers of trusting strangers like Seth Grover, and she'd seen Jess and Addie off on their way back to Whitman Falls, Amanda returned to her room at the boardinghouse. Her head was spinning with everything that had happened that day—from the time she'd spent with the Baxter twins to Addie's news about her father to her visit to the jail.

She knew she should have been disgusted by what she had seen there, but the truth was that once she got past the shock, she felt energized. Here was a cause she could champion. Her sympathies for Minnie Price—and what she assumed were other women just like her living right down the street from the boardinghouse—kept her awake long into the night. She wished she had more time to talk to Addie about what they might do, especially for these women she had once heard referred to as "soiled doves." She thought about the woman who owned the saloon in Whitman Falls, Miss Lillian. She was ashamed by how often she and others had been guilty of crossing the street simply to avoid having to pass the saloon.

She took out pen and paper and wrote a long letter to Addie, laying out her feelings and seeking her friend's advice for how they might work together toward better lives for these women. Tomorrow she would go to the drugstore and introduce herself to Mr. Matthews and his daughter. Together they would take up Addie's cause and make it a complete success.

Exhilarated, she found sleep impossible, and abandoned it in favor of sitting on the window seat by the garret window. She was thinking of ways she might inspire the Baxter twins to get involved in the cause when she noticed someone scurrying across the flat roof of the Baxter home. She leaned closer to the window, trying to get a better look, and wondered what she should do. What *could* she do? By the time she might reach the house and pound on the front door to raise the alarm, the culprit would be long gone. Besides, the person was moving away from the house, climbing down a trellis, and disappearing from her view, obscured from her sight by the adobe wall that encompassed the property.

She wished Seth were in his room. He would know what to do. But Seth was at the jail. She strained to see the alley below and saw the same person leading a horse from the property—a horse that made no sound, because its mouth and hooves had been muffled with cloth. The person led the horse down the alley. He was stealing one of the Baxter horses! She had to do something.

She grabbed her robe and ran barefoot down the stairs, through the kitchen and past the door that led to Miss Dooley's quarters. She peeked out the back door, moving the lace curtain aside only enough to see where the culprit might be, and gasped.

The man—or rather boy—guiding the horse was none other than Eli Baxter. She recognized him by the fringed jacket she'd seen him wear before.

Her shock at this discovery paralyzed her long enough for him to mount and ride away. She opened the kitchen door and stepped outside in time to see him crest a hill and disappear. In the alley she saw a piece of wool and knew it was one of the mufflers he had used on the horse's hooves. She picked it up and rolled it into a ball. It would possibly come in handy when she and Eli had yet another standoff.

Not surprisingly, when Amanda arrived at the Baxter house the following morning, she found Ellie sitting alone at the table. "Where is your brother, Ellie?"

The girl kept her eyes on the closed book before her. "Sick," she mumbled.

Amanda was hardly shocked. She had no idea when

the boy had returned home, but since it had been well after midnight when she saw him leave she doubted it had been much before dawn. "I see. Has Mrs. Caldwell been told?"

"Yes, Miss Porterfield. She's with him now."

"And your father? Has he been informed as well?"

For the first time since Amanda's arrival, the girl glanced at her. Her eyes were wide with fear. "No. I mean, Eli pretended to be all right until Father left for the bank, but then…"

"I see." She did not have to ask why the charade for their father's benefit. She placed a consoling hand on Ellie's shoulder. "Hopefully, Eli will be up to joining us later in the day. In the meantime, why don't you choose a Psalm to read before we pray?"

She handed Ellie her Bible. To her surprise, the girl did not hesitate, but turned to Psalm one hundred, stood, and read it aloud with feeling. Amanda suspected that when her brother was present, Ellie took her cues from him, but on her own she was far more confident. After they had prayed together, Amanda followed her usual protocol of writing the day's work on the chalkboard. She returned to the table to see that Ellie had laid her completed homework assignments out for review. She seemed disappointed when Amanda did not immediately attend to them.

"Ellie," Amanda said as she took the seat where Eli normally sat across from Ellie. "I have been wanting to speak with you about the essay you wrote that first week of class. The one where I asked what you would do if you could do anything?"

The girl's cheeks flared bright red, and she looked as if she might burst into tears at any moment. "You mustn't pay that any mind, Miss Porterfield. I mean, I just started writing because…well, I thought if I filled up a bunch of pages, you would tell my father that I had done good work and—"

"Are you saying what you wrote about becoming a novelist and traveling the world to gather your stories was not true?"

"No, miss. I mean, yes, miss, it's true. I do love to make up stories, but Father says…"

"Oh Ellie, never concern yourself with what others may say when it comes to following your heart's desire. Have I ever told you about my younger brother, Trey?"

Ellie shook her head.

"Trey was not well when he was a boy. In fact, he spent much of his childhood in bed or sitting in his room watching what happened outside his bedroom window. When he was around eight or nine, he began drawing little sketches of what he saw from that window. As his health improved, his passion for art grew as well, until just a few weeks ago he left home to spend several months in the wild. There he will sketch the things he sees, and those drawings are to be published—first in the Tucson newspaper, and eventually, Trey hopes, in a book."

Ellie's expression was rapt with interest, but then she frowned. "I don't understand why you told me that, Miss Porterfield."

"I told you that because, in spite of others in our family belittling Trey's dreams, he has remained steadfast

in following his heart. I told you about my brother
with the hope that you might consider how truly passionate you are about your dreams for the future. Do
you have what it might take to pursue them? I mean,
what if members of your family do not approve? What
if you write a novel, or two or three, and no one reads
them? Would you continue to write? Perhaps a more
pertinent question is, are you writing now?"

"No, but…"

"Then you must begin. While I go speak with Mrs.
Caldwell about your brother's condition, I want you
to write."

"Write what?"

"A story—a little story about anything. You must
have ideas buzzing in your head. Choose one, and get
it down on paper." She pushed the inkwell, a pen, and
a sheet of clean paper across the table. By the time she
had walked to the door, Ellie was bent over the table,
scribbling away.

Amanda smiled and went in search of Kitty
Caldwell.

"I can't find a thing wrong with the boy," Kitty
admitted, "but this much I know—he cannot keep his
eyes open for longer than a few minutes."

Amanda wasn't surprised, but she decided not
to share the information she had about Eli's post-
midnight ride. "Let him rest then, and perhaps after
lunch he will improve."

"I thought it was an act at first. It wouldn't be the
first time he's pretended to be sick, but this is different.
He was actually shaking when I went into his room."

"Is he running a fever?"

"Not that I can tell," Kitty said. "I made him some hot broth, and he took a couple of sips, then curled back under the covers."

Amanda worried Eli had encountered something—or someone—that had threatened or frightened him. She had to come up with some way of warning him that his adventures could end up getting him hurt, and again she thought of Seth. Perhaps Eli would respect a man like Seth warning him about the peril he was putting himself in.

Kitty continued to talk, although Amanda's mind was too occupied to really listen, until she heard the word "baseball." Of course. She had identified Ellie's love of storytelling and hopefully set her on a path to pursue that dream. Eli had written in large childish letters that his dream was to play baseball. But what did she know about the sport? As usual, she thought of Seth. Surely he would have some idea of how she might help Eli pursue that safer path.

"Let Eli sleep until lunch, and then tell him I expect him in the library."

For the rest of the morning, Amanda gave Ellie assignments she could complete on her own, and when Eli came downstairs later, she did the same with him. He seemed well enough, but subdued. While they worked, she scanned the hundreds of titles that lined the shelves of the library, looking for something that might engage each child's special interests.

Choosing something for Ellie was easy. She chose a copy of Louisa May Alcott's *Little Women*, hoping that, even if she had already read the novel, perhaps Amanda might help her connect deeply with the character of Jo March. But what would hold Eli's interest enough to keep him safe at home? She rejected book after book—science books, books on geography, books on the breeding of horses. And then she saw a thin volume almost lost among its wieldy shelf-mates. She pulled it out, first taken by the fact that it had fewer pages and therefore would be less daunting for the boy. The title was *Chadwick's Base-Ball Manual for 1871.* It was the perfect choice.

Toward the end of their day together, she collected the children's work and told them that, in light of all they had completed in class, their only homework assignments would be reading.

Eli groaned and drummed his fingers impatiently on the table. Ellie looked worried as usual. "An entire book in one night?"

"Fifty pages at a minimum. If you go beyond that, so much the better." She handed Ellie her book. "I want you to pay special attention to the character of Jo March."

Ellie nodded solemnly while her brother rolled his eyes. But when Amanda handed him the book on baseball, he had a good deal of trouble hiding his surprise. "Where did you find this?" he asked.

"Oh, Eli, there are many treasures to be found in a library. You just have to be willing to look."

With something that approached reverence, he slowly turned the pages of the small volume. Ellie looked up from her own exploration and gasped. "Mama bought that book for you, Eli. It was to be your present for our birthday the year she..."

"She died," Eli muttered. "The day before our

birthday," he added, more to himself. "So why didn't Father give it to me?"

"Perhaps in his grief—" Amanda began, but Eli interrupted.

"His grief didn't stop him from giving Ellie her present." He continued to stare at the book, only now it seemed to Amanda as if he looked at it with disgust.

Amanda sat next to him. "Eli, I do not know the story behind how this book ended up on these shelves. What I do know is that you have a love of the game of baseball, and according to your sister, your mother was aware of that as well. If I were you, I would look upon this as a belated birthday gift from your mother—one she made sure has finally reached you."

Eli sat very still for a long moment, fingering the cover. Finally, he nodded and carefully placed the book in the leather folder he used to carry his homework assignments and books to and from his room upstairs. "May I be excused?"

"Yes. We are done for the day. You both did excellent work, and I will make sure to relay that message to your father."

As she did every school day once the twins had been excused, Amanda stayed on writing the report she would leave on Mr. Baxter's desk before she headed back to the boardinghouse. She was so engrossed in choosing exactly the right words for praising the children without appearing naive about what the future might bring that Ezra Baxter entered the house—and the library—before she was even aware of his presence.

"You've stayed late today, Miss Porterfield. Was there a problem with the children?"

Amanda stood out of respect for her employer, although it annoyed her that his first assumption was that his children had caused trouble. He walked to a cabinet next to the fireplace, took a key from his vest pocket, and unlocked it. As he waited for her reply, he removed a crystal decanter from the cabinet and two glasses and poured a small amount of amber liquid into each.

"Well?" he said, offering her one of the two glasses.

"Thank you, no," she said primly, and picked up her report. "As for the children, today was our best day to date. They have made remarkable progress, sir. You should be very proud of both."

"Even Eli?"

"Especially Eli. I am aware that he has his problems when it comes to discipline, sir, but my theory is that they arise from boredom. He needs to be challenged."

He watched her closely as he drained the liquor in the glass he held, set that aside, and did the same with the glass he had offered her. "You do not approve of my sending the children away in the fall, do you, Miss Porterfield?"

"I believe families should stay together," she replied.

"Of course, if the children remained here, you would continue to be employed. Does that not factor into your thinking?"

She bit her lower lip to stop the words she wanted to say from tumbling out. Words like *I don't need this job.* Or *If you think for one minute that…*

To her shock, the man smiled and indicated that she should take one of the two chairs facing the fire. "Please join me, Miss Porterfield."

It would be rude to refuse. "Miss Dooley is quite strict about mealtimes," she said as she glanced at the clock on the mantel.

"You have a few minutes. After all, the board-inghouse is practically in my backyard." Again, he gestured to the chair, and when Amanda perched on the edge of the seat, he sat down in the other. "I have been most impressed with your handling of the children, Miss Porterfield. Perhaps I misjudged the importance of a female influence once my wife died."

"They have Mrs. Caldwell," she reminded him.

The smile reverted to the more familiar scowl that lined his face most of the time. "Mrs. Caldwell is a servant, Miss Porterfield. She is hardly of the class I would choose for influencing my children."

Of all the arrogant…

"You, on the other hand, come from a fine family—an educated family—and one of means and social standing in the region."

Amanda glanced at the clock. It showed she had five minutes to get from here to the boardinghouse dining table or suffer the wrath of Miss Dooley. She so wished he would come to the point.

"It is for that reason, Miss Porterfield—Amanda—that I would like to propose we make our arrangement one of permanence."

Her head was spinning with what excuse she might offer Miss Dooley for her tardiness, but as Mr. Baxter's words broke through her thoughts she froze in mind and body. Surely, he could not be suggesting…

"I propose that we wed, Amanda, for the good of the children."

That brought Amanda to her feet and had her backing away from him as she gathered her belongings. "I have to go, Mr. Baxter. I…thank you for…I have to go."

He stood—a bit unsteadily, she noticed. "I have shocked you, my dear. I apologize. Please consider my offer, for I assure you, it is not made lightly."

She had reached the doorway of the library. Ten more steps, and she could be out the door. She glanced toward the kitchen, where she could hear Kitty preparing the family's supper, and then a movement at the top of the stairs caught her attention. She caught a glimpse of Ellie's skirts as the girl fled back to her room and closed the door. Amanda hesitated, her instinct telling her to go to the girl and let her know that her father had not been himself, had surely not known what he was saying. And then she felt Ezra's hand on her arm, squeezing tight.

"Please," he whispered, and leaned in as if to pull her closer. Amanda wrenched her arm free, grabbed her cloak and satchel, and fled from the house.

❧

The first thing Seth noticed when Amanda came rushing into the dining room was that she was ghostly pale. The second was that when her sleeve crept up to expose her forearm as she reached for her chair, there were red marks that were obviously fresh. They would possibly leave welts or bruises. Had the Baxter boy attacked her? If so, that kid was going to get a lesson in how to treat a lady.

"So nice of you to join us, Miss Porterfield," Miss

Dooley said as she paused for a moment to give Amanda time to sit down and bow her head.

When the silent prayer had ended and the boarders began passing dishes around the table, Amanda turned to their landlady. "I do apologize. My employer came home early, and he wanted to talk about the children."

"And how are they doing?" Mrs. Rosewood asked.

Seth saw Amanda visibly relax as the conversation turned to the twins and their studies. Her previous reluctance to discuss her work had disappeared, and she was filled with enthusiasm. Clearly, she no longer had a problem with the boy. In fact, after telling them about finding the baseball book for Eli, she raised the question of whether anyone knew if there might be some man in town who would be willing to practice the game with Eli.

"I mean, one can only learn so much from reading a book," Amanda said as she settled her gaze on him.

Seth had no idea why the next words he heard were his own. "I used to play," he said, and the way his admission made her eyes sparkle had him offering information he should have kept to himself. "Some say I was a pretty good hitter."

"There's a group of men who come to the saloon regular, and two or three times a week, they get a game going out back of the place," Ollie said.

"I cannot see Ezra Baxter allowing his son to join a game that takes place behind an establishment like the Blue Parrot," Miss Dooley said.

"Don't see why not, since Baxter himself is there most every night," Ollie muttered.

"Mr. Baxter plays the game?" Amanda asked.

Ollie snorted. "Naw, he's too highbrow for the likes of a game where he might get his hands a little dirty. Might get those fancy duds of his messed up as well. My guess is he's not keen on letting the boy play either."

Seth watched Amanda wrestle with this information. He could practically see the wheels of her mind turning and was pretty sure that whatever she was thinking could lead to trouble. He glanced at her arm again, and when she saw him looking, she pulled at her sleeve to hide the marks. But Seth was already working it out. If Eli hadn't hurt her...then who? She spent all her time during the day at the Baxter house, so with the banker coming home early and keeping her late, Seth could come to only one conclusion. And it was one he fully intended to do something about.

❧

Amanda used her excitement about the twins as a shield to hold herself together as best she could until supper finally ended. Then she retreated to the seclusion of her room where the full impact of Ezra Baxter's words struck her. To her surprise, as soon as she had closed the door, she began to shake. She sat at her dressing table and released the tears she hadn't realized she was holding at bay. They leaked down her cheeks in silence as she stared at herself in the mirror and replayed the incident, looking for any way she might have contributed to the sheer madness of it.

What on earth could have possibly given the man the idea that they might wed—that she might have the slightest interest in being his wife? She barely knew him, and other than that first dinner, they had not exchanged more than a dozen words. And yet he apparently felt he knew her well enough that he could make such an absurd proposal. And how much had Ellie heard? And what might she tell Eli?

What was she thinking? Her position with the Baxter children was over. How could she possibly return to that house after this? But if she didn't complete the term, if she didn't guide the children through the work so that they might succeed in passing the entrance examinations to the private school their father had mentioned, then what might their futures be?

She wiped away the tears that had dripped onto the front of her shirtwaist, staining it with moisture, and stared at her reflection in the mirror. She would not abandon those children. There had to be a way she could tutor them without having to endure the unwanted advances of their father. Of course, given the two glasses of whiskey he had consumed in quick succession before making his proposal, perhaps he might not recall his actions—or he might pretend not to remember. He might be as embarrassed as she was. If that were the case, they could both go back to the way things had been.

But just before she had broken his hold on her arm, he had mumbled something beyond the word, "Please." Now, as she recalled the encounter in detail, she realized what he had murmured was, "I have come to care for you, Amanda."

Ridiculous! The man knew nothing of her. Other than reading her daily reports on the work the children had completed, what could possibly be the basis of his feelings?

She paced the room, but soon felt as if she had to escape—not only the room, but the clutches of Ezra Baxter. She needed air. Back at the ranch, she would think nothing of going for a walk no matter the hour. Here in town, such an action had to be clandestine.

She heard the clock in the parlor strike eight, heard Miss Dooley turn the key in the lock on the front door, and finally, heard the landlady close the door of her room at the back of the house. Down the hall she heard the bathroom door open, and then Miss Jensen's door close after wishing Mrs. Rosewood a good night. Everyone was settled in for the night. Ollie Taylor was at work, and more than likely, Seth was out as well.

Amanda started to undress. What choice did she have but to also go to bed? But then she saw the shirt and pants she had brought with her from the ranch, thinking she might need them should she decide to take the children out for a ride or a trip away from town. An old hat that had belonged to her younger brother hung on the post of the bed. Her riding boots were lined up side by side in the bottom of the wardrobe.

If she disguised herself as a boy, who would think twice seeing her out and about at this hour? She needed to think, and she had always done her best thinking late at night under a starry sky. It took her less than ten minutes to change, slip out of the room and down the stairs. Once again, she left the back door unlocked and stepped outside.

As she stood on the back stoop, trying to decide her next move, she realized that for the first time in days, she felt the reality of the independence she had sought when she left home. She smiled as she headed down the alley, picking her way behind shops and the back entrance to the Blue Parrot until she reached the edge of town, where she stopped.

Now what?

This was not the ranch where she knew every inch of the land, where the creek that ran through their property was always there as a place of refuge. This was Tucson—and what lay beyond its shops and homes and other buildings was a vast unknown. She must have been out of her mind to think she could escape the bonds this place had put on her.

Defeated, she prepared to retrace her steps, but before she could someone grabbed her, placed a gloved hand over her mouth, and wrestled her to the ground.

For the last three nights, Seth had been aware of someone following him as he went from the boardinghouse to the saloon and sometimes down the alley to the rear of the bank, where he looked for signs that anyone had been checking out the entry to the place. His stalker was good, keeping to the shadows of the closed shops and wearing dark clothes to further blend into the darkness. But sooner or later the guy would make a mistake, and when he did, Seth would be ready. If somebody in town had figured out Seth wasn't who he pretended to be, that was a danger he couldn't risk. He also wanted to snare whoever was following him in order to learn if that was the cowboy who had left the note about checking out the Frost ranch.

In the night he'd spent watching over Jess's prisoner, he'd picked up one key piece of information. The prisoner, who went by the name of Rusty, had heard some talk about a gang coming south, hoping to make a big strike before escaping across the border into Mexico. None of this was news to Seth, but he'd resisted the urge to press the man.

"You planning on hooking up with them?"

Rusty had looked at him and laughed. "I'm in jail. Does it look like I'm getting ready to meet anybody?"

"I just meant…"

"I was scoping out the town of Whitman Falls for them when the saloonkeeper caught me stealing a bottle of hooch from behind her bar and called the marshal on me."

Seth had smothered a grin even as he imagined the ruckus Lilly must have raised. "She's not somebody you want to mess with," he agreed.

Rusty looked at him with interest. "You know her?"

Seth shrugged. "Had some dealings of my own with her. I came out on the short end pretty much the same as you."

"Then you know that town?"

"Just passed through. I noticed it was on the way to the fort, and that made me think any payroll coming that way would have to pass right through town."

Rusty leaned closer and lowered his voice to a soft whisper. "That's what I was gonna tell the Stock boys."

"Before you got arrested," Seth added.

Rusty bowed his head. "They're gonna think I double-crossed them. My life won't be worth a plug nickel."

"How'd you get the beating in here?"

"That sheriff took a dislike to me right off."

"Did he say why?"

"Just said he was giving me fair warning to keep my mouth shut." For the first time, he seemed to realize that he was talking freely to a complete stranger. "Aw, gol-darn it. I'm a dead man for sure."

"I've got an idea. What if you wrote the Stock brothers and told them what you'd found out, and I delivered that message for you?"

Rusty stiffened. Slowly, he reached for the lantern and raised it so he could get a better look at Seth. "What's your business in this, mister?"

"Let's just say, like you, I'm not what people think I am."

The lantern light glinted off a gold cap on Rusty's front tooth as he grinned. "You thinking on joining up with them boys?"

Again, Seth shrugged. "You want the deal I'm offering or not?"

"Can't hurt," Rusty said, "except I can't for the life of me figure out what's in it for you."

"Well, you have to tell me where to deliver your message, don't you? And I'm thinking since you did your part, maybe I can pick up what's owed you while I'm delivering it."

Rusty snickered. "That or get yourself killed. Well, better you 'n me. You got paper and pencil?"

In the end, Rusty had scribbled a message and told Seth the gang could be found at the same abandoned ranch he'd checked out earlier. He'd gone there twice now. The first time, he'd left Rusty's note under a tin cup in the falling-down house. He'd waited for hours, but no one came. The second time, the note had been gone. Neither time had he found any sign of human life, but nevertheless, he'd had a sixth sense that told him he was being watched.

From the far end of the alley behind the bank, he heard muffled footsteps and pressed himself into a doorway across from the back door of the building. He watched as a small figure dressed in dark clothes darted down the alley, head bent and features hidden under the wide brim of a hat. The person moved like a kid, and Seth thought he'd finally found his brother.

He let the scoundrel reach the end of the alley before following. When he turned the corner at the edge of town, he froze.

It wasn't Sam—too small and slender. Also couldn't be the bulky Baxter kid. Whoever this was just stood there, staring off into the black of the countryside. Seth waited. The guy didn't move a muscle. Seth touched the butt of his gun and then decided not to draw. He saw no sign that the kid was armed.

Stealthily, he moved nearer until he was close enough to strike. In one swift movement, he muzzled the boy with one hand while wrestling him to the ground with the other. All the while, he hoped against hope this was his brother Sammy. And all the while, he knew he was wrong.

Seven

AMANDA FOUGHT HER ATTACKER WITH ALL HER MIGHT, ineffectually flailing away with both fists. Then, realizing her nails and teeth were better weapons, she raked his neck, even as she bit down hard and got a mouth filled with the taste of her attacker's leather glove for her trouble. She struggled to free herself from his solid, muscular body. He had pinned her to the ground by straddling her. She went completely still, hoping to surprise him, but he hauled her to her feet, leaving her hat in the dirt and her hair falling free of the pins she'd used to hide it under the crown of the Stetson.

"Amanda?" Seth Grover was breathing hard and staring down at her, one hand still holding the front of her shirt. She took pride in the realization that she'd put up enough of a fight to leave the man breathless. On the other hand, he was practically touching her breasts, which were heaving noticeably after the exertion.

"Explain yourself, Mr. Grover," she demanded as she planted both hands flat on the solid wall of his chest and shoved him away. He let go, but the sound of fabric ripping told her he'd taken the top buttons of the shirt with him. When she saw his eyes riveted on her exposed skin, she covered herself with crossed hands and felt heat race through her body. "Well?" she hissed, aware that they were standing outside, and anyone might pass by or hear them.

"I thought…are you following me, Amanda?"

"Do not flatter yourself, Seth. Miss Jensen might keep tabs on you, but your comings and goings are of no interest to me whatsoever." She dusted off the seat of her pants, then realized she'd once again exposed herself to him by letting go of her shirt front. "A gentleman would avert his eyes," she said, "or at the very least offer a lady the cover of his coat."

He chuckled. "Have to say I'm not much of a gentleman, ma'am, but if you're feeling a chill…" He shrugged out of his coat and draped it over her shoulders, allowing his hands to linger until she stepped out of reach.

"Thank you." She bent to retrieve her hat and slapped it against her thigh as she'd seen her father, brothers, and cowboys at the ranch do more times than she could count. The gesture made her feel tougher and taller at the same time. She shook her hair back from her face and planted the hat, tugging at the brim until the fit was snug. "I'll leave your coat outside your room. Good evening, Seth."

"I'll walk you back." He fell into step beside her. "Shall we take the street or the alley?"

He was mocking her. She remained silent but picked up the pace.

"Oh, then we're going to race back?" He matched her step for step, an easy feat given his long legs.

"Will you please…"

He took hold of her arm, forcing her to stop walking. "I am not leaving you alone, Amanda. You shouldn't be out at this time of night." His tone bordered on patronizing. He sounded like her brother Jess, and that irritated her.

"Why do you care?" she snapped and meant it to be a challenge, but found that she really wanted him to tell her. "You hardly know me."

He was still holding her upper arm. She could feel the heat of his fingers through the coat and realized he'd removed the leather gloves. While she processed this thought, he led her to a small lane that passed between the pharmacy and the milliner's shop. There he took hold of her other arm and pulled her closer.

She was sure he planned to kiss her. She was also sure that she had never wanted anything in her life quite as much as she wanted to find out what kissing Seth Grover might be like. Here, at last, was the true adventure she'd come to Tucson to find.

"Listen to me, Amanda. You're looking for trouble, and I won't always be around to make sure you don't find it, so fair warning. You need to stop these midnight wanderings. You need to stop getting yourself dressed up to look like a boy. You need to…"

So, kissing her was clearly the last thing on his mind.

She wrenched herself free of his hold. Not that he fought to hold on. "I can take care of myself," she muttered as she massaged her arms, although his touch had been firm but gentle.

"Really?"

"Really," she snapped, and started to walk away.

He caught her hand, and then before she knew what was happening, she was pressed up against the side of the building by the length of his body. He had his other hand over her mouth again—this time without his glove. His skin smelled like leather though. She struggled, and he tightened his hold on her. His face was so close she could feel his breath, hot against her cheeks.

"Wake up, Amanda. You are no longer residing on your family's ranch where no doubt you had others looking out for you. You are alone here in Tucson, and you need to take care." He removed his hand from her mouth but did not back away. "Honestly, woman, you can be the most…"

Amanda had no idea what came over her. Maybe she just wanted him to stop telling her what she already knew. She cupped his face with her hands and *kissed him*.

And then suddenly, he was kissing her back, gathering her into his arms. He pulled away for only a brief moment, looked at her, shook his head as if fighting off a notion, and then kissed her in a way she had never experienced. He teased her by nibbling her lower lip, and when she moved to have her lips meet his head-on, she felt his tongue brushing against her lips and teeth. She gasped, melting as he placed one hand behind her head, drawing her closer still.

The kiss seemed to go on forever, yet ended far too soon. When he pulled away a second time, actually moving a step away, their breaths came in gasps, as if they had run a race. "Amanda," he said softly, as he leaned in to kiss her again.

This was getting out of hand. She ducked free of his hold and scampered away, fighting to collect her wits. "As I was saying, Seth Grover, I can take care of myself."

She ran all the way back to the boardinghouse, listening for his footsteps following, but realizing he had given up without a chase. The truth was, he had made his point. How easily he had subdued her. She shuddered to think what a less scrupulous man might have done before she could get free, and by the time she had crept to the top of the stairs and reached the safety of her room, she was trembling so much that she had to sit down. But her thoughts quickly turned to the kiss. No longer would she need to fantasize about what kissing Seth Grover might be like. Now when she closed her eyes, she had that moment to relive, and whether he wanted to admit it or not, she was not alone in Tucson. She had Seth Grover watching out for her.

She pulled Seth's coat tight around her as shaking turned to laughter, and she lay back on her bed, savoring the scent of him surrounding her as she covered herself with his coat.

⁓

Seth swore as Amanda dashed off, but he knew she'd done the right thing. One more kiss and…

He watched until he saw her enter the boardinghouse, then returned to the livery to try and sleep. But he lay awake imagining all sorts of things that might have happened had she encountered one of the ruffians that frequented the saloon.

If he was going to be completely honest with himself, then he had to admit that he had wanted to kiss her pretty much from the minute he'd revealed her identity. And then she surprised him by taking that first step.

"Admit it, Grover. You've been thinking about kissing her since you first laid eyes on her back in Whitman Falls," he muttered, disgusted with himself for letting her get to him in more ways than one. With a growl of frustration, he left the livery and walked back to the boardinghouse.

He couldn't figure it out. She was pretty, all right, but that had never been the deciding thing for Seth when it came to a woman. He'd seen women a lot more beautiful than Amanda Porterfield. Hell, he'd *had* women more beautiful, and more worldly. Amanda was an innocent when it came to how things went between a man and a woman. He'd bet everything he owned on that. Sure, she'd been raised on a ranch, so she had to have some idea of the mechanics. Even so, the mating of animals was a far cry from the elements of heart and mind that passed between a man and a woman while making love. No way she understood that.

But if she insisted on taking these midnight walks and thinking she could handle herself, she was going to learn—and it was likely to be a hard lesson. It was likely to be a lesson that could destroy her.

That thought pulled him up short. This business of thinking so much about Amanda distracted him from the real reason he'd come out here tonight: to confront whoever had been following him.

It wasn't Amanda—he was sure of that, but having gotten himself mixed up in trying to talk sense into her, he'd forgotten all about whoever it might be. That was dangerous, and if there was one thing Seth was good at, it was his job.

In the years he had worked for Wells Fargo, not once had anyone unveiled his true identity. Time to concentrate on the job he was in Tucson to do. At sunup he would head to the abandoned ranch, find a spot where he wouldn't be seen, set up camp, and observe the place for activity. Miss Dooley wouldn't be happy about him missing breakfast and supper without giving proper notice, but so be it. It was high time he got back to work.

He used his key to open the front door of the boardinghouse and took the stairs two at a time. His coat was hanging on the doorknob of his room, and before he could stop himself, he had lifted it to his face, hoping to catch the scent of Amanda lingering there.

❧

"You were certainly up late last night, Miss Porterfield," Lucinda Jensen said at breakfast the following morning. "I do hope you weren't ill."

Amanda had finally pulled herself together enough to return Seth's coat and wash away the dirt, grime, and tears in the shared bathroom. "I'm sorry if I disturbed you," she said, refusing to offer any explanation.

"So you are not ill?"

"I am fine. Thank you for asking." Amanda turned her attention to their landlady. "Miss Dooley, you seem to know everyone in the area. I am still seeking a gentleman who enjoys baseball. The Baxter boy is quite a fan of the game, and I am convinced that encouraging that could also inspire him to take his studies more seriously."

"His father should be the one to work with him on that," Miss Dooley replied.

Ollie Taylor snorted. "Ezra Baxter wouldn't know a baseball from a wad of chewing tobacky."

"I thought Mr. Grover had volunteered," Mrs. Rosewood murmured.

"He seems to have once again been called away on business," Amanda replied. "I need someone I can rely upon to work with the boy over the next several weeks."

Miss Dooley frowned. "Well, there's Jim Matthews. He owns the drugstore across from the courthouse. I suppose you could ask him."

For the first time since kissing Seth the night before, Amanda accepted that she had probably made a fool of herself. Moving forward with her part on the jailhouse project was just what she needed to distract her from that fiasco. "I need to introduce myself anyway," she said. "He's been working with Dr. Porterfield on the jail reforms, and now that I'll be standing in for Addie…"

"Are you saying, Miss Porterfield, that it is your intention to actually work with prisoners in the jail?" Mrs. Rosewood asked. It was evident she did not approve, and it was obvious that Lucinda Jensen seconded her disapproval.

"Yes. In a few weeks, my position with the Baxter children will come to an end, and I have promised to help Dr. Porterfield while she takes care of a family matter."

"Yes, we are all saddened to hear of her father's illness," Mrs. Rosewood continued, "but really, Miss Porterfield, have you thought about how your working with those people might affect the rest of us?"

"Clearly not. Please enlighten me," Amanda said tightly. Oh, how she wished Seth had not skipped breakfast. As relieved as she had been when Miss Dooley announced he had left a note stating his intention to be away for a few days, now she wished he were here to stand with her.

"The prisoners are filthy, and they no doubt carry disease. Certainly, those women held there do, and…"

"Hold on just a durn-tooting minute," Ollie exploded. "The girls over at the Blue Parrot are clean as—"

"Stop this right now!" Miss Dooley shouted. Then she turned her attention to Amanda. "Do you see what you've done? If you hadn't insisted on conversation at meals, nothing like this would happen." She looked around the table. "Forthwith, there will be no conversation at meals. This is my house, and I will decide what we will and will not do. Anyone who takes issue with that is free to find other accommodations." This last was directed at Amanda.

"Please excuse me," Amanda said. She knew she had to leave the room or risk saying something that would get her banished from the house altogether.

She collected her satchel and cloak and crossed the yard to the rear entrance of the Baxter property. Kitty was scrubbing a man's shirt on the washboard she kept with the laundry supplies outside the kitchen door. "Well, you look like a horse that's been rode hard and put away wet," she said, pausing to study Amanda's flushed face and clenched hands.

"What do you know about Jim Matthews?"

"The druggist? Good man. His wife walked out on him and their four young'uns when the oldest was not yet seven. He's raised three boys to be upstanding citizens, two of them ranching and the third running his own business over in Phoenix. The girl, Ginny, is of age to marry, but prefers to help at the drugstore and write articles for the local paper now and again. Why?"

Amanda repeated what she'd told the others about needing to meet the man so they could continue the work Addie had begun for reforms at the jail. "And I understand he might know a thing or two about baseball."

Kitty paused in her scrubbing, stared at Amanda for a long moment, and then chuckled. "Don't know where my brain is these days. Shoulda seen this one a week or more ago."

"So you think asking him to work with Eli on the rudiments of the game is a good idea?"

"What I think, missy, is that you and Jim Matthews make the perfect match, and if it takes asking him to come over here and play ball with Eli to get things started, then that's a great idea."

"Kitty, be serious. If I have any hope of getting Eli to the point where he will pass those entrance examinations, I need to do something. My hope is that I can use baseball as a reward to inspire him to work harder."

Kitty frowned and returned to her scrubbing. "Well, the way I see it, you won't have much of a problem. That is, not until Mr. Baxter realizes things might go beyond Matthews coming over to pitch a ball or two with his son."

"Do Mr. Baxter and Mr. Matthews not get along?"

Kitty looked at her with a sly grin. "Oh, they do now, but once Mr. Baxter realizes he's in competition with Jim Matthews for your affections, things could get ugly fast."

Amanda sighed. "You are no help at all," she grumbled as she entered the house and went straight to the library. Eli and Ellie were arguing about something in heated words and hoarse whispers.

"I'm telling you what I heard," Ellie said.

"And whatever it was you heard, Ellie, I do hope it was firsthand, because repeating information you were not directly privy to is gossip."

"I heard Father ask you to marry him," Ellie shot back.

"You're lyin'," Eli said.

Amanda set down her satchel and faced Ellie. "The only habit that is at least as bad as gossiping, young lady, is eavesdropping."

"You're sayin' it's true?" Eli shouted.

"Do not raise your voice to me, Eli. What your sister overheard was a private conversation between your father and me. And if she wishes to pursue the matter further, then she will do so with her father. Understood?" She removed the Bible from her satchel and set it down firmly in the middle of the table. "Our Father..." she began, and paused while the twins halfheartedly bowed their heads and joined in. Their recitation of the Lord's Prayer was no more than a series of mumbled words, but Amanda decided to let it pass.

She turned to the chalkboard and posted the day's work. The first item on the list was *book report*. To her delight, both Ellie and Eli were prepared—not only prepared, but enthusiastic. She had chosen well, and that made her set aside the events of the night before and the upsetting incident at breakfast. Ellie had clearly fallen in love with the character of Jo March and admitted that she had stayed up late into the night to finish the book. As Amanda listened to Eli give a veritable treatise on the game of baseball as illustrated in Chadwick's book, she decided she would go to the drugstore while the twins had their lunch with Kitty. No doubt Kitty would give this plan her blessing, although her purpose and Amanda's were quite different.

To her delight, it occurred to her after meeting Jim Matthews and his daughter Ginny that introducing the Baxter twins would be a victory on two levels. Ginny was Jo March come to life and would be a wonderful role model for Ellie. Jim Matthews was a gentle soul who laughed easily and, apparently, was as devoted to the game of baseball as Eli. When Amanda asked if they would be willing to work with the twins, they enthusiastically agreed.

"You go now," Ginny instructed her father. "I can manage here. The afternoons are always slow." She fairly pushed them out the door.

On the walk back to the house, Amanda brought up the jail reform project. She told Jim about the feelings of the other boarders—or at least the women.

He was a good listener, and she had expressed more outrage than she'd intended by the time they reached the Baxter house.

"I apologize," she said. "Usually, I can control my tongue, but—"

"Not at all," Jim interrupted. "It's refreshing to hear someone speak their true feelings." He grinned. "Especially when they are so in line with my own."

Amanda laughed. "And it is doubly refreshing to talk so freely. I'm afraid I was raised to speak my mind, but I have discovered that doing so when your audience is family and doing so among strangers is very different."

"Well, then, let's be clear about one thing, Miss Porterfield—it seems we have a good deal in common. Both unafraid to say what we think. Both friends with Addie. Both dedicated to making the world a better place. And—if I do this right—my guess is by the time I'm finished talking baseball with the twins, you'll be a fan of the game as well." He stuck out his hand. "Friends?"

Amanda laughed and shook his hand. "Absolutely," she agreed. "I mean, as long as you don't hold me to that baseball part."

He chuckled, and she found she liked it. She realized there was a lot to like about Jim Matthews, from the way his straight sandy hair fell over his forehead, to how he matched his long-legged pace to her smaller steps, to his smile, and the twinkle in his eyes. She liked that she didn't feel unsettled around him.

Maybe Kitty had the right idea. She certainly hadn't given Seth Grover a thought since meeting the druggist—unless she counted comparing the two men for all the ways Seth was different.

❧

When Seth returned to town two days later, he deliberately timed his arrival so breakfast at the boardinghouse would be done, and everyone living there would be off doing whatever they did during the day. He climbed the stairs after asking Bessie to let Miss Dooley know he was back, but he might sleep through supper, so not to count on him.

On his way to his room, he glanced at Amanda's closed door and imagined her standing at the chalk-board in the Baxter house next door, lecturing the twins on something or other. He was glad, and at the same time disappointed that he would probably not see her until breakfast the following morning.

On the other hand, he'd discovered something that could affect her while scouting out the abandoned ranch. Both nights he spent there, he had observed the Baxter boy ride that way in the hours just before dawn. The boy slid from his horse and went inside the cabin for less than a minute, then mounted, gave a whistle, and rode back toward town. Both times Seth had waited for someone to show up at the cabin to retrieve whatever the boy had left there. Both times he'd observed an old prospector with a pack mule enter the cabin and leave again.

Between the kid's leaving and the prospector's arrival, there was no time for Seth to risk checking the cabin. He'd have to come back later. He thought of tailing the prospector—it would be easy enough—but he felt certain that there were others watching all of this as he was, and he didn't dare reveal his position, so he stayed put.

When there was no further action over the next two days, he decided his best bet was to return to town, corner the Baxter boy, and see what he knew. He was frustrated with the lack of progress, and as he rode back to town, the thing most on his mind was a hot bath and several hours of uninterrupted sleep. He was truly grateful that Miss Dooley's father had installed running water and a claw-foot tub long enough to accommodate his six-foot frame.

After soaking until the water turned gray and tepid, he dried himself off, wrapped the towel around his hips, and prepared to shave the beard he'd grown while on the trail. The bathroom had a small window that overlooked the Baxters' backyard, and when Seth heard an unfamiliar voice shout "Strike one!" he raised the window enough to give him a view.

The very proper Amanda Porterfield was standing at one corner of the yard, a baseball bat resting on her shoulder. The housekeeper stood on first base, the daughter was out in the field, the boy was pitching, and James Matthews, the local druggist, crouched behind Amanda in the catcher's position. Matthews was also the one calling the plays.

"Strike two," he shouted as Amanda took a mighty swing that missed the ball by several inches.

Matthews placed Amanda's hands closer together on the handle of the bat, then stood behind her—far too close to be proper, as far as Seth was concerned—and pantomimed swinging the bat.

"Keep your eye on the ball, Miss Porterfield," Matthews instructed as he assumed his catcher's crouch. Seth felt jealousy roll through him like a desert dust storm.

Amanda nodded. Seth could not see her features clearly, but everything about her posture told him she was determined not to miss again. Eli Baxter took his stance, glanced over his shoulder at his sister, and then back at Amanda, then fired a fastball toward Matthews.

Crack! The unmistakable sound of wood connecting with the leather of the ball seemed to startle everyone, most of all Amanda, who stood frozen in place, the bat dangling from one hand.

"Run!" Matthews instructed as the housekeeper rounded second, and the Baxter girl scrambled to retrieve the ball, juggling it and dropping it twice before succeeding. By that time, the housekeeper had headed for home, and Amanda had gathered her skirts in one hand, exposing more of her calves above her high-buttoned shoes than anyone would think proper, and she too was headed for home plate.

Eli Baxter pleaded with his sister to throw the ball, while Matthews and the housekeeper urged Amanda to score. The Baxter girl might not have been much of a fielder, but she had a good arm, and her pitch to her brother arced high against the blue sky.

Jim Matthews stood, his shirtsleeves rolled back to expose his forearms, his light hair blowing in the hot breeze as he watched Amanda race toward home—and him. Eli held out his glove, and the ball plopped into it. He turned to tag Amanda, but she had flown past him and straight into the waiting arms of the druggist.

Even though Seth understood that Matthews was only making sure that Amanda didn't fall, to his way of thinking the man held onto her a lot longer than necessary. And what about the fact that Amanda had asked Seth to play ball with the Baxter kid?

Three sharp knocks sounded on the bathroom door, followed by the rattling of the knob, and Ollie Taylor's irritated voice asking, "You drown in there, Grover? A guy's gotta take a leak."

"One minute," Seth replied as he scrubbed the remaining lather from his face and pulled on a pair of jeans before unlocking the door.

"Hotter than hell in here," Ollie grumbled as he brushed past Seth and shut the door. Seconds later, he heard Ollie shout, "Hold it down, will ya? Some of us have to work tonight." The window slammed shut, silencing the sounds from the yard next door. But nothing could shut out the image of Amanda looking at Jim Matthews and laughing as the druggist assured her she was safe.

Seth lay down on the cool sheets of his bed. Even though his room was at the front of the boardinghouse, away from the Baxter property, with the window open he could hear the faint aftermath of the game— the boy chiding his sister, the housekeeper suggesting cold lemonade, and most of all, Amanda's laughter. The likelihood that he would get any sleep now was probably not good. On top of that, he could smell the chicken and peppers Bessie was preparing for supper. He wondered if she'd told Miss Dooley he was back. He wondered if he might be able to change his mind about joining the others for the meal. He wondered if he would be able to eat while listening to Amanda regale everyone with details of the baseball game.

Later, when he reached the dining room, he needn't

have worried about the evening's conversation. There was none. He glanced around the table and saw everyone focused on the food. Bessie came and went, removing dishes and bringing dessert. Ollie muttered something and left for work. Mrs. Rosewood went to her room. Miss Jensen tried to gain his attention, but Amanda kept her eyes on her dish of butterscotch pudding, scraping the last remnants of the dessert from the sides of the small glass bowl before dabbing her napkin to the corners of her mouth and standing.

"Lovely meal, Miss Dooley," she said. "I think I'll take a short walk before turning in."

Seth saw his chance and hastily devoured the rest of his dessert before rising as well. By the time he grabbed his hat and reached the street, Amanda was at least a block ahead of him. She walked with purpose, nodding to the few people she passed along the way. He had crossed the street to keep her in view and was about to break into a trot to catch up when he realized she was not just out for a walk. She was entering the drugstore—Jim Matthews's drugstore. As soon as she was inside, someone—Jim, he assumed—shut the door and turned the sign that dangled from a string to read *Closed*.

Seth slowed his pace to a stroll. He crossed the street again, mostly deserted at this time of day, and continued down a side street. As he passed the alley behind the row of shops, he noticed the back door to the drugstore was open. It wouldn't hurt to check on her—to be sure Matthews wasn't taking advantage.

He edged his way closer to the rear entrance and heard Amanda's laugh. There was another female voice, and he realized that Jim's daughter Ginny was also inside. He let out a breath he hadn't realized he was holding.

"I'm sure Mr. Grover…" The rest was lost to the sound of a wagon rattling by on the side street. By the time the creaking vehicle passed, Ginny was the one talking. Her voice was high-pitched with excitement, and again he heard Amanda laugh. "Slow down," she said.

So this was a meeting to plan something—but what? Knowing Amanda, she was about to place herself and Matthews and his daughter in some situation that could turn dangerous in a hurry. Should he make his presence known? Act as if he'd just been passing by and thought maybe he might buy an after-hours sarsaparilla to ease the lingering heat of the day?

How about tending to your own business, Grover? How about concentrating on the fact that something is going down soon, and you don't yet know what it is? How about you stop mooning over Amanda Porterfield and do your damn job?

Resolutely, he turned away from the shop and headed back to the boardinghouse. He would leave Amanda a note about the Baxter kid's midnight ventures then collect his jacket—and his gun. Not once since coming to Tucson had he forgotten to strap on his gun belt whenever he left the boardinghouse… until now. This fascination with Amanda had to stop before he got himself shot.

◈

As she joined the others for breakfast the following morning, Amanda used the silence to recall her meeting with Jim and his daughter the evening before. She had no doubt that Jim Matthews was the kind of man her mother would think of as a perfect match. "Opposites attract," Constance Porterfield often preached to her four children. "Just look at your father and me—two more different people never walked this earth, and yet never was there a love story like ours."

It seemed ever since Amanda's father died, her mother had been on a mission to find proper matches for her children, Chet for Maria, and Addie for Jess. Now Amanda supposed it was her turn. And the truth was she found Jim appealing—as a friend, and someone with whom she could discuss anything. She knew that working with him on the jail reform project would not only be productive, but also fun. He had great ideas, and his daughter Ginny was a fireball of energy. The way he'd immediately agreed to Amanda's idea of working with Eli on his baseball skills showed him to be a man of kindness. Oh yes, her mother was going to love Jim Matthews.

The problem was that Amanda still spent a good deal of time thinking about Seth. Whenever she was around him, she found herself paying far too much attention to the way his shirt stretched across his shoulders, or the way his hands seemed hardened by work, but at the same time could handle one of Miss Dooley's crystal glasses as the fragile thing it was. His eyes fascinated her—the way he appeared to notice everything without seeming to be looking around. And those dimples! The way he didn't have to deliver a full-blown smile to bring them to life. She refused to allow herself to consider his mouth, because that inevitably led to images of those lips meeting hers. The way her breath quickened whenever she had such thoughts told her she was unlikely to abandon the memories kissing him stirred.

And that would, of course, be a disaster. A man like Seth Grover had no doubt made love to a string of women. He certainly would not be satisfied with a couple of kisses.

"Are you unwell again, Miss Porterfield?"

Amanda roused herself from her thoughts when Mrs. Rosewood dared raise this question in spite of the mandate not to speak during meals. Everyone around the breakfast table looked up from their plates and stared at her.

"Because you are quite flushed, my dear," Mrs. Rosewood continued. "I do hope you will have the good sense to isolate yourself if you are coming down with something—no doubt something you picked up from those children or your new friends at the jail."

For an instant, Amanda's gaze settled on Seth. He was watching her intently, a slight frown marring his handsome features. Did he agree with the widow? Was he afraid she might be carrying some malady that could infect him and the others?

"I am well," she murmured, embarrassed to have attention called to her, especially when she was all too aware that any rosiness in her cheeks had been brought on by thoughts of kissing Seth. Well, what else was a girl to do but daydream when normal conversation had been banned? "If you will all excuse me, I have a busy day ahead of me," she announced as she stood and placed her napkin on her chair, then left the room.

As she climbed the stairs, she could hear the others speculating on her health.

"Did you not think she looked feverish, Mr. Grover?" Mrs. Rosewood demanded.

Amanda paused on the stairs, curious in spite of herself to hear Seth's reply. "I find Miss Porterfield to be one of the liveliest and most energetic people I've ever met," he said. "Perhaps, as she said, the tasks ahead of her today were on her mind and caused her some momentary discomfort."

Good heavens, the man was talking about her as if she were livestock—lively and energetic, indeed. She heard Miss Dooley clear her throat, a definite signal that this particular discussion was at an end. In the ensuing silence, Amanda went to her room, shut the door, and sat on the edge of her bed trying to control her ire at Seth's analysis of her.

She saw the folded piece of paper lying just inside the door and immediately recognized the handwriting as Seth's. "What now?" she muttered as she bent to collect the note.

We need to talk. Name a time and place. S

Who did he think he was? Did he really think she would dance to his tune? Well, she wouldn't.

She unfolded the paper fully and noticed an addendum.

It's about the Baxter boy.

What could Seth have to tell her about Eli? He'd already passed along Ollie's warning, and indeed,

Amanda was aware of Eli's mischievous side, which bordered on something far more serious. But getting him involved with Jim Matthews might be the solution she had hoped for. Eli now came to class with his homework done, and he fully participated in the work she assigned. Of course, that was because she held out the carrot of time for baseball worked into the day's schedule.

She turned the paper over, just in case Seth had provided other information. The back was blank. She refolded the note and tapped it against her palm. She really could not afford to ignore Seth, if indeed he had information about Eli.

Tomorrow was Sunday and her day off. She had planned to rent a horse and ride back to the ranch to surprise her family. At breakfast, she would state her intention and hope that Seth picked up on the hint.

Sure enough, she had barely left Tucson behind on the following morning when she saw a lone rider coming across the desert. The man was dressed in black, but this was not Seth. This man was larger, heavier. Once again, she had allowed her impulsive nature to overrule her common sense. She thought of Seth's warning that night he'd found her walking alone.

She spurred her mount and the roan took off at a trot. She had foolishly believed that dressing in her brother's clothes might allow her to pass anyone she might meet unnoticed. But that had not exactly worked that night in town. Glancing over her shoulder, she saw the stranger spot her and turn his mount in her direction. Her heart pounded as she tried to decide what to do.

She knew that Fort Lowell was only a couple of miles away, but the other rider was closing in on her. "Oh please, let someone come," she whispered as she urged the horse to a full gallop.

Her prayers were answered when she saw a prospector walking across the range, leading a pack mule. She turned her horse and rode toward him.

"Hello!" she called, then immediately realized the need to lower the tone of her voice, if she was going to be seen as a boy.

The prospector looked at her and then at the rider coming her way. He waved, but it was not a greeting. He seemed to be waving her away, as if to warn her. She hesitated, saw the other rider turn toward the prospector, and used the opportunity to ride away as fast and as far as she could get from the two men.

Still, she was not so far away that she missed hearing the single gunshot, and when she looked back, she saw the prospector lying on the ground, and the other rider headed back the way he'd come. Amanda reined in her horse.

She felt bile rise in her throat and her entire body shook. A man had been shot. What should she do? Her instinct was to go to the prospector's aid. But what if the other rider came back?

Well, she couldn't just leave the man lying there. She turned her horse's head and rode back to where the prospector lay moaning, blood pouring from the shot that had hit him in the chest. "Oh no, you don't," she muttered as she slid from her horse and ran to him. "You are not going to die if I can help it, do you understand?"

The man opened his eyes, then smiled and closed them again. "Made it straight to heaven," he whispered.

"Not yet, you didn't," Amanda grumbled as she searched for something she could use to stem the flow of blood. She pulled the prospector's blanket free of his pack mule and wadded it into as tight a ball as she could, then shoved it against the wound, the way she'd once seen her father do when one of their horses had gotten tangled in a barbed wire fence. The man let out a yelp of pain that echoed across the barren land.

"Sorry." She sat back on her haunches and saw dust in the distance—a sure sign of somebody coming their way. She prayed it was not the shooter returning.

"Lie still," she instructed the man. "Help is on the way." She hoped she wasn't mistaken as she shielded her eyes with one hand and waited for the dust to clear. It was a wagon, so not Seth—or the shooter.

"Stay put," she said again as she mounted her horse and headed toward the wagon, praying the vehicle did not represent even more danger. She was thinking of her father, who had been left to die alone, and she no longer saw the prospector lying there. She saw her father.

"Help!" she shouted as she rode toward the wagon. "We need help."

To her relief, the wagon slowed, then turned in her direction. Two people were on the seat, one of them female. Surely, that was good. Amanda let out a breath. "Over here!" she shouted.

As the wagon came closer, she realized the driver was Jim Matthews, and Ginny was with him. She felt her breathing steady for the first time since she'd spotted the rider in black. She jerked off her hat and waved it high above her head. "He's been shot," she shouted, pointing to the prospector. "He needs a doctor."

Jim pulled his team to a halt and leapt down to examine the situation. "What on earth happened?" he asked as he checked the man's shallow breathing and instructed Ginny to bring him the tablecloth from their picnic basket. Amanda filled him in on the bare details.

"If we could lift him into your wagon, we're closer to Whitman Falls, and I'm sure Addie could help. Of course, my family's ranch is even closer, but we'd still have to wait for Addie and…"

"Ginny, you take Amanda's horse and ride ahead to town and get Addie. Meet us at the Porterfield ranch—Addie will know the way. Amanda, let's get this old-timer bandaged up as best we can and into the wagon." He gently pulled the blanket free of the wound, but the man still cried out in pain. "Check his pack, Addie. My guess is there will be a bottle of whiskey in there somewhere."

She did as he asked and found a full pint-sized bottle to bring him. "Should I try to get him to drink it?"

Jim nodded. "But just as much as it takes for him to pass out. We'll need the rest to clean the wound."

Amanda knelt next to the prospector and lifted his head. Eagerly, he sought the bottle, and she had to take care the precious liquid didn't spill down his chin. "Easy there," she said softly. Meanwhile, she heard Jim ripping the tablecloth into strips.

"What are you and Ginny doing out here?" she

asked as she doled out the whiskey in small sips. To her surprise, Jim smiled.

"Ginny had this idea that we should go on a picnic, and then she suggested we stop by the boardinghouse and see if you might want to join us. When Miss Dooley told us you'd gone home for the day, nothing would satisfy my daughter but that we set off after you. We could be company for you on the ride back to town."

"And you fell for that?" Amanda said as she recapped the bottle of whiskey and eased the prospector's head to the ground.

"Let's just say I didn't object."

Their eyes met for a long moment, and Amanda thought again what a good man this was and how she might make a good life with him. "You do understand that Ginny is matchmaking?"

"Yes, ma'am," he replied, not taking his gaze off her. "Like I said before, I didn't object."

The prospector's loud snore broke the moment, and Amanda passed the whiskey bottle to Jim, who soaked a larger piece of the tablecloth with the potent liquid and pressed it onto the wound. The man startled but did not cry out, so Amanda and Jim wrapped and bandaged the wound with strips of cloth. As they worked, their heads were close together and their hands brushed often. Amanda was aware of Jim's long fingers, his freshly shaven face, and the scent of piñon soap.

And once again, she could not stop herself from making comparisons—ones that still had Jim Matthews coming out the loser.

❧

On his way to get his horse and catch up with Amanda, Seth ran into Rusty, the prisoner from the jail.

"Hey, Grover," Rusty called out. He kept glancing over his shoulder as he skulked close to the shade provided by the shops. He was obviously more than just nervous. The man was scared.

"Rusty." Seth acknowledged him but kept his tone brusque on purpose. "I see you got off."

"Yeah, well, they don't fool me. That sheriff's got it in for me, so I might as well be dead. And that ain't all. That stuff I talked to you about? You done anything with that?"

"Look, I have an appointment I need to keep, Rusty. Good seeing you." Seth attempted to move past the man, but Rusty stepped in front of him, blocking his path. "You need to move now," Seth told him.

"I'm begging you, man. Take me with you wherever you're heading. If they see me with you, they'll think everything's jack. They been watching you, but the kid they've got with them told them he knew you from some jobs pulled back north."

Seth had to work hard not to react to this bit of information. The man had to be talking about his brother. "Look, I don't know who 'they' are, but my advice would be to put some distance between you and whoever you think might want to see you dead. Other than that, I can't help you."

"I helped you—told you what you wanted to know." The man was near tears.

"You didn't tell me anything I didn't already know." He pulled some coins from his pocket and pressed them into the man's palm. "Stagecoach will be through in an hour. I suggest you get yourself a ticket and be on it when it pulls out. Now, let me pass."

Rusty studied the money. "Okay," he whispered. "Yeah, okay."

Seth walked the rest of the way to the livery, where he collected his horse and rode out of town, trying to make up for lost time. He was familiar with the trail that led to Whitman Falls and pretty sure that was where he would catch up to Amanda. Once he did, he intended to tell her about the Baxter boy's adventures and leave it at that. He had more important work to do than to worry about the banker's kid. Now that he had his best reason yet to believe that Sam was part of the gang, he needed to focus his attention on making sure his brother didn't end up dead.

He took a couple shortcuts cross country to lessen the distance between them and ended up riding along the ridge above an arroyo with an expansive view of the countryside. He scanned the horizon, looking for a lone rider. Instead, he saw a wagon plodding along with two people on the seat and somebody curled up in the back. A pack mule was tied to the rear. Since these folks were the only sign of life he'd seen, and they were squarely on the trail Amanda would have taken, he decided to ride down and see if they might have seen her.

But the closer he got, the more familiar the two people sitting up front on the wagon got. He recognized Amanda's hair first and then realized Jim Matthews was driving the wagon. The whole scene made no sense. Where was Amanda's horse? Had he misunderstood her message at breakfast? Was she really headed to the ranch—and with the druggist?

Jealousy ate at him like an attack of fire ants. He considered riding on, but when Matthews glanced his way, he decided there was little choice but to meet up with them. Amanda said something to Jim, and then the druggist pulled the wagon to a halt and waved. Seth waved back and kicked his horse to a gallop to make up the distance between them.

"Miss Porterfield ran into a bit of trouble," Matthews said when Seth came alongside. "Somebody shot the old man back there. We're headed for the ranch to meet up with my daughter, and hopefully Addie." He snapped the reins, and the team started forward. Seth and his horse kept pace.

"You found him like this—shot, I mean?" Seth asked, keeping his eyes on Amanda. He'd gotten a better look at the man passed out in the rear of the wagon, recognized the clothing, and knew this was the same man he had seen going into the abandoned shack after the Baxter kid came and went.

"Not exactly," she replied, squinting and focusing straight ahead as if she were trying to see her way through a dust storm.

Seth remained silent, his gaze fixed on her. Matthews glanced from him to her and back again. "There was a rider who apparently had a beef with the prospector. According to Amanda, he shot the man and rode off."

"Did he see you?" Seth asked. Again, he was speaking only to her.

"Maybe. I guess." She shook her head like a horse ridding itself of a pesky fly. "What does it matter?

There's a man back there who's been shot, and we
need to get him help and—"

"Ever occur to you that you might have been the
one shot?" He watched as she slowly turned her face
to look directly at him.

"Ever occur to you that this is none of your business?" she challenged. "Either help us or—"

Matthews chuckled uncomfortably. "What are you
doing out this way, Grover? Come to check on that
property over in Whitman Falls?"

Seth took the lifeline. "Exactly," he said, and grinned
at Amanda. "You don't mind if I ride along with you,
do you? It can get pretty lonesome out here."

If looks could kill, Seth would have been a dead
man.

Eight

WHEN THEY REACHED THE RANCH, INSTEAD OF RIDING on as Amanda had hoped, Seth insisted on staying with them all the way to the house and helping Jim carry the prospector inside. Of course, that prompted her mother to insist that Seth stay for the noon meal, although Amanda had not missed the way her mother's eyebrows had lifted in surprise at the sight of him riding alongside the wagon. Ginny and Addie arrived shortly after they had gotten the old man settled. Amanda made sure she stayed close to Addie, fetching whatever she might need to treat the prospector's wounds. But once Addie had pronounced the man in critical condition, Amanda worried that she had not done enough.

"You did what you could," Addie assured her. "Now come, eat something. There's nothing more we can do here."

Seth sat across from her at the table, wolfing down Juanita's menu of chicken enchiladas with rice and beans, announcing this might be the best meal he'd had since leaving home.

"And where is 'home' exactly, Mr. Grover?" Amanda's mother delivered the question with a tone of polite conversation, but also a piercing glance that told everyone paying attention that she intended to gather information about Seth Grover.

"Chicago," he replied.

That launched Addie into a long stroll down memory lane of the days she and Jess had spent there on their honeymoon. "I got my medical license there," she told Seth. "An actual license."

"Congratulations," Seth said, and flashed her those dimples.

Amanda pushed away from the table. "I just want to… I just… Excuse me, please."

She fled the room, reaching the open courtyard and gulping in fresh air as if it were manna from heaven. *I cannot breathe when that man is around,* she thought, and then she gasped. *He quite literally takes my breath away.*

"Oh, for heaven's sake, get a grip," she muttered as she stalked off toward the creek and plopped down on a flat rock. But it was true. Seth Grover did not need to be within ten feet of her to feel his presence, see his handsome face, imagine what it might be like if they were to…

"Amanda? Are you unwell?"

She did wish people would stop asking that as she turned to see Jim Matthews coming her way and forced herself to work up a smile. "I'm fine," she said, and patted a place on the boulder next to her. "I guess the chaos of the last few hours became a little overwhelming. Join me?"

He sat down next to her. "Addie says Jess sent word

to Fort Lowell. Since the range is under their jurisdiction, they'll send somebody to question the patient about what happened—if he makes it."

"And they'll want to question me as well, I expect."

"No. Jess kept you out of it. Your mother suggests you stay the night, but Ginny and I should be getting back."

Amanda nodded. "I'm so glad you came along when you did, Jim. I really don't know what…" She fought the tears she tried to hide with her smile.

Jim wrapped his arm around her and pulled her to him so her head rested on his shoulder. "You would have figured it out, but I'm glad I could be there."

It had been a long time since she had felt so comforted, so safe. And the fact that Jim didn't seem inclined to take advantage of her vulnerable state made her like the man all the more. Maybe she was being foolish in rejecting the idea of allowing their friendship to blossom into something more.

"You and Ginny have a long trip ahead of you," she said as she sat up and faced him. "You should probably get started."

He nodded, but made no move to leave. "Amanda, about Ginny's mother…"

It was a statement out of the blue. "Your wife," she confirmed, realizing that a romance with Jim Matthews came with its own problems.

"When she left us, Ginny was only six. I had no idea where Essie had gone, or if she might return, so I took things day by day, waiting and trying to make sure Ginny and my boys understood that their mother's leaving had nothing to do with them."

"You're telling me that she's been gone—what? Ten or twelve years?"

"Eleven, to be exact."

"And in all that time, you never…"

"I wrote to her regularly in care of a sister in California, but never got an answer. Her sister would remember birthdays and send Christmas greetings, but never a word about Essie. And then two years ago, a package came with the news that Essie had died, killed in an avalanche on her way to Oregon."

"How horrible. What was in the package?"

"Some personal items—her Bible, a few trinkets of jewelry, and a picture of Ginny as a baby." He drew in a long breath. "Until now, there seemed to be no reason to tell others about Essie's passing. Ginny and I had settled into a good life. Still, it's past time for Ginny to follow her dreams and find a man who will love her. But I know she worries about me. I've tried to assure her I'll be fine, but the truth is I've been dreading letting her go."

"She won't be gone altogether. My mother has always said that…"

"I know." He played with a small stone, rolling it around in his hand, coating his palm with the red dust that covered it. "Look, I know we've just met and spent very little time together, and it's far too soon to consider that there might be something beyond friendship for us, but…if Ginny thought I had found…"

She did not understand why, but she knew she had to stop him from saying more. She placed her hand on his, trapping the stone between their palms. "Jim, you are someone I know I can rely upon. I am so grateful for the help you have given me with the Baxter twins, and I truly look forward to working with you on the jailhouse project, and…please, can we let it be just that for now?"

He smiled, but kept his eyes on her hand, now covering his. "Yes. All right." He turned her palm up and placed the stone in it. "A symbol of our everlasting friendship," he said before pushing himself to his feet. "Ginny and I will see you back in Tucson," he added, and walked away.

Amanda watched him go and saw her mother observing the scene from the courtyard. Constance Porterfield would have questions about her relationship with James, but she would not raise them. She would simply let her personal preference for James over Seth be known through veiled statements and comments about what a solid citizen he appeared to be and how she still had her doubts about Seth. But in the end, when it came to matters of the heart, Amanda's parents had always believed that they needed to allow their children to find their own ways and trusted them to seek guidance when they were lost.

She waved to her mother, a signal that all was well. Then she walked along the banks of the creek, allowing precious childhood memories to wash over her—she and her siblings had played there, and she and her father had gone fishing together. She walked for some time, following the winding trail of the water, listening as it splashed over rocks, and savoring the certainty that whatever choices she made in life, this would always be home.

She was farther afield than she had realized when

she heard footsteps behind her—boots that crunched over the ground with purpose. Secure in the knowledge that she was still on Porterfield land, she stopped and prepared to face whoever was coming.

Seth Grover strode across the land as if he'd walked there a thousand times before. He did not hesitate and choose one path over another, but came straight to her, his face shaded by the brim of his black hat. "The old man died," he said.

"Did he suffer?"

"No. Doctor Porterfield said he never regained consciousness—just slipped away." He placed his hand on her forearm. "There was nothing you could have done, Amanda."

She walked toward the creek.

"We have to talk," he said, following her.

"So you said in your note. What can possibly be so urgent that it cannot keep until tomorrow?"

"Sorry about that. I misread your comment at breakfast. I had no idea your real plan was to meet up with Matthews."

"That was not…" She shook off any attempt to offer an explanation. Let the man believe whatever he chose. "Well? What is it we need to discuss?"

He removed his hat and ran his fingers through his thick black hair. He squinted at the sun, then back at her. "Mind if we get out of this sun?" he asked, nodding toward a cluster of cottonwoods that anchored a bend in the creek.

"Very well, but I do have to get back to the house." She picked her way through brush and tall grass toward the creek.

"Too late. Matthews and his daughter pulled out already."

"Will you please not concern yourself with my personal life? You don't like it when I question your activities, so please show me the same simple courtesy."

"Fair enough." He indicated an old cottonwood tree that had fallen so it jutted into the creek. "Okay if we sit a minute?"

She sat and released an audible breath of exasperation. He leaned against the trunk. "Eli Baxter has been making midnight forays into the countryside."

"I know." His look of surprise pleased her. "I saw him one night. He sneaked out of the house and took a horse and left. The following morning he was—not surprisingly—too *ill* to attend class."

"Did you mention this to his father?"

"No. Ezra Baxter has a temper, Seth. I have seen the marks of that temper on his children, and it goes beyond acceptable discipline. I decided to let the matter stand unless it became clear that Eli had made a habit of these outings."

"And how were you going to judge that?"

She sighed. "If he'd continued to miss class, especially in the mornings, then I was going to do something about it. I would have spoken to him first, with the warning that if I learned of any more forays, I would report it to his father."

"But you never had that conversation."

"I didn't feel the need. Eli has been a model student, especially since Jim agreed to work with him."

Seth's mouth tightened at the mention of Jim's name, but he shook it off and pushed himself away from the tree—and her. "Here's what you need to know. Eli has not only continued his rides, he's gotten mixed up with pretty bad ruffians in the bargain."

"How do you know this?"

He smiled. "Now, there you go again, Amanda, asking questions you know I can't answer."

"Can't or won't?"

He stared at her for a long moment, as if trying to make a decision. Then he reached out and touched her cheek with his forefinger, tracing a feather-light line along her jaw. "Both," he said softly.

He seemed to gather himself, pulling his hand away as he put on his hat. "That's all I wanted to say, Amanda. The kid is headed for trouble. Hopefully, you—and Matthews—can get him back on the right trail."

He turned to walk away, but she grabbed his arm. "Wait a minute. If you know all this, why not speak to him yourself? He would certainly pay attention to someone like you. You, of all people, could convince him…"

He went so still that she felt a tremor of fear rocket through her. When he looked down at her hand on his forearm, she released him. "Someone like me?" It was a raspy whisper. "Is that how you see me, Amanda? As someone people should fear? As someone not quite right for polite society? As…"

"I don't know what to think. One minute you're mysterious and standoffish, and the next you're sweet and caring and…"

He took a step closer, his eyes dancing over her face. "And which do you prefer, Amanda?"

"Both," she replied. She did not retreat as she knew she should have. This was a moment she had thought about a good deal. She had feelings for this man that had gone unexplored for too long, and now, as he studied her, reached for her, and folded her into his embrace, she understood that nothing she felt was one-sided. In this moment, at least, he was every bit as curious as she was about taking that next step and kissing her again.

❧

Seth had kissed his fair share of women, but kissing Amanda Porterfield was different. As he had that night in town, he felt the expected carnal urge to take her then and there in the tall grass along the creek, and yet in the light of day, there was a stronger feeling—a confusing mix of the need to savor and protect, as well as the sense that one time would not be enough. A thousand times would not be enough.

He was touched by her sweetness and inexperience, and at the same time, driven by her willingness to go wherever he might lead. When he pressed his mouth to her lips, she settled in to learn the dance he silently proposed. She pushed his hat off and buried her fingers in his hair, tugging him closer. He could feel the pounding of her heart through the fabric of his shirt—or maybe it was his own heartbeat he felt.

Only the need to take in air could make him release her for so much as an instant. And when he did, they stood toe to toe, breathing as if they had run miles as they stared at each other. With both hands, she framed his face and allowed the pads of her thumbs to stroke his cheeks, the stubble of his beard.

"Amanda," he said, and his voice was hoarse with

wanting. "You don't understand… We can't… I'm not…" Words failed him as he felt the riptide of those emerald eyes surround him and pull him under.

"Then make me understand, Seth," she pleaded.

In the distance, he heard the laughter and whoops of the cowhands coming in off the trail. The interruption brought him to his senses. Gently, he moved his hand from her back to her upper arms, and stepped away.

"I have a job to do, and when that is done, maybe then you and I can talk about where this might lead. But in the meantime, I'm urging you to take a serious look at Matthews. He'll be good for you—good to you."

"And you wouldn't be?"

"That's not the point, Amanda. The point is that what just happened here can't happen again. I won't allow it." He looked around for his hat, found it, and held it in both hands. "Now let me walk you back to the house so I can say good-bye to your family and head back to Tucson."

"I know the way back, so I hardly need you to walk me there," she said, and this time she was the one to take a step closer. "I also know, Seth Grover, that you have not seen the last of me. Whatever it is that Eli is mixed up in has something to do with you and *your* mysterious midnight rides. Let me in, or I will take matters into my own hands until I can figure out what's really going on."

"No!" Seth saw the full extent of the danger she could not possibly realize. "You will stay out of this. I will talk to the Baxter boy and make sure he doesn't get hurt, all right?"

She had her hands planted on her narrow hips and tapped one foot impatiently. "And what if you get hurt?"

He tried to laugh off her concern, but could not deny it felt damned good to have someone this worried about him. "I can handle myself."

"I'll bet that's exactly what that prospector thought," she said, and stalked off toward the house.

He could have easily overtaken her, but he gave her time to make it all the way back before he followed. His plan was to stop briefly to express his thanks to Mrs. Porterfield and then head to Tucson. But when he got to the ranch house, Amanda was waiting for him. Her horse was saddled, and her mother was looking at Seth as if he were the devil incarnate.

"My daughter believes she needs to return to Tucson tonight. She says she needs to be with her students tomorrow—something about a special assignment she forgot she gave them."

Seth wasn't sure what any of this had to do with him, and to tell the truth, he was probably as upset as Amanda's mother about this sudden turn of events.

"I am entrusting her safety to you, Mr. Grover, given that Mr. Matthews and his daughter are already well on their way. I will be honest and tell you that I do so with some concern. I do not for one minute believe that you are a businessman, and I have no idea what it is you are hiding behind that ruse, a fact that gives me pause. But my son tells me I have no need to worry, and I certainly cannot allow Amanda to go off on her own at this time of day."

Just then, Amanda's brother Jess strolled into the

courtyard, his eyes on Seth, repeating his previous warning to stay away from his sister. Seth wondered if either mother or brother would be surprised to understand that the last thing Seth wanted—or needed— right now was to spend the next several hours alone with Amanda.

"Maybe I could talk to her—offer to carry a note back to Mr. Baxter and his children, explaining her need to stay over."

"No! I'm going now—with or without you," Amanda announced as she checked the cinch on her horse's saddle one last time.

She had to be one of the most pig-headed females God ever gave the breath of life. He knew what she was up to, why the sudden need to get back to Tucson at once. In spite of his plea to allow him to handle the matter, she would confront Eli Baxter. At least he hoped that was her plan and not something more dangerous.

Seth turned his attention to her. "Now, Miss Amanda, I could take care of this for you, and you could stay here and enjoy some time with your family."

He saw the way she bristled at the way he called her *Miss Amanda,* but she recovered quickly, batting her lashes and smiling as she said, "Oh, that is so sweet of you, Mr. Grover, but really, the children will be disappointed, and their father made it quite clear that he expects me to put them first." She climbed into the saddle, settled herself, and turned to look back at him. "Coming?"

Seth glanced at Mrs. Porterfield who threw up her hands in exasperation, while Jess folded his arms across his chest and glared at Seth. Talk about being between a rock and a hard place.

"You go on, miss. I'll catch up," Seth said as he strode toward the corral to get his horse, hoisting his saddle off the fence as he went.

"Ma, this is a bad idea," he heard Jess say.

"I thought you told me he was not…dangerous, so how is this a bad idea?"

"Trust me. It is," Jess grumbled.

"Then either you go with her, or talk her into staying," Mrs. Porterfield replied as she returned to the house.

Seth was aware of the marshal headed his way, but he concentrated on saddling his horse. He was already mounted when Jess reached the corral. "I thought we had a deal," he said.

"We did, and I'm doing my best to keep it, but unless you want your sister riding out there where the varmint who shot the prospector is still at large, I suggest you let me catch up to her and see that she gets back safe and sound."

"And once you do, that'll end it?"

Jess's wife Addie was walking their way. "Stop badgering the man, Jess, and let him be on his way. Seems to me whatever might be going on with him and Amanda is a two-step dance, and you've got no say in it, so back off and let your sister make her own mistakes."

At first Seth had been flattered by Addie's comments, but when she said that part about letting Amanda make her own mistakes, he understood that *he* was that mistake. Well, she had a point. A guy like him—working undercover and moving from one place to the next—was not exactly the addition to the family that folks like the Porterfields would want. The truth was that he tended to agree.

As he headed cross-country, he met up with a small detail of soldiers coming to question the prospector. He stopped to fill them in on the old man's death, told them what he knew of the shooter, and answered their questions about how he'd come to be involved. Finally, they let him go.

He spurred his horse to a gallop, certain he would catch up to Amanda quickly, but as the sun sank lower in the western sky, casting the landscape in shades of orange and rust, he saw no sign of her. There was only one main trail between Whitman Falls and Tucson, and right now, she didn't appear to be on it. His heart hammered as he pulled his horse to a stop and looked around. Where could she be? What if the guy who'd shot the old-timer had seen her riding alone?

Seth slid from his saddle and searched the trail for signs of recent tracks. Up ahead was a cluster of aspen trees near a creek, probably the same creek that ran through the Porterfield property. He thought he saw movement and then recognized Amanda's horse. He climbed back in the saddle, and once again urged his mount to a gallop, not yet relieved. He saw the horse, but he didn't see *her*.

❧

For the first mile or so, Amanda fully expected to hear Seth's horse coming behind her at any moment. But she saw no one and heard nothing except the muffled beats of her horse's hooves hitting the soft dirt of the trail. The sun was lower in the sky now—not yet setting, but late in the day. By her calculation, Tucson was at least an hour's ride away, assuming she kept pace. As the shadows of the hills lengthened and stretched across the range, she imagined she saw movement, and her anxiety grew in direct proportion to the fading light.

She had been so certain that Seth would come. What could be keeping him?

When she saw the place where the creek narrowed and all but disappeared, she turned her horse in that direction. At least the animal would have water, and she would have cover where she might observe the trail. Of course, if she lingered there too long, it would be dark, and then what would she do? She thought about the prospector. If she hadn't been there...if she hadn't witnessed...

And that, of course, was the problem. *The shooter had seen her.*

She dismounted and led her horse to the edge of the narrow stream. She took advantage of the clear water to wash her face and hands. She was tightening the cap of her canteen after taking a long drink when she heard two things—a horse coming down the trail, and the telltale rattle of a snake not two feet away from where she stood.

Her horse shuffled behind her, clearly aware of the danger. The snake remained coiled on a rock at the edge of the creek. The hoofbeats came closer, and at this point, she really didn't care who the rider might be. The rattle sounded again—a warning—as the snake seemed to lock eyes with her. She stepped back slowly and bumped into the side of her horse, which whinnied and shifted. In fascination, she watched as the snake's body began to move, its muscles rippling as it prepared to strike.

"Please," she whispered, unsure of whether she was uttering a prayer to the heavens or a plea to the snake.

She no longer heard the rider behind her. Had he passed her, unaware of her presence? She couldn't recall. And then suddenly, she was shoved aside as a shot rang out, and when she opened her eyes, Seth was standing over the corpse of the rattler, and he was furious—at her.

He yelled, his voice carrying across the deserted land. "Are you satisfied? Two times in one day you could have gotten yourself killed, and still you insist on going out looking for trouble. You are an impulsive and mulish woman, Amanda, and sooner rather than later it's going to get you killed. I have known some characters when it comes to taking unnecessary risks, but you take the cake. I mean, what was the point of…"

She really didn't know whether to laugh or cry. She decided to do neither. Instead she stood, brushed herself off, and headed for her horse.

"Well, it certainly took you long enough to catch up," she said. "Thank you, by the way. That could have turned out badly."

His mouth dropped open. *"Badly?"*

He mocked her as he holstered his gun and kicked the carcass of the snake aside. Of course, he was right—she had been foolish to take off on her own like that, especially so late in the day, but the prospector's violent death had stirred memories of what her father must have once suffered, and she knew she couldn't stay one more minute at the ranch. Of course, she wasn't about to admit that to Seth or let him see how truly terrified she had been.

"We should get going," she said as she put her canteen away. "It'll be dark before long and——"

Before she could utter another word, he had taken hold of her and pulled her close. "Stop doing this," he said, his voice husky.

"What do you mean by 'this'?"

"Scaring the bejesus out of me," he replied as he tilted her face so she looked at him.

He still held her. She could feel his heart beat against the palm she pressed to his chest in a half-hearted attempt to put some distance between them. She felt her own heartbeat quicken at the very suggestion that he might care.

But then he went and spoiled the moment. "I don't have time for this, Amanda."

Now, she struggled to put space between them. "Nobody is asking you to do anything. Thank you for killing the snake, of course, but other than that…"

To her surprise, instead of loosening his hold, he tightened it. Now his handsome face was so close she could count each whisker of the stubble on his jaw. "Do you really not have the good sense God gave you to be afraid when danger is staring you in the face?"

"The only thing staring me in the face at the moment is you," she snipped. "Now——"

He cradled the back of her head with one hand and kissed her—kissed her as she had never in her life been kissed. This was no boyish, experimental slobber meant to test the waters. This wasn't even that first, truly adult kiss they'd shared earlier. This was a kiss that announced, loud and clear, his desire and his intention to act on that desire, unless she stopped him.

So what did she do? To what she was well aware would be her mother's horror, she kissed him back, giving what she was given. When his lips parted, so did hers. When his teeth collided with hers, she did not pull back. When he stroked her teeth with his tongue, she opened wide to allow him the access he was clearly requesting, and when she heard him exhale, she could not help but feel as if she had won. Everything about the way he deepened that kiss told her he did care—he cared far more than he had allowed himself to admit. She had no doubt of that, and definitely no doubt that she cared as well.

Instead of pulling away, she leaned into him, allowing his arms to wrap her in his strength. For the first time in a long time, she felt shielded from the fears and anxieties about what the future might hold, which she'd held inside since her father's tragic death. She had found her future in this man's embrace. She had never been more certain of anything in her life.

He broke the kiss finally and gently stroked her lips with his thumb. "Amanda?"

"Right here," she said softly, and snuggled closer to him.

"We can't… I mean, this is insanity and…"

She framed his face with her hands and pulled him to her. "Kiss me again and then tell me about insanity," she whispered as she pressed her lips to his.

❧

Seth was pretty sure that giving in to Amanda Porterfield's kiss was possibly the most dangerous thing he had done in a long time. He understood that kissing her would satisfy his need to have her, to make her his, for only so long, and then he'd be ready to move on to serious lovemaking—ravishing the rest of her as he was currently ravishing her sweet mouth.

He had already managed to pull her hair free of the pins that held it. He could smell the pine of the soap she had used to wash it. He imagined her soft hair streaming over his bare chest as they lay together. Feeling her full breasts pressed against his chest, he thought about what she would look like naked—that skin, so fair in the few places exposed to the world, would be like milk. The image made him groan with desire.

"I want you," he whispered as he feathered kisses along her brow, waiting for their breathing to ease back to normal.

"Yes," she said.

"But…"

"Seth, I said yes. It's almost dark. Let's build a fire and stay here by the creek, and we can…"

Gently, he set her away from him and then removed his hands from her shoulders and held them stiffly at his sides. "You don't know me, Amanda. You would be making love with a stranger."

"I do know you, and you know me. We may have met only a few weeks ago, but—"

"I've lied to you and the others, Amanda."

"I don't understand. Are you telling me your name is not Seth Grover?"

"No. I mean, that's my name, but who I am and who I pretend to be—that's the lie." He could see she was near tears, the stress of the day and the depth of her passion for him taking its toll. He wanted to tell her the truth, but he'd sworn an oath, and until this job was done and he was free to walk away and live the life he hadn't realized he wanted, he could not break that oath.

"Tell me," she pleaded, her eyes growing wide with doubt—in him and herself.

"I can't do that now. You have to trust me. There are good reasons, and one day soon, I promise I'll be free to tell you everything." He took a step toward her and knew when she retreated that it was a mistake.

Abruptly, she turned away and began unsaddling her horse. "It would be foolhardy to try to make it back to town in the dark," she said. "I believe I know you well enough to trust you are a gentleman, and if we stay here until first light, nothing will happen. That is, there can be no repeat of…"

"I'll take first watch," he said as he unbuckled his horse's cinch, pulled the saddle free, and carried it to a place where he could keep a lookout. "You bed down over there and get some rest. Those Baxter kids will be waiting for you in the morning." He worked hard at keeping his tone light, trustworthy, that of a brother or good friend. He even put a twang into his words, hoping to give her some comfort.

"Oh, for heaven's sake, Seth, you don't have to treat me like I'm fragile crystal. We kissed and got momentarily carried away. Fortunately, we both managed to come to our senses. Wake me when it's my turn to watch."

She spread her saddle blanket on the ground, lay down, and tried unsuccessfully to wrap the cover around her.

"Here," he said, taking his blanket and opening it as he walked toward her. She didn't protest when he placed it over her.

She also didn't protest when he bent down to pull it over her shoulders. Unable to stop himself, he touched a curl of her hair, allowing his fingers to sift through it as if it were sand—or strawberry gold.

"Get some sleep," he said before returning to where he'd propped his saddle against the thick trunk of a tree near the creek.

As the night deepened, he stared up at the stars and thought about the future. What he had wanted when he left Chicago three years earlier had changed. Problem was, what he wanted now didn't fit with the life he'd made for himself. What he wanted now was the life he'd seen as boring when he thought about his parents—a home and family and a woman at his side who would be there no matter what.

A woman like Amanda.

"No," he whispered to the dark. "Not a woman *like* her. Only Amanda."

He could tell neither of them was sleeping. She moved restlessly, as if trying to find comfort on the hard ground. He got up and, although he was fairly certain he was making a mistake, went to her.

"Amanda?" He knelt next to her.

"What?" she grumbled, pretending he had awakened her as she pushed herself to a sitting position and covered her shoulders with the blanket.

"I don't want to fight with you."

"No," she admitted. "Me neither. I just wish…"

"I trust you—more than trust you, Amanda. The truth is I think I'm falling in love with you." He ran his knuckles over her cheek. "Couldn't come at a less opportune time, but there it is. Look, I know I'm not what your family wants for you, but…"

"Shhh," she whispered, silencing him by placing her finger on his lips. "You are the man I want for me, and that is all that matters." She ran her fingers through his thick hair. "In time we'll find our way, but for tonight, Seth, let's not waste the one chance we may ever have. Teach me how to love you."

He settled himself beside her and guided her hands to the buttons on his shirt. Following his lead, she opened each in turn, and then spread the fabric to expose his bare chest. He placed her palms on his skin. She leaned closer so a trail of her kisses could follow the path of her hands exploring him. She started to open the shirt she wore, pulling it free of her riding pants.

"Let me," he said, his voice raw with need. He opened each button and then pushed the garment off her shoulders, exposing her breasts pressed against the lacy fabric of her chemise.

He lay down next to her, and instead of caressing her or kissing her as she had expected, he opened the closing on her pants, pushed them down, and slowly began his sweet torment—stroking her inner thighs—up and around her womanhood, until she squirmed with pleasure.

Seeking to give as good as she got, she thrust her hand down the waistband of his trousers and clutched his manhood. His gasp of surprise and pleasure was all she needed to keep going. She opened the buttons of his fly and pushed at his clothing, wanting it gone. He had bundled her riding pants around her knees.

"Help me," she said as she sat up and pushed her pants to her ankles. He pulled them free, cast them aside, then shed the rest of his clothes. She followed his lead.

They stopped, their breathing like the exhaust of a train as they stared at each other's naked bodies.

"I knew you were beautiful," he said, his voice a rasp of passion, "but, honey, never could I have even begun to imagine…"

She held out her arms to him. "Shut up and love me," she pleaded.

But still, he hesitated. "Be sure this is what you want, Amanda. No regrets when dawn comes."

"No regrets," she whispered. "Not ever. No matter what happens."

Her willingness to go wherever he might lead inspired him. Their first time was an explosion set in motion by the buildup of desire they had fought since the day they'd met. But later, after they had dozed in the haven of each other's arms, he woke her with a kiss. She turned and pressed her body to his. She reached to touch him, but he gently pushed her hand away. "Your turn," he said as he kissed her throat, suckled her breasts, moved lower until he was kissing her most vulnerable and intimate core.

She writhed beneath him, tugging, pleading with her hands and gasps to end the sweet torment. And when he entered her and held himself back, she lifted her hips to meet his, insisting on this new dance she had learned all too well, and he was lost. And afterward, as she lay beside him, curled into the shelter of his body, he heard her whisper, "It's almost dawn—the dawning of the first day of *us*."

Nine

AMANDA SQUINTED INTO THE RISING SUN AND STRETCHED her legs. Overnight her muscles had stiffened. She giggled. Served her right after what she and Seth had done throughout the night. She pushed herself to a sitting position and looked around. Seth was standing on the top of a rise. He was fully dressed and staring out at the landscape.

"Good morning," she said softly.

He took a sip of water from the canteen he held and grinned. "Ah, Sleeping Beauty." He wiped the rim with his bandana and passed it to her. "You should get dressed and get a head start, so there are no questions once you reach town. I'll keep you in sight just to be safe, but come in later."

She took a swallow and made a face. The water tasted like minerals.

He hesitated before crouching close to her. "Look, Amanda, there's a good deal I can't tell you, but what I *can* tell you is that you need to keep the Baxter kid in town. He's asking for trouble riding out the way he does. Talk to his father if you have to, but…"

"His father would beat him badly. I will not be responsible for that boy enduring more abuse."

"Then talk to him, because he's asking to get himself killed if he keeps doing what he's doing."

"Why do you care?"

"He's a kid."

"It's more than that," she argued. "Tell me why you care so much what happens to a boy you barely know."

He let out a breath that showed steam in the chill of the morning air. He stared toward the distant hills, then finally looked back at her. "I've got a younger brother his age, okay? Kids that age think nothing can happen to them."

"Were you that way at their age?"

He gave her a half smile and stood. "Worse," he said as he walked away to lead her horse closer to their camp. "Go wash up. I'll saddle your horse. You've got more than an hour's ride ahead of you. Best get started."

He'd said nothing about their passion of the night before other than that stupid joke about Sleeping Beauty. Did it mean so little to him after all? She splashed cold water from the creek on her face and twisted her hair into a knot that would fit beneath the crown of her hat. When she stood and turned away from the creek, he was watching her.

"What?" she said irritably.

"Do you have any idea how beautiful you are?" he said softly, and she had the oddest feeling that he was unaware he had spoken aloud.

"I'm a mess," she countered as she strode to her horse and mounted. "With any luck the others will be at breakfast, and I can slip by and get changed before they see me."

He had been holding the reins to keep the horse steady. As he handed them to her, he took her hand. "Amanda, there's something I need to finish, but once that's done…"

The last thing she wanted was an empty promise of *someday*. "Yeah, well, you know where to find me," she replied, and pulled her hand free as she kneed the horse's flanks.

She was halfway back to the main trail when she heard him shout, "Talk to the Baxter boy!"

Without turning to look at him, she waved and urged her horse to pick up the pace. The very idea that there could ever be anything more than one night of passion between them was ludicrous. He kept secrets, and on top of that, her family would never accept him—not her mother, and certainly not Jess. After all, she had known what she was getting into—one night was all she had asked for, and now, she'd had that. Best put the whole business behind her, she thought as she drove her mount hard to make up time.

Later that morning, after she had washed and changed and brushed the tangles his fingers had created from her hair, she made her way to the Baxter house and was stunned to find Ezra Baxter waiting for her.

"Good morning, Amanda," he said, dropping all pretense at the formalities usually observed between employer and employee. "How is your mother?"

"She is well, thank you." She felt the need to offer some explanation for not getting back to town until that morning. "In fact, my entire family had gathered, and we were…"

"No need to explain yourself, Amanda. I am pleased you enjoyed the time with them." He cleared his throat. They were still standing at the gate where he had intercepted her before she could reach the back entrance. From the corner of her eye, she was aware of Kitty watching them under the pretense of hanging laundry.

Apparently, Ezra was also aware of his housekeeper's curiosity. "Shall we?" he asked, indicating the front porch.

"Of course."

Once they were seated on two straight-backed chairs made of cypress wood, Amanda folded her hands in her lap and waited for him to explain why he had chosen not to go to the bank at his usual hour. When he did not speak, but instead relaxed into the chair and stared at the main street, she felt something must be amiss. "Has something happened, Mr. Baxter? Are the children…"

"The children are fine, Amanda. I am so pleased with their progress that I gave them the day off."

"I see."

"I thought we might spend the day together, you and I. After all, not to pressure you, my dear, but you have not yet given me your answer."

"My answer?"

"To my proposal of marriage. With you at my side, there would be no need to send the children east." He chuckled. "When I spoke of this to them, they were delighted. It seems they have grown quite fond of you."

Amanda could barely find words. "You...surely you can see that what delights them is the idea they will not need to leave their home. You hardly need me to marry you for that." She stood and reached for her satchel. "I believe we have had a serious misunderstanding, Mr. Baxter."

"Ezra," he said calmly.

"I am Eli and Ellie's tutor, sir—nothing more. As for you and me, we are employer and employee— nothing more. I barely know you, and you most certainly do not know me. Either we speak no more of this idea that you and I might ever..."

"I could ruin you," he said in that same calm, singsong way she'd heard him speak to people on the street. He might as easily be saying, "Have a nice day."

Amanda froze and slowly turned to face him. "Are you threatening me?"

"Do you care at all for the happiness of my children?" he countered.

"Of course I do."

"Then may I suggest that at the moment your reputation is in question all over town—those evening meetings with the pharmacist, bringing him here to my home at midday under the guise of teaching my son some game? At the moment, marrying me rather than James Matthews would be the wiser choice, clearing up any question of your character. In addition, making a home for Eli and Ellie, living here in this house with the freedom—and finances—to do whatever you want in terms of furnishing the rooms, taking your rightful place as one of the community's most respected women..."

It hit her that he had said nothing about Seth. He thought she was romantically involved with Jim Matthews. It explained his sudden urgency to get her answer to his proposal. "I was unaware that my personal life was a factor in my employment, Mr. Baxter. If that is the case…"

His breath came in a rush of exasperation, and his hands, while they remained in his lap, tightened into fists. "Why do you insist on provoking me, Amanda? I should not need to remind you that your future is at best precarious. I am offering you security."

I don't want security. I want romance, adventure, love.

"I appreciate that it may be difficult for you to understand, Mr. Baxter, but times are changing—women, in particular, are changing when it comes to how they view the future and their lives."

The man's face went nearly purple with horror. "Please do not tell me that you have become infatuated with those women who insist on the vote and such."

He had given her the opening she needed. "Could you not marry such a woman, Ezra?" She took care to frame her facial expression in a concerned frown.

"I could not." He was practically blubbering. "Under no circumstances could I ever stand for such foolishness. A woman belongs…"

"In the home?"

"Precisely."

She picked up her satchel. "Then we have nothing further to discuss, Ezra. May I assume you would prefer that I no longer tutor Eli and Ellie?"

She understood by his expression that his first instinct was to terminate her employment, but the children were so close to achieving the goals he had set. Furthermore, if she would not marry him, then he would send them east, after apparently telling them they did not have to go. She almost felt sorry for him and decided to ease his pain.

"May I suggest that since we are nearly at the end of the school semester, I could complete the work with the children? Of course, there would be terms."

"Terms?"

"There would be no more talk of a union between us."

He smirked. "You took care of that with your obvious enchantment with those foolish suffragists."

"And there will be absolutely no discussion of my personal life," she added.

He sighed. "I suppose your politics and those of the druggist are a better match, although why you would turn your back on a house like this, and all the money you could ever hope to have, puzzles me."

What puzzled *her* was where he planned to get all that money, since town gossips repeatedly hinted that the bank was in trouble. "I have one final condition."

He scowled at her the way he had before he got it into his head that they might wed. "Do not push your luck with me, young lady."

"I wish to be paid what I am owed to date, and going forward I wish to be paid—in full—weekly."

He stood and faced her. His anger was visible in his flushed cheeks, his bulging eyes, and the way his breath wheezed through his flared nostrils like a bull preparing to charge. She had the sudden image of Eli's black eye and the bruise on Ellie's arm. She had never known his wife, but a vision of a woman enduring his abuse flashed through her mind. Every bone in her body pleaded to take a step back.

Instead, she straightened to her full height, eye to eye, and refused to blink or flinch. "Do we have an agreement, Mr. Baxter?" She thrust out her hand, and to her shock, he took it, pumped it once, and then brushed past her on his way down the street to the bank.

She had won. She had stood her ground, kept her wits about her, and won.

The feeling was incredible, and she wanted to share her triumph with someone.

Not just someone, she thought. *Seth*.

❧

The first person Seth saw as he rode into town was the banker. Ezra Baxter was leaving the house, slamming his derby onto his head. He hurried down the street, oblivious to traffic as he crossed the rutted road. He looked upset, but then Seth tried to recall if he had ever encountered Ezra Baxter when he didn't look like he could chew nails. Word had it that his bank was on the verge of failure. This was gossip, and most people paid little attention, but Seth had his sources.

As he neared the boardinghouse, he spotted Amanda, standing at the adobe entrance to the Baxter house. She waved, and that surprised him, since they really hadn't parted on the best of terms.

The woman constantly surprised and confused him. He was a man who prided himself on his ability to read beneath the surface and get to the heart of what a person thought or felt. With Amanda he was never quite sure. Of course, that was part of the attraction—that, and the fact that she was impossibly beautiful, and making love to her had been like nothing he had ever experienced.

He tipped two fingers to his hat and rode to the boardinghouse. He was aware of her watching him, but when he made no move to ride in her direction, she returned to the Baxter house and went inside. Knowing he should be relieved, all he really felt was disappointed.

"Grow up, Grover," he grumbled as he tied his horse to a hitching post and climbed the steps to the front door. He made it past the parlor and up the stairs without running into anyone. When he reached his room and opened the door, the first thing he saw was another note.

Bank. Rooftop. Saturday night. Nine o'clock.

Okay, this was either a setup or a way to distract him from whatever was really going down. The confusing thing was that the timing and place in no way matched with when the garrison's payroll wagon would be headed for the fort, or the schedule of the train. It had nothing to do with the abandoned Frost ranch and the activity he'd observed there. He really needed to talk to the Baxter kid and find out what he knew.

He glanced out the window that overlooked the backyard of the banker's home. The housekeeper was sweeping the tiled steps that led into the kitchen. There was no sign of Amanda or the children. He saw movement behind the row of three windows framed in painted wood toward the front of the house. A glimmer of white reminded him of the blouse Amanda often wore. She was teaching. The windows were the library.

After changing to a clean shirt and tucking it in, he ran down the stairs and out the door. Circling around to the back of the house, he crossed into the Baxter yard and knocked lightly at the kitchen door, hoping no one would be there. He was in luck.

He entered the kitchen, where he spotted the boy's baseball and glove and picked them up. As he passed the corridor that led to the bedrooms, he could hear the housekeeper moving around down there. When he reached the library, the doors were closed, but he could hear Amanda's voice.

He stopped outside the door to listen.

"I understand that your father is so pleased by the progress you have both made that he's given us the day off. I have to agree that the research you've done on your studies of the geology of the area has been exceptional, Eli. Of course, you have a way to go to equal your sister when it comes to your writing skills. As for you, Ellie, that story you wrote for Friday's assignment was poignant and lovely. You've both done excellent work."

Seth admired the way she complimented the kid without leaving out the sister's accomplishments as well. He heard a boy's voice shifting between the registers of adolescence and adult.

"Do we get time outside then, Miss Porterfield?"

"You do indeed. However, I'm afraid Mr. Matthews

will not be able to join us today. He sent word that he has no one to mind the store."

Seth slid the door open just wide enough for him to sidle through. He tossed the ball in the air and caught it. "Maybe I could be of help?"

Amanda's blush fueled his desire—his desire to impress her. Eli watched him with mixed emotions. He really wanted to play ball. On the other hand, he clearly recognized Seth, and the expression in his eyes was one of wariness.

"You're that man," the girl blurted. "Father said we should stay away from you. He would be upset to find you here. He doesn't like you, mister."

"I'm sorry to hear that. Maybe if he got to know me…"

"What are you doing here?" Amanda asked in a low voice meant only for his ears.

He tossed the ball again, caught it, and then lobbed it to her. In spite of herself, the Baxter girl giggled.

"Are you any good?" The boy seemed to have found his nerve. He had stretched himself to his full height, which came close to equaling Seth's.

"Why don't we find out, Eli?" Seth handed him the glove and headed for the door. When the three remained as still as statues, he grinned. "Well? You coming or not?"

Outside, he took the ball from Amanda and tossed it to Eli. "Show me what you've got," he said as he crouched into a catcher's position.

"You'd better take the glove," Eli said.

"Just throw your best pitch." Seth held his hands to receive the ball. Eli wound up and then threw a blistering fastball that Seth dropped as soon as it struck his hand. "Pretty good."

"Pretty good?" Eli held out the glove again. "You want this now, or do you want me to burn you again?"

Seth stood and met the boy halfway to get the glove. "Sure. Thanks."

While Amanda and the girl sat on a banco outside the kitchen door, Eli threw pitches to Seth, who sometimes gave him a pointer on making it more effective, and sometimes received the pitch with a grin before lobbing it back.

After about half an hour, the housekeeper emerged with a tray loaded with glasses and a pitcher of lemonade. "Come have something cold to drink," Amanda called.

Seth walked to the makeshift pitcher's mound on the pretense of handing Eli his glove and ball. "We need to talk," he said softly. "I need to know what you mean by that latest note you left me." It was a shot in the dark, but he saw by the way the boy's eyes widened in surprise that he'd guessed right. "You're playing a dangerous game, kid. Let me help you."

"You can't," Eli said. "Nobody can." And with that, he stalked off toward the house. Without breaking stride, he said something to Amanda and his sister as he passed them and entered the back door.

"What happened between the two of you?" Amanda demanded after she'd sent Ellie back into the kitchen for napkins.

"Leave it be, Amanda." Seth pasted on a grin as Ellie emerged from the shadows of the house and placed a stack of cloth napkins on the table next to the plate of cookies the housekeeper had left.

"Mrs. Caldwell said Eli was upstairs lying down—too much sun. She was fixing him some ice water."

Amanda filled and distributed glasses of lemonade. "I expect we could all use something cold to drink."

Seth drained his glass in one action. "Well, ladies, it's been fun, but I have work to do. Ellie, be sure and tell your brother I hope he gets to feeling better. I look forward to seeing him again soon." He tipped his fingers to his hat. "Miss Porterfield," he said by way of parting.

The fact that she wanted to question him further was written all over her face, but until he'd had time to sort things out with Eli, he had no answers to give.

⁓

Amanda didn't have much time to ponder what might have transpired between Eli and Seth. After she sent Ellie to her room to get her bonnet and gloves with a promise of visiting some of the local shops that afternoon, Kitty cornered her.

"What's going on?"

"I don't know—"

"Don't play dumb, Amanda. You and the mister had a serious talk this morning, and before that he told me to prepare for a large party he wants to host on Saturday—he's invited a bunch of important people, from the district attorney to Judge Ellis himself. Their wives as well. That man hasn't hosted so much as a Sunday dinner since his wife died, and when I suggested such a gathering could get expensive, he said—and I quote—'Spare no expense.' Now you tell me, is that not strange?"

"Very strange." Amanda's first thought was that Ezra had been so confident she would accept his proposal that he had gotten the cart well before the horse. No wonder he had been so upset. "He may change his mind."

"Not likely. He hired the Tucker boy to hand-deliver invitations yesterday. So far, there have been no regrets. Everybody's coming—including James Matthews and his daughter. You coulda knocked me over with a feather when I heard that one. If there's one person Mr. Baxter has butted heads with in this town, that would be Jim Matthews. He can't stand the man, especially the way he built that business of his even after Mr. Baxter turned him down for a loan."

Amanda's head was spinning. This was a disaster in the making, and she felt compelled to put a stop to it. "Kitty, would you tell Ellie to meet me at the millinery in half an hour? I forgot an appointment I need to keep." She didn't really wait for the house-keeper to agree, but ran across the yard and into the boardinghouse instead.

From her room she grabbed her satchel and then hurried to the bank. Ezra's secretary, Mr. Fitzhugh, looked up in surprise at her entrance.

"I'm afraid Mr. Baxter has requested no appoint-ments today, Miss Porterfield. Is there some way I might be of service?"

"Oh, Mr. Fitzhugh, this is about the children, and I'm quite sure Mr. Baxter will want to see me." Before the little man could protest—or indeed, move from behind his desk—she had swept past him, and opened, then immediately shut, Ezra's office door.

Ezra stood and glared at her. "This is not the time—"

"Kitty has told me about the party," she interrupted. "Forgive me for presuming that you planned that as an event to announce our…"

She saw by the way he slumped into his chair that not only had she guessed right, but also that he had completely forgotten about the party.

"I can't cancel," he mumbled. "It will ruin everything."

"What if I have a plan so the party can go forward, and you will not lose face?"

He straightened and scowled. "I'm listening."

"Have the party be a celebration of the children— the work they have accomplished."

The scowl changed to a frown of concentration, but he was definitely listening.

"Over the next couple of days, I could have Eli and Ellie prepare a little program. Ellie could read one of her stories or poems, and Eli could explain the geology project he's been working on. Think how impressed everyone would be that you were able to bring your children through their grief for their mother to become the model students they were when she was alive."

"And you would attend as well?"

"Of course. I am their teacher." She placed her satchel on a chair and removed some papers. "Just look at what your daughter has written, Mr. Baxter."

He waved the papers away as he stood and paced from one side of the room to the other. "It might work," he said, more to himself than to her. "And with the children providing the evening's program, I could cancel the musicians I hired." He paused and pivoted to fix his gaze on her. "There can be no mistakes," he told her. "I'll need a program that entertains our guests for at least half an hour."

"I'm certain that the twins and I can easily—"

"I suppose you expect extra wages for this."

She was insulted that he thought for one minute money might be her motive. She was saving the man from embarrassment, after all. "I am delighted to have Eli and Ellie receive the praise and credit they deserve. This party is the perfect opportunity. And that is remuneration enough." She glanced at the wall clock above his office door. "And now, if you will excuse me, I promised Ellie I would meet her at the milliner's."

"Just a minute more, Amanda." To her astonishment, Ezra Baxter opened a small safe and removed an envelope. "Buy Ellie something she can wear to the party, and get a new shirt and a vest for Eli as well." He pressed the envelope into her hands. "If you have anything left, buy something for yourself—perhaps something for your lovely hair."

Amanda glanced at the envelope so stuffed with money it would not close properly. "Thank you, but I cannot accept that. If there is anything left, I can give it to Mrs. Caldwell to pay the expenses for the party."

"Do as you like," he said gruffly, and turned his back to her.

"We won't disappoint you, sir—the children and I," she assured him as she gathered her things and opened the door. "I'll keep you informed on the progress."

Outside the bank she realized she was still clutching the money. She decided to return to the boardinghouse before meeting Ellie. Tomorrow she would take the twins shopping. The one thing—perhaps the *only* thing—she felt sure of was that she was not about to allow Ezra Baxter to use his money to buy her something pretty for her hair.

❧

The party Ezra Baxter was hosting was the talk of the town. Certainly, the residents of the boardinghouse seemed incapable of discussing anything else, whether or not they had received an invitation, although only Ollie had been left off the list. To no one's surprise, Seth was also not invited, and that would work to his advantage. The party was the same evening he was supposed to get to the roof of the bank for the mysterious meeting.

Eli Baxter continued to deny that he had written the note, although he did finally admit to delivering it. Seth had confronted him one night when the boy made one of his midnight rides to the abandoned ranch. "You need to stop doing this, kid. You have no idea what these men are capable of, if they have reason to believe you've crossed them."

"So don't put me in that position by talking to me and coming to the house to play baseball, mister. I know what I'm doing."

"Let me help you. Tell me what's going on. Do you know where the Stock boys and their gang are hiding?"

The kid's reaction had told Seth he'd guessed right. It was dark, but there was no denying the way Eli tensed at the mention of the gang. "I gotta go." He turned his horse away from Seth, but Seth reached out and took hold of the bridle.

"The old prospector got shot in broad daylight. He died. Do you think they would hesitate for a second to do the same to you?"

"And what's it to *you*? Everybody in town thinks you're up to no good. How do I know you're not in cahoots with the gang, spying on me? I heard Sheriff Richter tell Judge Ellis he was pretty sure you were on the wrong side of the law."

Seth took this as good news. If people with power thought he was an outlaw, then his cover was protected. If anybody thought he was working the other side of the fence with a plan to prevent a robbery, he might as well pack up and leave Tucson. "Maybe I am. Maybe that's why your mysterious note sender told me to meet him there—maybe we're in cahoots."

"I gotta go," Eli said again, and this time Seth released his hold on the horse.

"Stay away from this, kid."

Eli snorted with derision. "Who's gonna stop me?" He rode off.

Seth watched him go. Suddenly, Sam wasn't his only concern. Eli Baxter was in this thing up to his neck.

Seth fingered the note in his pocket. Maybe he was being lured to the meeting. They were on to him and intended to eliminate him. The party the banker was throwing would be the perfect cover—the saloons would be as rowdy as ever, and in addition, most decent citizens would be at the Baxter house. In effect, the town would be deserted.

Later that evening, he waited until everyone had

left the boardinghouse, Ollie for his shift at the Blue Parrot and all the women for the Baxter house. Admittedly, he had lingered near the window, waiting to see Amanda. She wore a modest, pale-blue gown, a dress appropriate for a teacher. From talk at the boardinghouse, he knew the party was a celebration of the progress the Baxter twins had made in their studies. The others, however—Mrs. Rosewood, Miss Jensen, and their landlady—had apparently decided to take full advantage of a social outing. They were dressed in finery suitable for a ball.

He watched the four women make their way along the path from the boardinghouse to the Baxters' front gate. Other guests arrived by carriage. Ezra Baxter and his children were at the gate to greet them all. Seth cringed when he saw Baxter place a proprietary hand on Amanda's waist as he introduced her to Judge Ellis, and then was clearly taken aback when Ellis apparently let the banker know he and Amanda had already met.

Seth waited for the last guest to arrive and for the Baxter family to enter the house and close the door before making his move. His plan was to be on that roof well ahead of whomever he was supposedly meeting. He would lie in wait for his attacker—or attackers.

Making certain he was not followed, he made his way down the alley, past the drugstore and Miss Jensen's millinery shop. He checked all side lanes and doorways—anywhere an attacker might hide—and saw no one. At one end of the street, he could hear the honky-tonk piano from the Blue Parrot. At the opposite end, he was aware that the Baxter party had spilled into the courtyard because the weather was so fine. He glanced up. The sky was full of stars and a sliver of a moon. With any luck, tonight would mark the completion of his final assignment for Wells Fargo. He would foil the Stock brothers and be free at last to begin a proper courtship of Miss Amanda Porterfield.

When he reached the bank, it occurred to him that with the place closed, he had no way of reaching the roof. Why had his mysterious confidant designated *this* as their meeting place? That was a sure sign something wasn't right, but he didn't have a choice. He hesitated, then ducked between the bank and the mercantile next door. As he headed for the street, he noticed a side door to the bank ajar—a door that should have been closed tight and locked.

Because he was early, he decided to take a chance and step inside, where he found himself at the foot of a steep, narrow stairway. It had to go to the roof. He closed the door that led to the street, but did not secure it. Whoever was coming would find it unlocked as expected, and Seth would hear the door open and shut again. He would be ready.

He started up the steps, keeping close to the wall, his hand on his gun. The steps were iron, and it was hard to keep from making a sound as his leather bootheels connected with metal. The door at the top of the stairway had been blocked open, allowing light from the street and surrounding buildings to filter into the confines of the dark corridor. He listened for footsteps and watched for shadows, but other than distant music from the saloon, all was still and silent.

He waited for several seconds once he reached the top step before slipping over the threshold and onto the flat surface of the roof. His senses were on high alert, and he immediately picked up the scent of sweat and—of all things—oranges. Somebody had gotten there ahead of him, and when he heard the slurp of somebody eating the orange, he knew he had the advantage.

Turning toward the direction of the scent, he stepped onto the roof, gun drawn. He heard a scrambling, like a rat scuttling across a floor, and saw a shadowy figure struggle to his feet. "Jeezel Pete, Seth, you're early. Put that thing away."

It was a voice he knew, but had almost given up ever hearing again. "Sam?"

His mind raced with a myriad of thoughts—he had found his brother and had the urge to wrap his arms around him and hold him tight. It would embarrass them both, but the feeling was still there.

He took a step forward, lowering his pistol as he did, but stopping short of returning the weapon to its holster. "What going on, Sam?"

"They're gonna rob the bank tonight." Apparently oblivious to his older brother's wariness, Sam stepped closer and offered Seth a section of an orange. The sweet, tangy smell hung in the air between them, but Seth waved him away.

"Talk to me, Sam."

"I've been on the inside now for the last several weeks."

"You sent the notes?"

"Yeah, the kid was like a regular carrier pigeon. I figured, why not get a couple of messages to you?"

"Eli?"

Sam shrugged. "Don't know his given name, just that he's the banker's kid."

"Where did the prospector fit into all this?"

"He was the one supposed to be getting information about what was going on at the fort and the movement of the payroll. But then the brothers got suspicious about him after somebody saw him talking to that marshal there in Whitman Falls. They thought he was setting them up, so Rudy Stock—he's a hothead if ever one walked the earth—just took off to find him. That's when they changed the plan from robbing the payroll for the fort to robbing the bank. Orson Stock and the banker grew up together, so he went into town one day and had a little talk with his old friend. Pointed out to Baxter that his bank was up to its eyeballs in trouble. I guess he's been borrowing from Peter to pay Paul, as Ma would say. Anyway, Orson told him that as an old friend, he'd be willing to help him out."

"Okay, this is making no sense," Seth said as he put away his gun. "If the bank's in trouble, then what makes it worth robbing?"

Sam sighed and stuffed a quarter of the orange between his lips, sucking the juice free. He spit out the seeds. "It's complicated, but they stand to make a huge haul, if they pull it off. Yesterday, the sheriff persuaded the captain at the fort that the payroll wagon was going to be hit, but if he would let him store the actual money in the bank and replace it with cut up paper and rocks, they could catch the gang and not lose the money."

"You're telling me that the money meant for the fort is in this bank?"

Sam grinned. "On its way, I reckon. The colonel agreed to send the money here tonight, so Rudy and Orson figured while they wait for the payload to show up, they might as well help themselves to what's already in the bank. Pretty brilliant, right?"

"And you're saying the sheriff had a part in this?"

"*Has* a part. The sheriff and the banker—they were promised their cut, of course."

"And the messages Eli has been carrying were instructions for his father?"

"Nope. For the sheriff. The kid didn't know nothing about his pa—he thinks he's *saving* his pa. The sheriff needed a courier. The kid's part was to deliver the messages to that lady at the boardinghouse, so she could get word to the sheriff. Not the notes I sent you, of course. I sort of snuck those in there when I thought it was safe and paid him extra to slip them under your door."

"What woman?"

"I don't know. What I do know is that she's related to Orson and Rudy somehow."

Seth thought of the women in the house—the widow lady? Could be an aunt or even the Stock boys' mother. Same with his landlady. But both were so proper that he had a hard time imagining either being part of something so sordid. Of course, the milliner could be a sister or girlfriend, but then why not deliver the messages to the shop? That left Amanda.

Sam was still talking. "I knew we had to meet up tonight if we were gonna have any chance of stopping this. The Stock boys have got this thing planned out down to the minute. They're gonna hit while the banker's party is going on and then ride hard all night for the border. You ask me, they've got no intention of paying anything to the banker or the sheriff." He polished off the rest of his orange and licked his fingers.

He was so damned young, Seth thought. How on earth had he gotten himself mixed up in something like this? "What's your role?"

"Horses. I hold 'em and have 'em ready to run soon as the job's done."

"You understand that if you don't get yourself killed tonight, Ma is gonna do the job herself?"

Sam chuckled. "Her and Pa think I'm still just a kid, but it's time, Seth. I want my chance to do what you're doing. Chicago is boring, but out here there's adventure around every bend. And if I do this right, then Wells Fargo will take notice. We could work together."

Seth wondered if he had ever been quite so naive. "Here's the way we're gonna play this, little brother. You are going to leave here now and head for the fort. Hopefully, you'll intercept the payroll detail on the way and can warn the captain of the plan and let him take matters from there. You'll stay put until I come to get you. Understood?"

But even as he laid out the instructions, he knew it was already too late—he heard movement at the entrance to the alley two blocks away. Before Sam could protest, Seth held up his hand for quiet and crept to the edge of the roof to see what was going on below. He saw half a dozen riders, their horses muzzled.

"Are they expecting you to be here?" he whispered.

"Yeah. It was my job to slip into the bank and hide until after closing, so I could open the side door, and then take hold of the horses while they move the money. They're early though." He sounded surprised and confused—and very, very young.

"Okay, give me your hat and jacket." Seth shrugged out of his own garments and handed them to his brother. "I'll go do your part. As soon as they are inside the bank, you head for the fort."

"They'll have two acting as lookouts," Sam protested.

That explained the large number of men. Two outside to keep watch, while four pulled off the heist. *Think, Grover!*

He wished Amanda's brother were around, or that he could at least count on the district sheriff, but Richter was part of this whole business. It was Sam and him against six members of the gang *and* probably the sheriff.

"Hey, Seth, maybe I can jump from here to that roof next door and then shimmy to the ground and then…"

Seth's instinct was to immediately reject the idea. But then he looked at the roof of the mercantile. It was flat and slightly lower than the bank's roof. The gap between the buildings was maybe six feet.

"I'll do it," he said as he handed Sam back his hat and jacket. "You follow the original plan they laid out for you, but when I show up, you get the hell out of there, do you understand me? No heroics. Just grab a horse, mount up, and ride hard for the fort."

"But the payload detail must be getting close to town already."

"Then you'll warn them off. I'll handle things here."

The movement below had stopped. He heard men arguing in low voices. They had reached the bank.

"Now go on, and do whatever you were told about the door." He shoved Sam toward the stairway and watched him hurry down. He waited until he heard voices below.

"Where were you, kid?" a rough-talking man demanded in a raspy whisper.

"Right here, Rudy—just like you told me."

"Come on," another man said. "We don't got all night."

Seth peered over the edge of the roof and saw Sam emerge into the alley and take hold of the horses. To his credit, he resisted the urge to glance up. Two men spread out to watch from either end of the alley, while the other four entered the bank carrying saddlebags.

Seth hurried to the far side of the roof, took a running start, and jumped.

Ten

AMANDA WAS TIRED, ANNOYED, AND DESPERATELY IN
need of an escape from Ezra Baxter's hand.

It appeared that the banker had packed as many
people as possible into the over-furnished and already
crowded rooms of his home. The dining room table
was laden with food, while in the parlor several
guests were relegated to standing or perching on chair
arms and ottomans to enjoy the refreshments. In the
library—where Ezra insisted that Amanda stand in a
receiving line with him and the children—there were
so many people talking at once she could not hear
herself think.

On top of that, she had now been standing for
over an hour, and Ezra kept touching her—his hand
at her waist or on her arm. Once he had even dared
to touch her cheek on the pretense of brushing away
an errant curl. She had no doubt that it was his intention to send a message of ownership to anyone who
took note of these intimacies. And she was aware that
tongues were wagging.

Furthermore, the windows and doors were closed,

and there was a fire blazing in the corner fireplace on a night when the air outside might be cool, but would certainly be a welcome relief for those crammed into the small space. Amanda was quite certain that if she didn't get some air soon, she was going to pass out.

"Father, please," Ellie pleaded when there was finally a momentary break in the throngs of guests around them, "can we have something to eat?"

"Yes, Father," Eli added. "It seems like hours."

Amanda saw Ezra hesitate. He had been enjoying his position as host and his children's as the center of attention. She decided this might be her only opportunity. "I believe if Eli and Ellie could get some refreshments and circulate among the guests, that would make an even deeper impression, Ezra." She had deliberately elected to call him by his given name, knowing it would soften him.

"Yes, yes," he said, waving the children toward the dining room. "Feed yourselves, but do not go far. I want you here for the special announcement I have planned."

The twins glanced at each other, their curiosity evident. But in the end, their appetites won out, and they headed for the dining room. When Amanda started to follow them, Ezra caught her hand. "I don't believe I gave you permission to leave your post, Amanda."

And when Judge Ellis and his wife approached, and the judge asked how Amanda was doing with the jail improvements work, she was aware that Ezra did not release her hand. The sweat from his palm as he gripped her fingers sickened her. It occurred to her that based on their behavior, Eli and Ellie were unaware she had refused his proposal, and she feared his "special announcement" was that they were to wed. He would bank on her not wishing to cause a scene in such a gathering.

She forced a smile as she focused her attention on the judge. "We are making some progress at the jail, sir," she told him, and then saw her path of escape. "As a matter of fact, Mr. Matthews's daughter has come up with some quite innovative ideas. I'm sure she would love to have your opinion, sir. Allow me to introduce you."

She wrenched her hand free of Ezra's and led the judge and his wife across the room to where Jim and Ginny were talking to Miss Dooley. Behind her she saw three local businessmen surround Ezra, and they did not look pleased.

This was her chance. As soon as the Matthews and the judge were engaged in conversation, she excused herself and slipped down the hall to the kitchen and out the back door.

Outside she turned her face to the sky and closed her eyes as she allowed the fresh air to wash over her, as if it were a welcome rain shower on a hot summer day. The streets were deserted as she hurried to put some distance between herself and the house ablaze with light, buzzing with the muted conversations of Ezra's guests. In the distance, she could barely hear the music from the saloons at the far end of town.

The sky was clear, the air cool on her face. She wondered what might happen if she simply returned to the boardinghouse, changed clothes, and went for a long walk. Of course, that would be the final straw for Ezra. She would be fired, but so what? He was going to send the children away soon, and she would no longer be their teacher.

Behind her she heard the front door of the Baxter house open and close. She moved into the shadows, not wanting to be seen or questioned. She was sure Ezra had come to find her, and she was about to fake a spell of sickness, when she realized the person coming her way was not Ezra. It was Eli, and so intent was he on whatever his mission might be that he had walked right past her without realizing she was there. He had also changed from his Sunday best to the rougher clothes he wore for riding. He headed down the main street past the plaza and then ducked into an alley.

Amanda gathered her skirt in one hand and followed him.

⌒

Seth limped across the roof of the mercantile, nursing a sprained ankle he'd suffered in the jump. He was no good to Sam if he was injured, so he gritted his teeth and put the pain out of his mind.

What he needed now was to get to the Baxter house and raise the alarm. Ezra Baxter might be up to his eyeballs in this robbery, but among his guests would be Judge Ellis and the district attorney, and any number of locals who would do whatever it took to foil a robbery that could include their life savings. He had no doubt that the Stock brothers would see the opportunity to include whatever money was already in the bank, in addition to the payroll, in their take.

He shimmied down a ladder the store owner used to display blankets and other handwoven items from the local pueblos, dropped to the ground, and started running, bum ankle and all. But he stopped dead in the middle of the deserted street when he saw what he was pretty sure he couldn't possibly be seeing—a flash of blue gown and a certain strawberry blond hurrying down the alley toward the back of the bank.

Amanda?

He thought about how the contact for the gang's messages to Baxter and the sheriff was "some woman in the boardinghouse."

He felt sick and betrayed and furious. There had been a time when he'd given his heart to another woman, been ready to give up everything for her, only to learn that the whole time she'd been part of the gang he'd been chasing. That had been the one and only time Seth had failed in his job. That woman and, as it turned out, her brother had robbed a train and gotten clean away, and it had all been Seth's fault. The Stock boys were not part of Amanda's family, so what was the connection?

He thought about her decision to move to Tucson about the same time he had learned that Tucson might be the site of the crime. He thought about the way she had been standing there that night at the edge of town. He thought of how often she had demonstrated a passion for adventure. Maybe somewhere along the way—long before he'd met her—she'd met up with one of the Stock boys, and she'd seen in them the exciting life she clearly craved. He thought about the questions she'd asked about him and his work. And he battled the idea that either Rudy or Orson could be her lover. Doubt and distrust outweighed everything in his mind, even as his heart tried to tell him this was different. *She was different.*

The fact that she had not stopped to change out of her party dress told him she was acting on impulse. But it could still mean that because she knew this was the night, she had decided to go now, rather than wait to meet up with her lover later. He hesitated, uncertain whether he should see what she would do, or raise the alarm as he'd intended.

In the end, he followed Amanda. He needed to know for sure—to see for himself. He had fallen in love with her, and on this night his heart trumped his mind and common sense.

By the time he reached the entrance to the alley, she was nowhere to be seen. But the lookout outlaw had hold of Eli Baxter, wrestling him down the alley toward the rear entrance to the bank. The kid struggled and shouted something unintelligible until the outlaw slugged him hard, and he crumpled to the ground. The outlaw left him lying there and ran to the far end of the alley where a wagon pulled up to the entrance to the bank.

Seth was about to go to the kid when he saw Amanda step out of the doorway to the pharmacy and hurry to the boy's aid. Acting purely on instinct—and his hope that no way could she be part of this—he joined her.

"Seth," she whispered. "Eli's hurt and…"

The kid moaned, and his eyes opened in slits as he focused on her. "Stop them," he pleaded. "They're gonna ruin my father." He tried to sit up, but failed.

Seth pulled Eli to his feet. "Take him home, Amanda. Go back to the party, and raise the alarm."

To his relief, she didn't argue. Instead, she wrapped her arm around Eli's waist and led him away. Relieved that his instincts about her innocence were right after all, and satisfied that for once she would do as he asked, Seth turned his attention to the far end of the alley. The two outlaws who had been the lookouts were holding the soldiers accompanying the payload at gunpoint while the rest of the gang hurried to the back of the wagon to unload the money, placing bills and bags filled with coins in saddlebags. He didn't see Sam, but there was a lot of activity, and maybe...

He heard a click and felt the barrel of a gun press hard into his back.

"Hello, detective," a woman's voice whispered. "Let's take a walk."

"Sure. Where do you want to go?" He thought he knew the voice but couldn't place it.

The gun poked his back. The woman carrying it remained silent.

⁓

Eli wiped blood from his lip, which had puffed up to double its size. He stumbled along until he finally found his footing, and Amanda could release the hold she had on his waist.

"Are you gonna tell my father?" he asked.

Amanda could not believe this was his focus. "Eli, those people back there. Who are they?"

"Outlaws. I guess they mean to rob the bank."

"You guess?"

"Okay, I know. I've been working for them."

Amanda's head was spinning. "Start at the beginning.

Does this have something to do with those rides you took at night?"

"Yeah." His tone announced he was clearly surprised that she knew of those outings. "Did the Grover fella tell you that?"

"No one had to tell me, Eli. I saw you." They were nearly at the entrance to the house. Inside, the party was still going on. "Why were you helping the outlaws?" She had a sudden memory of Eli's black eye. "Was your father forcing…"

"My father knows nothing about me," Eli muttered. "He especially doesn't know I was trying to save him. Of course, now he will, and that I failed—again."

The door opened, and Ezra stood there for a moment, speechless, as he looked at his son. "You left the party and got into a fight?" He made a move toward the boy that was more threatening than concerned.

"We don't have time for this," Amanda said, stepping between father and son. "Eli, go around to the kitchen and let Mrs. Caldwell treat your lip. Then go to your room and stay there."

Eli limped away. Ezra started to stop him, but Amanda placed both hands on his chest. "Your son was acting on your behalf," she told him, "so leave him be."

Ezra turned his attention back to her. "What are you talking about?"

"Outlaws are in the process of robbing the bank. Eli somehow knew about the plan and went to stop them."

"And they hit him?" Ezra was incensed.

"Did you not hear what I said? A gang of outlaws is now robbing the bank." She had never met a man who seemed to have such tangled priorities. "We need

to raise the alarm." For a long moment, Ezra stared at
her. It was as if he were trying to make sense of her
words. "Ezra? We have to…"

"Yes, of course. Leave it to me. You, my dear, have
placed yourself in danger. You must immediately go
back to the boardinghouse and wait for me there."

"No, I…"

"Do as I say, Amanda."

She could stand there and argue, or she could let
him raise the alarm and stop the robbery. "All right,
I'm going, but you should know that Seth Grover is
already there, and he is not one of the outlaws."

To her shock, Ezra smiled. "Then why is he
there?" It was clearly a rhetorical question because he
turned and entered the house, apparently satisfied that
Amanda would follow his instructions to wait for him
at Miss Dooley's.

And she did walk back to the boardinghouse, where
she stood on the porch, expecting to see a throng of male
guests leaving the party and heading toward the bank.
When they didn't, she returned to the Baxter house, and
as she passed a front window on her way to the entrance,
she saw Ezra in conversation with the judge, but the
two men were laughing. Ezra wasn't warning anyone.
Was he in on this, and what of the judge?

There was no time to figure out who was involved.
If she ran inside and shouted the bank was being
robbed, would Ezra pretend it was all a hoax? There
had to be a reason he hadn't done as he'd promised,
but instead returned to the party as if nothing were
amiss. It was up to her to do something.

Trying not to trip over her gown, she ran down

the street, intent on the saloons where there were men gathered as well—men who might actually do something to stop this madness. But as she passed the plaza, she saw the bell tower used to raise the alarm in the event of fire, built by Miss Dooley's father because of his fear that his Victorian frame house would be far more vulnerable to fire than its adobe neighbors.

She climbed the rungs of the ladder, reached for the rope, and pulled it with all her strength.

❧

The clang of the fire bell distracted the woman with the gun enough that Seth was able to spin around, pin her arms to her sides, and make her drop the weapon. He kicked it away and then grasped the woman's jaw.

Mild-mannered Mrs. Rosewood glared back at him with a fury and hatred he could not have imagined she possessed. "Who are you really?" he demanded.

"None of your business." She practically spat the words. "Now, let me go."

Her demand was ridiculous given the circumstances. "Or what?"

"Or I'll blow your damn head off," a gruff male voice replied.

Seth raised his hands, releasing Mrs. Rosewood, and slowly turned to face his latest enemy. "Rudy Stock," he drawled. "It's been a long time."

The outlaw ignored him. "You okay, Ma?"

"You let me worry about that. Didn't you hear the fire bell? Before we know it, this town is gonna be crawling with folks. How the hell do you think we're gonna make it out of here?"

Rudy hesitated.

"She's got a point, Rudy," Seth said. "Those saddle-bags filled with loot are heavy, and they'll slow you down." He glanced down the alley toward the bank, hoping to see Sam, hoping to signal him to get going.

"Move," Rudy instructed as he positioned his gun at the base of Seth's neck.

Mrs. Rosewood—or whatever her real name was—led the way. "Where's Orson?" she demanded when they were within ten feet of the others.

"Right here, Ma." The other Stock brother emerged from the shadow of the bank's side door, one arm wrapped tight around Sam's throat. "Got ourselves a traitor here. What do you think I should do with him?"

"Oh, for Pete's sake, Orson, shoot the boy or wring his fool neck, whichever is quicker. We need to move." She took the reins of a horse and, with an agility that Seth would not have believed, hoisted herself into the saddle, pulling the skirt of her gown high over her knees to give her the access she needed. "And do the same with this one," she added, pointing to Seth.

"One question," Seth said. "Back there, you called me 'detective,' and I want to know how you knew. Your sons have always thought I was an outlaw—at least a gambler. One of their kind."

She relaxed in the saddle, the reins still wrapped around the horn. "Your friend Miss Lillian has—"

"I don't believe you."

"Let me finish. I was about to say she has this bartender, Pete? Well, Pete Townsend is my uncle—he works with us. He figured it all out."

"Pete wouldn't betray Lilly." Seth took a step closer.

"Oh, but he would," she replied, and laughed. "Everybody has a price, Mr. Grover." She turned her attention to her eldest son. "Are we done here?"

"Just have to clean up these last details, ma'am." Orson wrestled Sam back into the bank, and Rudy shoved Seth to follow.

Once Seth and Sam had been pushed against the wall, Rudy pressed his gun to Sam's temple. "How about you watch me shoot little brother here, Grover?"

Seth could see that Sam was trembling with fear, but there was little he could do about that. "How about you shut your filthy mouth, and listen to me— the both of you?"

"Okay," Orson said, "we're listening. I'd sure get a kick outta hearing you beg, but make it quick."

"You're being double-crossed," Seth said, even as he racked his brain for some plausible story to back up that statement. He gained time when both brothers burst into laughter.

"You don't say," Orson managed finally. "I think you've got things backward, Grover. We're pulling the double-cross here. The banker thinks he's gonna be all right, but he's gonna find out different."

"Then how did I know where and when to be here tonight? And ask yourself if I would be so stupid as to try to take on half a dozen of you without backup." He paused and pretended to listen intently. "It's gotten mighty quiet out there where your ma is waiting."

Both Stock brothers turned toward the door that led to the alley. That was Seth's chance. "Go to the roof," he ordered Sam as he rushed at both outlaws, pushing them into each other and the door, praying Rudy would drop his gun. He heard the clatter at the same time one brother threw his elbow into Seth's face, and he heard a bone cracking.

Oblivious to the pain and the taste of blood that told him he'd been cut or his nose had been broken, he fought on as the two outlaws found their footing and fought back. He was aware of the sound of Sam's boots on the metal stairs and nearby voices in the alley, shouting as horses whinnied and snorted. He hoped Sam had made the leap to the mercantile and managed to get to a horse, and was now racing for the fort. Knowing he couldn't beat both men, he tried edging his way to the stairs with the intent of following Sam, but Rudy's gun was still on the floor.

He had backed his way up three steps when Orson came for him, and he saw Rudy pick up the gun. Gripping the iron railings to either side of the stairs, he catapulted himself toward Orson, striking him full in the chest with his boots and sending him staggering back into his brother.

The sound of the gun going off was like an explosion in the small, dark hallway. Orson slumped to the floor, his body blocking his brother's escape. Seeing his chance, Seth hurried up the stairs to the roof, where he found Sam curled into himself in a corner, sobbing.

"Come on, Sam, we gotta go," he said gruffly, hoping it would spur his brother to action. Eventually, Rudy would realize he'd shot his brother, and he would be furious. He would come after Seth, and nothing would satisfy him but killing Sam—a brother for a brother. Seth understood that. Some things in the West were unwritten but inviolable laws.

Seth dragged Sam to his feet and to the far side of the roof. "Take a running start, and then jump," he ordered. "It's not as far as it looks, and it'll be over before you have time to be scared." He gave Sam a shove, and to his relief the kid took off, sailing through the night sky and disappearing.

Seth held his breath until he heard the thud of Sam landing on the roof of the mercantile, then he followed. Just as he flew through the air, he was pretty sure he smelled smoke and saw flames below.

∞

After she had rung the bell long enough to rouse interest from the saloons at the far end of town, as well as the concern of guests now pouring out of the Baxter house and into the street, Amanda climbed down the ladder. But halfway down her dress got caught, and she was forced to waste precious moments freeing it. Her intent had been to direct both the men from the saloons and the party guests toward the alley, blocking off either end, so the outlaws could not escape. Instead, everyone was headed toward the plaza.

With a last desperate tug that ripped her dress, Amanda freed herself and ran toward the men from the saloons.

"Where's the fire?" Ollie Taylor hollered.

"It's the bank!" she yelled back. "It's being robbed!"

As the two groups met and shouted to be heard above each other, suddenly there was the sound of a shotgun blast, and everyone froze. Sheriff Richter stood on the second rung of the bell tower ladder and fired the gun a second time to assure he had everyone's attention.

"Folks, I don't know what's going on here or what kind of prank this little lady thinks she's pulling, but there is no fire, and from where I'm standing, the bank looks just fine. Now everybody go about your business, and enjoy your evening."

Amanda was dumbfounded to realize they believed the sheriff. Several men brushed past her and muttered rude comments, and she could hear Ezra's guests gossiping about her as they slowly walked back to his house.

Meanwhile, across the way she saw the flicker of flames reflected in the side window of the pharmacy. "Fire!" she shouted, and pointed as Richter gripped her upper arm. "Fire!"

Thankfully, a few people looked back, saw what she'd seen, and took up the cry. Jim and his daughter ran toward the store, and Amanda took advantage of the sheriff's momentary confusion to wrench free and join them.

Blessedly, the fire was not coming from inside the shop. Rather, they could see the flames through the open back door that led to the alley. Fumbling with his keys, Jim finally got the door unlocked, and the three raced toward the rear of the store, where the back door stood open.

When they reached the alley, Eli Baxter was emptying bottles of German bitters and Lydia E. Pinkham's Vegetable Compound—both full of alcohol—to fuel the fire already burning hot and spreading fast.

"Eli!" Amanda screamed, although she knew he would not hear her above the chaotic scene. Horses reared and pawed the air in panic as men yelled directions that went unheeded.

"Don't go out there," she heard Jim say, but she saw Seth running toward her.

"Go back!" They shouted the same words at the same time—each ordering the other to return to safety while both ignored the instructions.

Amanda was nearer to Eli. If she could just grab him and pull him inside the drugstore... But she had forgotten she was wearing a dress—a dress with a full skirt and layers of material. And as she screamed Eli's name and held out her hand, she was too busy to notice that the flames had begun lapping at the hem of her gown, until Eli turned and dropped the bottle of Pinkham's tonic. His eyes went wide with terror, and he froze as the fire spread around him.

"Take my hand," Amanda begged, aware that her breathing was shallow, and her eyes stung. From behind her she felt two strong hands grab her waist and drag her away from Eli. "No!"

"Stop fighting me, Amanda," the voice she had come to love ordered. He flung her into waiting arms, and before she knew what was happening, she found herself on the floor as Ginny Matthews batted at the smoldering dress, and Jim doused her with water from a bucket he kept near the back door.

"Seth!" she shouted as she peered through the smoke and haze to see what was happening. A moment later, two figures stumbled into the drugstore, and Jim shut the door behind them.

Seth had Eli slung over his shoulder. He lowered the boy onto the counter and turned to Jim and Ginny. "You got this?" he demanded, and when they nodded and turned their attention to Eli, Seth knelt next to Amanda. "Woman, you are going to be the death of me yet. Now will you please stay put and let me handle this?"

Amanda coughed and felt her chest burn as if the fire had infiltrated her body. "Stop bossing me around," she managed to croak. "I could have saved Eli, if only—"

"It's not Eli I'm worried about. It's you."

"I don't see why. I am perfectly capable of—"

Seth pulled her close so their faces nearly touched. "You want to know why? How about because I care about you? How about because I'm in love with you? How about because I've been thinking we might spend the rest of the time we've got together? How about—"

All she heard before she passed out was *I'm in love with you.*

⁂

"She needs a doctor," Seth said as he eased an unconscious Amanda to the floor. "Do something." He could see that Eli Baxter sat upright, his face and hands blackened but otherwise seemingly all right, while Amanda's breath came in spurts and she wasn't moving. Meanwhile, he heard gunshots from the alley, and his first thought was of Sam. He stood and found himself face to face with the pharmacist. "I've got to… my brother's out there."

"Go," Matthews said as he opened the door just

enough for Seth to squeeze through without allowing too much smoke in. "That fire's getting close. We'll get them both back to the boardinghouse. Go...I won't let Amanda..."

The two men looked at each other for one split second, and in that instant, both understood that the other loved Amanda, and that Amanda would be the one to choose.

Another gunshot, and Seth was surrounded by smoldering debris that had fed the fire and a heavy fog of smoke that made seeing what was happening impossible. He eased his way down the alley until he could make out the players outside the bank. Behind him he heard the clang of the fire wagon and the cries of the townspeople as they formed a bucket brigade to squelch the inferno. Ahead he saw the limp bodies of the soldiers who had delivered the payload and the outlaws mounting their horses as they prepared to make their escape. He did not see Sam, and that made his mind run wild with scenarios he did not want to consider—most ending with some version of Sam being dead.

He saw a figure exit the side door of the bank and then a second man—a man he recognized as the sheriff. He moved closer. The first man was Rudy Stock, shaking hands with the sheriff as he handed Richter a fat envelope Seth suspected was stuffed with currency. They clasped hands, and then the sheriff turned to go.

Richter hadn't gotten three steps when Rudy shot him in the back. Calmly, the outlaw twirled his six-shooter and replaced it in its holster as he walked to the sheriff's lifeless body, kicked it with the toe of his boot, and then bent and retrieved the envelope of money.

"Let's ride, boys!" he called out as he mounted his horse and passed the envelope to his mother.

The far end of the alley was unobstructed. Everyone was focused on the fire. Eli's ploy had backfired, and now the Stock gang would get away clean. Seth knew he had to do something, but what? He had no horse. His ankle had swollen so much he certainly couldn't run.

But he had a gun. And he knew how to use it.

He hurried forward and took aim at the outlaw most likely to cause the others to stop. The very woman he had sat next to at meals for the last several weeks.

Seth squeezed off a round and smiled when he saw her hat go flying through the air. She yelped and ducked. Of course, that startled her horse which, having already endured gunshots and a fire, was inclined to rear or bolt.

Seth ducked as the horse leapt over the wagon and raced down the alley.

"I'll kill you with my bare hands," he heard a voice shout, and the next thing he knew he was on the ground, wrestling with Rudy Stock.

Eleven

"Where's Seth?" Amanda asked the minute she regained consciousness. Ginny and Jim knelt next to her. "I need to…" She started to get to her feet but began coughing and sank back to the floor. Her chest felt as if it had been filled with wet mud, her throat like it was lined in sand.

"He'll be fine," Ginny assured her just as they heard a gunshot followed by a horse's shrieks and hoofbeats pounding past the door of the pharmacy.

"Help me up," Amanda pleaded. "I have to know. I have to see."

Using Jim's shoulder as support, she pushed herself to her feet and stumbled to the door. When she stepped into the alley, Ollie and other men from town were moving toward her, sloshing water onto the remains of the fire.

"They're going to get away," she managed to say, although surely, since she was waving her hands wildly in the direction of the horses gathered at the other end of the alley, her message should be clear.

She was just able to make out Seth's familiar form when she saw a large man throw himself on him.

"No!" she choked as she stumbled forward, unheeding of the footsteps behind her and the pleas for her to wait. "Stop!"

"Oh, Amanda, thank heaven," a woman cried. "These horrible men were taking me as their hostage, and who knows…"

Still dazed, Amanda peered into the darkness. "Mrs. Rosewood?"

The next thing she knew, someone had his brawny, smelly forearm around her neck and was dragging her backward. "Ma, this here's the one saw me shoot the prospector."

Ma?

Amanda's eyes sought and found Seth, who looked as if he might be ready to singlehandedly take on the gang—and their mother. "Let her go," he growled. "You need a hostage, take me. Wells Fargo will pay the ransom."

None of this made sense to Amanda. Mild-mannered Mrs. Rosewood was the mother of outlaws? And why would Wells Fargo care in the least what happened to Seth? She needed answers, but she could hardly breathe, much less raise questions, with her body pressed against the outlaw.

Recalling a stage tactic that a friend had once shown her for faking a faint, she allowed her body to go limp, and in the instant it took for the man holding her to adjust to this shift in her weight, she drove her elbow into his midsection with all her might as she twisted away from him. The air came out of him with a satisfying whoosh.

What happened next was a blur of motion and noise. Gunshots as Jim and others dove for cover. Seth coming toward her as he fell face down in the street. Behind him, Mrs. Rosewood slowly lowering the gun still smoking from the discharge.

Amanda dodged the outlaw's attempt to recapture her.

"Leave her," she heard Mrs. Rosewood order. "I should never have believed you boys could pull this off. Now mount up, and let's get out of here before that mob strings us all up from the nearest tree."

To Amanda's surprise, all the men followed her orders, mounting their horses and riding away hard and fast. At the far end of the alley, she saw shadowy figures moving toward her through the smoke from the extinguished fire. She knew they were calling to her, but she couldn't make out their words.

All she knew for sure was that if Seth was dead, then she had lost everything she had ever dreamed of having in her life. And if that was the case, what did she care if outlaws got away? What did she care about anything? Without Seth, she had no future, and Amanda had spent far too much time daydreaming about her perfect future to let anything—or anyone—stop her now.

∼∞∼

Seth felt the balm of water, drops that dotted his face and trickled down his cheeks to his neck. He was cradled against someone—a woman—and for an instant he thought maybe in death a fellow returned to his youth, and the days of being held by his mother. That was comforting.

He struggled to open his eyes, wanting to see what things were like on the other side. But the searing pain in his back made it impossible to focus. There was a woman all right, and she was crying, which explained the wetness on his face. There were others as well, crowding around, shouting orders, tugging at the woman holding him.

"Come on, Amanda," he heard a man say. "Let me take a look at him." Seth thought he knew that voice—the pharmacist.

He understood then that he was not dead, and the woman holding him was not his mother, but Amanda. He fought for full consciousness so he could reassure her that it would take more than a bullet in the shoulder to keep him from spending the rest of his days with her. But then he heard another voice, also male, but rougher. The banker.

"Amanda, pull yourself together," Ezra Baxter instructed. "Come, let me take you back to the house and…"

She tightened her arms around Seth. "Get away from me," she whispered in a feral hiss he barely recognized as her voice. "You belong in jail—you and the sheriff and…"

Afraid that she was about to get herself shot as well, Seth found the strength to touch her hand. As he had hoped, the unexpected sign of life ended her tirade and brought her attention fully to him. "Seth?"

"Right here," he managed.

"Oh, Seth, please don't die on me." The tears were a downpour now, as she placed kisses on his hair and forehead.

"Not planning on it," he whispered, and then things went black.

The next time he came to, it was daylight, and he was lying on a bed in a room with large windows that looked out onto the town. He was back at the boardinghouse, but this wasn't his room. .

He let his eyes adjust to the light as he scanned his surroundings and saw Amanda asleep in a rocking chair pulled close to his bedside. She was still wearing the blue party dress, now scorched at the hem, and her hair covered her shoulders and half her face, which was smudged with soot from the fire.

He heard footsteps in the hallway and turned his attention to the door. For one brief instant he wondered what had happened to his gun. For that matter, where were his clothes? He was shirtless and wearing only his underwear under the covers. When he tried to move, he saw his torso had been tightly wrapped in a bandage that looped over his left shoulder.

"Well, look who decided to come back among the living," Miss Dooley whispered as she tiptoed into the room and set a tray on the edge of the writing desk near the window. "Glad she finally lost the battle to stay awake." She jerked a thumb at Amanda then poured tea into a cup and brought it to him. "She was determined to keep her vigil, and my guess is she'll be madder than a—"

Amanda sat up suddenly. She looked at Seth, her eyes wide with panic, and he realized it was half a minute before she realized he was awake and sipping some of the bitter brew Miss Dooley called herbal tea.

"Mornin'," he croaked. If he had hoped she would

run to him, throw herself onto the bed and wrap her arms around him, he was sadly disappointed.

She scowled at the sunlight streaming through the large windows, then turned to Miss Dooley. "You let me sleep."

"I didn't 'let you' do nothin', missy. You're as human as the rest of us, and that means, sooner or later, you're gonna need to close those big green eyes of yours whether you like it or not."

Amanda's expression softened to one of tender concern as she stood next to the bed and brushed Seth's hair away from his forehead. "How's the pain?"

"It's there," he said, and tried to grin.

"I've sent for Addie. Jim was amazing in getting the bullet out, but you need to be examined by a real doctor. Addie will know what's best."

"We have doctors here in Tucson," Miss Dooley said.

Amanda and Seth ignored her.

"Any word from Sam?" he asked.

"Who is Sam?" The two women spoke in unison.

Seth shook his head to clear it and grimaced at the pain that shot up his side. "My brother," he managed, realizing there had been no time to let Amanda know that he had found his brother.

"He had a part in this business?" Miss Dooley eyed him suspiciously, as if she had not quite made up her mind if he could be trusted.

The jig was up, and he'd already decided to leave his job with Wells Fargo, so what would be the harm in telling them everything? But caution was inbred in him, so he ignored the landlady's question. "Did the Stock gang get away clean?"

"So far," Miss Dooley replied before Amanda could tell him anything. "Them and that woman. *Mrs. Rosewood* indeed," she huffed. "Well, I'll let you know soon as the doctor gets here. Meanwhile, Miss Porterfield, may I suggest you find time to make yourself a bit more presentable? You can use my room and the bath downstairs."

"Someone needs to stay here with—"

"I'll be all right, Amanda. Go on now." The truth was he needed time to think, to replay everything that had happened before he got shot. Where had he last seen Sam? And where was the kid now?

৵৩

Amanda gathered fresh clothing while Miss Dooley kept a close watch on her from the doorway. Taking things from her wardrobe with Seth lying there watching her seemed incredibly intimate in spite of Miss Dooley's presence. She had refused to leave Seth when they brought him back to the boardinghouse, but Miss Dooley had insisted it would be inappropriate for Amanda to be in Seth's room, and had finally agreed to allow him to lie in her bed—as long as the door remained wide open.

As she gathered her brush and extra pins for her hair, Amanda felt her cheeks and the back of her neck flush. She found it impossible to look at Seth directly as she bundled her things in her arms and left the room.

Downstairs, Miss Dooley instructed Bessie to prepare a bath for Amanda and to see that she had something to eat. Under any other circumstances, Amanda would have been tempted to linger in the warm water, even after she had soiled it by washing the grime and smoke from her hair. But now that Seth had regained consciousness, there were other matters that needed her attention.

Eli and Ellie topped that list. Kitty Caldwell had assured Amanda that, even as their father was led off to jail by the sheriff's deputy—the sheriff himself having been killed—she would stay with the twins and make sure they were safe. That had been a relief. On the other hand, Eli had clearly had a part in it all—even serving as messenger—and she worried that he might take matters into his own hands and make a run for it.

With a weary sigh, she climbed out of the tepid water, wrapped herself in a towel, combed her wet hair before braiding it, and then got dressed in the clothes she regularly wore for teaching.

"I need to see about the Baxter children," she told Bessie as she hurried through the kitchen on her way out the back door. "Please come get me as soon as Dr. Porterfield arrives."

To her relief, when she reached the Baxter house, she found Kitty and the twins clearing away the aftermath of the previous night's party. All three turned to her when she entered the dining room.

"Is he dead?" Eli asked, stuttering with fear.

"No. The doctor is on her way, and we will know more about the extent of his injuries once she has examined him. In the meantime, Eli, I would like a word with you." She pointed to the library, waited for him to precede her, and then closed the sliding doors with a soft click. "Sit down." She indicated the chair where his father usually sat and then took the chair opposite him. "You are an extremely intelligent young man, so I assume you have already realized the extent of the trouble that you and your father are in."

"I wanted to help my father. I heard him telling Sheriff Richter that the bank was about to fail, so I went to the sheriff, and he said I could help my father by running those messages to and from the old ranch."

"Are you saying that your father is guilty in this crime?"

"No!" Eli's eyes were wide with confusion. "They blackmailed him. It was the only choice. Sheriff Richter said that they would ruin him and the bank unless I did…"

The boy was near hysterics as he defended his father, who had struck him repeatedly and abused him verbally. There were some things about love that Amanda would never understand.

She reached across the space between them and patted his knee. "It's all right, Eli. I'm just trying to understand."

"My father is not a bad man, Miss Porterfield."

She wondered if Ezra had any idea how loyal and devoted his son was to him. "Then let's try and figure out how we can help get him through this. Start by telling me everything you know about the gang and the plan to rob the bank."

"I already told the detective all I know."

"The detective?"

"The guy that got shot. He works for Wells Fargo undercover, but the gang had him already figured out."

Amanda took a moment to digest this news. It made sense of the secrecy and the late night outings.

On the other hand... "Eli, do you know someone named Sam?"

The boy frowned. "Sam?"

"He'd probably be a little older than you, and he would be involved somehow in this mess."

"There was a kid—after the old prospector stopped being the one to leave the notes for me to pick up, it was that guy."

"He was a member of the gang?"

Eli shrugged. "All I know is one night when I picked up the messages I took to that woman at Miss Dooley's place, there was an envelope with my name on it, and inside was a message I was to deliver to Mr. Grover."

"And did you?"

"That's how he knew to be there last night at the bank." He refused to look directly at her.

"Eli, did you read that message?"

He nodded. "I know I wasn't supposed to, but I thought maybe..." He stopped talking and stared out the window. "I don't know what I thought, Miss Porterfield." He glanced at her. "What do you think will happen to Father?"

Eli looked so miserable that Amanda's heart went out to him. "I don't know, Eli, but while this gets sorted out, you must tell the authorities everything you know, everything you saw or heard in the weeks leading up to the robbery. Never has it been more important that you tell the truth, do you understand?"

"Yes, ma'am. Can I go now?"

"You may," she replied. "Just stay here. We'll work this out, and Ellie needs you more than anyone else right now."

Eli nodded and left the room. Amanda stayed seated by the cold fireplace. If the youngest member of the gang was Seth's brother, what would happen to him? And what would that do to Seth? He was in no condition to go after his brother and rescue him from the gang, and yet she knew he would try.

Kitty knocked lightly at the library door. "The lady doctor and her husband just pulled up."

Jess. Her brother would surely know how best to go about tracking down Seth's brother and getting him safely away from the outlaws. "Make sure Eli and Ellie stay here, Kitty," she said as she hurried away.

Jess and Addie were climbing the front steps when Amanda came running to reach them before they entered the house, where Miss Dooley or someone else might hear her. Her breath still came in short bursts after the smoke and fire. She told them about Seth's injuries in as few words as possible, and blessedly, Addie didn't wait for more information. Instead she grabbed her black bag and entered the house, but Amanda kept Jess from following with a hand on his forearm.

"I need your help, Jess." She told him about Seth's younger brother and her fear that the boy was mixed up with the outlaws. "I think Seth will try and go after him, and he's in no condition—"

"It's out of my hands, Amanda. I have no jurisdiction, even if I wanted to help."

"But, Seth will—"

Jess took hold of her shoulders and stopped short of shaking her. "Seth Grover is nobody you need to concern yourself with, Amanda. He's on the right side of the law, but he's not for you. He'll break your heart at the very least, and at the very worst, he'll get you killed if you insist on hanging around him. So stay clear, understood?"

He didn't wait for an answer, but released her and followed Addie inside.

Amanda remained standing on the steps, her mind working as she tried to think what her next move should be. Jess didn't know Seth the way she did. The man would take a bullet for her—*had* taken a bullet for her—and the only possible way to repay him would be to find his brother. Her decision made, she marched up the front steps and then to her room, where Addie completed her examination of Seth's injuries.

"Well?"

"He'll live," Addie replied as she replaced her stethoscope in the bag and stepped into the hall. "It's a flesh wound. Could have been a lot worse. That pharmacist of yours did a very good job bandaging him until he could get the stitches he needed."

"But he's going to make a full recovery?"

"It'll be awhile before he's back on his feet, especially given the damage he did to that ankle on top of getting himself shot, but he'll be all right."

"That's good."

"I gave him a sleeping powder," Addie continued. "The best medicine right now is rest, and under no circumstances should he try to get up—except for personal reasons, of course. What's he doing in your room instead of his own?"

Amanda wasn't in the mood to explain. "It just turned out that way. We didn't have a lot of time to think. He was bleeding and kept blacking out and—"

"He asked for you," Addie interrupted. "He seemed quite concerned that you might be in danger."

Amanda saw that her friend was studying her closely. "He has no need to worry."

"And yet worry he does. Perhaps it would be best if you stayed nearby. Being under duress will not help the healing."

"He's occupying my room. I have little choice but to."

"Jess and Bessie can help him move back to his room. I believe he will be more comfortable there—less likely to concern himself with the idea that he is putting you out. But he'll want to know you're nearby—and safe. So stay put."

"Perhaps I should sit with him until the medicine takes effect."

Addie smiled. "Perhaps you should. I think having you as his nurse would be very good for Seth's recovery. I also think it would be quite positive for your peace of mind."

"Stop playing doctor," Amanda replied, but she grinned at Addie as she returned to the chair near Seth's bed.

An hour later, Seth was settled in his room, half sitting against a stack of pillows. Jess stood nearby, his arms folded, his expression one of exasperation. "Are you gonna tell me what you know?" he repeated.

"Probably not," Seth replied calmly.

Jess threw up his hands and advanced a step closer to the bed. Knowing her brother's hair-trigger temper, Amanda moved between him and Seth. She could feel the edge of the bed pressed against the backs of her knees.

"Calm down, Jess," she said. "Addie says that—"

"Addie's done her job here, and now I need to do mine, so back off, Sis."

"You calm down first, and then we'll see." Behind her she heard something close to a snort and guessed Seth was covering a laugh. "And you," she continued, turning to face him, "are hardly in a position to hold secrets, so tell the man what he needs to know to hunt down those outlaws."

She looked from one man to the other. Both scowled as if she were somehow the problem. She placed her hands on her hips and tapped one toe impatiently to emphasize her point. "Well?"

Seth eyed Jess the way he might gauge the trustworthiness of a wild mustang. "My best guess is they're headed for the border."

Jess laughed. "Tell me something I don't already know, Grover."

"All right. My younger brother might be trying to trail them. He fancies himself a detective, working for Wells Fargo."

"Takes after you, does he?"

Seth shrugged. "Fact is, I couldn't give a hoot if Rudy Stock and his mama get clean away at this point. But my brother is another matter."

"You can't expect me to go after your brother when there's a gang of outlaws on the loose."

"I didn't think tracking down outlaws was in your jurisdiction," Seth shot back.

Amanda was fast running out of patience with the two of them. "For goodness sake, could we not argue the finer points here, and decide what's to be done?"

"You stay out of this," the two men said in unison.

Amanda could not help but smile. It was the first time her brother and the man she loved had agreed on anything.

⁂

Seth liked Amanda's brother, and he was pretty sure that if anybody could hunt Sam down and get him to safety, it would be the marshal. Problem was the marshal wasn't interested, and Seth understood that. Jess was not there to find some lost kid. He was there because dangerous outlaws were on the run.

He decided to tell him what he could. "I've been tailing them for a couple of years now," he said, and saw the tension in Jess's shoulders ease slightly. He also noticed how Amanda's expression radiated interest. "Amanda, could you get me some fresh water?" he asked, making sure to add a little grimace of pain to the request.

She was obviously reluctant to leave the room, but he was pretty sure her concern for his comfort would overcome anything else. She picked up the pitcher and headed for the door, then turned back. With a smile that dripped with sweetness, she said, "Whatever you tell my brother, be prepared to repeat it when I return."

As soon as she had shut the door, Jess chuckled. "My sister has a way of getting what she wants, Grover."

"Well, in this case, a little knowledge could be a dangerous thing. Unless you promise to help find my brother, Amanda will strike out to find him herself."

Jess's smile turned to a frown. "Then we'll tell her it's all arranged...right?"

"You're saying you'll look for Sam?"

"I'm saying I'll do whatever is necessary to keep Amanda safe, including lie to her. You, on the other hand, have a choice to make—your brother or my sister. If you tell her the truth, that I'm only interested in hunting down the outlaws, then you're right. She'll strike out on her own to find your little brother. On the other hand, if you love her—and I think you do— you'll go along with whatever I tell her."

Seth did not like the idea of lying to Amanda, but he could see that Jess was right. Lying would keep her safe. Telling her the truth would practically assure she'd put herself in danger.

"I'll make you a deal," he said, and saw Jess tense once again. "I'll follow your lead with Amanda as long as you keep an open mind when it comes to Sam. He's not part of the gang, and I don't want to see him get caught up in a shoot-out, should things come to that."

Jess hesitated then stuck out his hand. "Deal. I'll even go a step beyond that. If I hear news of your brother— someone has seen him or such—I'll make sure to get it to you. Have you got someone you can trust to follow up on leads until you're back on your feet?"

Seth accepted the handshake. "I've got some thoughts on that. Thank you, Marshal."

"Make that Jess. In spite of my concerns, I'm pretty sure one of these days—sooner rather than later—you and me might be family." He reached for his hat and opened the door just as Amanda returned with the water. "You been listening at keyholes again, Sis?" he asked, and without waiting for an answer, squeezed past her and hurried down the stairs.

Amanda filled Seth's empty glass before setting the pitcher on the table. "Well?" She handed him the water and waited while he took time to drink. He knew she was well aware that he was stalling, so he did the one thing he hoped would throw her off track.

As he swallowed the last of the water and handed her the glass, he said, "I was thinking maybe once I can do a proper job of it, I might ask you to marry me."

The glass clattered to the floor, but did not break. Amanda ignored it as she turned her attention to him. "I do not...I am not...how dare you?"

He shrugged, inwardly tickled at the way her cheeks had gone all pink, and how for once in her life she couldn't find words to express what she felt. "It's a pretty straightforward suggestion. Just wanted to see what you thought about the idea."

"You mean before you committed to a formal proposal? You mean in case I turn you down flat? You mean before you invest your hard-earned money in a proper engagement present?"

"Nope. What I'm saying is that it might be some time before I can do this right, and in the meantime, I want you to know my intentions. Now, if marrying me is not something that appeals to you, then we can—as my pa often says—cut bait and move on. On the other hand..."

Miss Dooley opened the door and surveyed the room. "The marshal has left?"

"Yes, ma'am," Seth replied, his eyes still on Amanda.

Miss Dooley flung the door wide open and advanced on Amanda. "And what have I told you, missy, about allowing yourself to be alone in a room with this man—any man?" The way she frowned at Seth, it went without saying that she was mentally adding *especially this one.*

"Mr. Grover was just in the process of proposing marriage," Amanda replied, her smile tight and her tone challenging as she gazed at him.

Their landlady was struck speechless, which was nothing compared to what Seth was experiencing. Amanda Porterfield had a way of turning the tables and doing the exact opposite of what he might expect.

Miss Dooley's mouth worked as she tried to find words. Then she giggled like a schoolgirl, and without saying anything, she left the room, closing the door behind her with a firm click. Her giggles faded as she descended the stairs.

"Well?" Amanda demanded.

The sleeping powder the doctor had given him was beginning to take effect. Seth's strength was ebbing and he was at a loss regarding what his next play should be. He was used to being in control, especially when it came to women. But Amanda was a different sort of woman. It was what drew him to her and drove him crazy at the same time. "Well what?" He could not help the irritation that crept into his tone.

She smiled. "You were bluffing," she crowed. "I knew it. My father was a fine poker player, Seth, and I used to hang around the table when he and the cowboys on our ranch played. I learned a thing or two."

"I was not bluffing," he grumbled. "Marry me. Don't marry me. I'm tired." With that he nestled under the covers and turned away from her. For a long moment, neither moved. Then he heard the rustle of her skirt as she crossed the room.

But instead of leaving as he had expected, she sat on the edge of the bed and reached over his shoulder to stroke his hair away from his forehead. "We're going to find your brother, Seth. You'll be needing a best man, after all."

And before he could digest those last words, she left the room.

Twelve

AMANDA COULD NOT RECALL A TIME WHEN HER WORLD had seemed so chaotic, and yet wasn't that what she had craved all those long, boring days back on the ranch? Still, she needed to put things in order.

There were the Baxter children to consider. With their father in jail, they might easily fall back into old habits. There was Seth's brother, who was no doubt in danger, and although she did not know the young man, he certainly deserved help. And finally, there was Seth's ridiculous marriage proposal. Of course, he hadn't meant it. He had been trying to throw her off asking what he had told Jess. Sometimes men could be so transparent.

But with everything she had on her mind, her greatest concern was Seth's welfare. Phony proposal or not, she loved him, and although Addie had assured her he would make a full recovery, her friend had given no indication how long that might take. The man had been shot. He could be bedridden for weeks. Every time he moved, his grimace told her he was in pain. And wounded or not, she had no doubt he would do whatever necessary to be sure his brother was safe, even to the point of jeopardizing his own health.

She knew her brother well enough to realize that stopping the Stock gang was his main concern, whether or not he had jurisdiction. Jess could not stand by and allow innocent people to be robbed of their life savings. No, he would not make finding Seth's brother a priority, no matter what he had told Seth.

Later that evening, she had dinner with Addie at the hotel where she and Jess had decided to stay the night. Addie told her that Judge Ellis was trying to convince Jess to take on the sheriff's job. They had even gone so far as to deputize him, but he was more concerned about making sure Addie got home as soon as possible to be with her father. Amanda had hoped she might persuade Jess to at least alert the militia to be on the lookout for Seth's brother.

"I have to say I never would have thought that sweet Mrs. Rosewood was somehow mixed up in this whole business," Addie said as they finished their dessert.

Mrs. Rosewood—of course.

The night of the robbery Judge Ellis and the district attorney had told Miss Dooley to lock Mrs. Rosewood's room after it had been searched for clues. But what if they had missed something? Later that night, she impatiently waited until Ollie had left for work, and Miss Jensen and Miss Dooley were sleeping, before using a hatpin to pick the lock on the widow's door. Before turning in for the night, Addie had administered Seth a dose of pain medication, and when Amanda checked, he was breathing deeply and evenly—fast asleep.

There was enough light from the streetlamps to allow her to move around without bumping into furniture or otherwise alerting others. On the bed lay an outfit of trousers, a shirt, and a man's jacket. The woman had intended to change. What had stopped her?

The dressing table was cluttered with hairpins and bottles of cologne and open jars of creams. More clothes hung in the wardrobe—the trappings she had used for her disguise as a grieving widow. It was as if she were a snake casting off one skin for another.

Amanda allowed herself a wry smile at the analogy. The woman was a snake, all right—and so were her two sons.

Disappointed, she was about to leave the room when she noticed a piece of torn paper on the floor just under the bed. She picked it up and took it closer to the window to read. It was part of a train schedule. At first she dismissed it as unimportant, but then she realized she had a clue that would help catch the gang.

She tiptoed out of the room, making sure to lock the door behind her, and headed straight for her room to change into riding clothes. She was just pulling on her second boot when she looked up and saw Seth leaning unsteadily against her door.

"Want to tell me where you think you're going?"

"You should be in bed."

He grinned. "Come with me, and I'll go."

"You are impossible." She finished dressing and stood.

"And you, my lady, are not going anywhere."

"I have news for Jess and the others."

"Jess is right down the street—no need for riding clothes."

"Jess and Addie left for Whitman Falls." It was a small lie. She knew they were at the hotel packing.

He hesitated. "What news?"

She handed him the scrap of paper. "I don't think the outlaws are on horseback or headed for the border. I think they knew that's what you and the others would think, so instead they planned to escape by train. The next train headed south is tomorrow at noon. I think they are still in the area."

She knew he agreed when he pushed away from the door and headed across the hall to his room, where he started to dress.

"Oh no, you don't," she told him, grabbing his shirt and clutching it to her chest.

"Then go wire Jess to come back, and get Judge Ellis over here. I'll not have you riding the countryside trying to find a bunch of thugs—and do not tell me that's not what you were planning to do. Once everybody's here, we'll figure out how we're going to stop the Stocks from boarding that train without innocent people getting caught in the crossfire."

❦

By the time Amanda returned, Seth had managed to get himself dressed, and he was sitting at the small desk in his room. He heard Miss Dooley's voice. "I'll make coffee," she announced with her usual tone of resignation. She was a good soul, however, one who cared deeply about the community her father had helped build.

To his surprise, Amanda, Jess, and Addie all crowded into the room. "Amanda said the two of you had left."

"Well, we're here, so let's get started figuring out a plan that will end this once and for all."

The two women sat on the side of the bed while Jess paced. "If they are still around here and planning to catch the train, there could be big trouble," he announced, as if they didn't already know this.

"I'm betting they've split up," Seth said, "with the bulk of the gang already heading south, and Rudy and his mother planning to take the train."

"I have an idea," Amanda said. "What if we let them board the train? Let them think they're getting away?"

"So innocent people on the train get shot instead of the folks here? Yeah, that's a great plan, Sis."

"Hold on," Seth said. He glanced at the small clock on the dresser. "We've got several hours before the train rolls into the station. They're bound to wait until the last possible minute."

"What's your point?"

Seth picked up the schedule Amanda had found and studied it. "The train makes one stop before it comes here. If we could intercept it at that stop…"

Amanda saw where he was going with this. "We could have passengers get off there and wait for another train," she said.

"And so," Jess said sarcastically, "an empty train rolls into town? Oh yeah, that should work. They won't be the least bit suspicious of that."

"Hold on a minute, and let me finish," Seth said. "We get the regular passengers off, but replace them with soldiers from the fort—armed and ready to take down the outlaws."

"You think they won't notice soldiers in uniform?" He gave a frustrated grunt and turned away.

"They could dress in regular clothes," Addie suggested. "Of course, there need to be some women aboard as well." She glanced at Amanda and smiled.

"Get that idea out of your head right this minute, Addie Porterfield," Jess said, alarmed.

"Then the plan can't work," Amanda said.

Jess paused in his pacing, and she could see that he knew she was right. "Well, maybe some soldiers could dress in women's clothing," he suggested.

"No time for that," Seth said. "We'd have to find clothes and make sure they shaved and…" His voice trailed off, and the four of them were sitting in silence when Miss Dooley arrived with coffee and biscuits.

"Well, this is a lively bunch," she muttered. Amanda filled her in on the plan as they served coffee.

"Whatever we decide, the first step is to stop that train," Seth said, "and alert the garrison at the fort."

"Maybe Eli Baxter could carry a message to the fort's commander," Amanda suggested. "It would be a way to do something that could help his father's cause when his case comes to trial."

"I'll have Bessie go get him," Miss Dooley offered.

As Amanda had expected, Eli was thrilled to take on this responsibility. He barely had the envelope with the instructions Addie had written for the colonel before he was out the door and down the stairs. The problem was that Ellie had come with him, and now insisted on being given some job to do as well.

"What if we disguise her as a visiting celebrity," Miss Dooley suggested.

"Yes, I'd be a good actress. Mother always said as much."

"To what end?" Jess asked. "Put the kid in danger? No."

"Too dangerous," Seth agreed. "We should dress up one of the younger men."

Ellie turned to Amanda. "Please, Miss Porterfield. You've taught us that we need to do what is right to help others. Well, surely this is an opportunity."

"Hold on," Addie said. "If there's some excitement at the station that attracts attention and delays the train, won't that make it harder for the Stocks to board and easier to be seen and captured?"

"She's got a point," Jess said.

"If I may contribute something," Miss Dooley said as she stepped fully into the room. "I have heard that the actress, Louise Goodfellow, is touring the area. She's very popular, and if word got out that she would be passing through…"

Jess rubbed his chin—a sure sign he was considering the idea.

"But not Ellie," Seth insisted.

On one hand, Amanda could understand the girl's desire to take on the role. On the other, Seth was absolutely right. She could end up in the middle of a gunfight, in which case Amanda would never forgive herself. "I have a way you could help without endangering your safety, Ellie."

Everyone was looking at her, waiting for her to explain her idea. If only she had one fully thought out.

"It seems to me," she began, "that we will need a signal when Rudy Stock and his mother approach the train station. That's when the musicians will start playing, and everyone will gather round to greet the train."

"They will want to stay well away from any activity," Seth added. "Most likely they will look for a car at the back of the train to board."

"And once they do," Amanda told Ellie, "you will let the rest of us know, so we can signal the conductor to get the train moving. By then, it will be too late for the outlaws to do anything but jump from a moving train once they realize the only other passengers are members of the militia."

"But where will I keep watch, and how will I let you know, and…"

Amanda looked to Seth for answers.

He glanced around the room and smiled. "That window there has a bird's eye view of the town—especially the train station. I chose this room for that very reason. You, young lady, will stay right here with me, and we'll keep a lookout together—providing I can persuade my jailers here to let me sit in the chair there." He glanced at Addie and Amanda.

"As long as all you do is sit," Addie said.

Amanda saw that this was a way to make sure Seth didn't become part of the action that would unfold at the train station. "I think that's a great idea. Two sets of eyes are always better than just one."

"So once we spot them, then what?" Ellie asked.

"You run to the drugstore across the street from the station, and when the marshal here sees that, he'll signal the conductor to move the train out."

"We still don't know who will pretend to be the actress getting off the train," Ellie pointed out.

"I am," Amanda announced, and before anyone could debate the matter, she took Ellie's arm and added, "Come and help me find a proper disguise."

"Amanda!" Seth and Jess spoke in unison, protesting her decision as Amanda closed the door behind her.

❧

To everyone's amazement and delight, the plan seemed destined to go off without a hitch. The crowd in the know gathered, soon augmented by curious bystanders. In the distance, the train whistle sounded a series of friendly toots. The crowd grew more excited as word spread of someone famous arriving. As one, they turned in the direction of the arriving train.

Of course, there were several details the bystanders did not know. They did not know the train was occupied by armed soldiers. They did not know that Amanda—disguised as the actress in an oversized feathered hat and an elaborate brocade gown more suited to the Blue Parrot than to teaching the Baxter children—was waiting in an empty boxcar on the track next to the one that would bring the train to town. They did not know that once the train had pulled to a stop, its engine wheezing and heaving as if trying to catch its breath, Amanda would simply move from the boxcar to a platform between two passenger cars and then out into the sunlight, where she would be greeted with cheers from those in on the scheme, as well as those who had no idea what was happening.

Seth focused his binoculars on the spot where he

knew Amanda would emerge then slowly scanned the surrounding scene. Ollie led a trio of musicians toward the station, positioning them on the platform, and then doing the same with four dance hall girls. The mayor, along with Judge Ellis and District Attorney Collins, stood waiting to receive the celebrated arrival. Seth also saw the pharmacist's daughter and Miss Dooley and others he recognized mingling with the bystanders.

And then he saw Rudy Stock and his mother—and Sam. They had taken his brother hostage and moved through the alley toward the rear of the train. Every muscle in Seth's body tightened. He thought of the promise he'd given his mother to make sure Sam was safe, and yet here he sat—helpless to do anything but watch as his brother was used as a shield.

"Ellie, could you get me some water, please?" He intentionally made his voice weak and clutched his bandaged side when the girl turned to look at him.

"It's empty," she said, holding up the pitcher and glass.

Seth was aware that he had drunk the last of the water. "Please?"

"I'll get some."

"Use the bathroom sink," he called as she started from the room. "And let it run so it's cold. I feel like my throat is on fire."

She hesitated, glancing at the window with a worried frown.

"I'll keep watch," he promised, and lifted the binoculars to make the point.

As soon as she was through the door, Seth struggled to his feet, thankful that he'd insisted on Jess helping him dress before he took his place in the chair by the window. He pulled on his boots, grimacing at the shots of pain that ricocheted through him with every movement. He grabbed his gun from the holster, tucked it into the waistband of his wool trousers, and stepped into the hallway. He could hear the water running and the clang of the metal pitcher as Ellie tried to fit it under the spigot. Holding onto the bannister for support, he hurried down the stairs, paused for a minute at the foot to catch his breath, and then opened the front door.

The difference between the shadowy light of his room and the bright sunlight took some getting used to. A wave of dizziness threatened to overpower him, and it took a full minute before the figures gathered around the station took solid form. He glanced from the crowd to the side street, where he could see Rudy's mother prodding Sam forward, while Rudy followed close behind, pulling a cart loaded with two valises. The three slipped behind the caboose, and he lost sight of them.

Seth made his way to the cover of the awning outside the drugstore and waited. The band struck up a tune as the train rolled to a stop. Everyone waited. Seth watched for Amanda to appear as planned. Once he knew she was safely out of harm's way, he would raise the alarm by firing his gun, knowing Jess and the soldiers would take action. But when she didn't step onto the platform, he saw Judge Ellis disappear into the shadows and then reappear a moment later, looking befuddled.

Seth pulled his gun from his waistband and limped

around the back of the train, where he saw Rudy Stock had shoved Sam aside and grabbed Amanda.

Mrs. Rosewood pulled off the large hat meant to serve as part of Amanda's disguise, and when Sam tried to come to Amanda's aid, Rudy struck him with the butt of his pistol. The boy dropped to the ground like a sack of potatoes.

The duo—with Rudy half-carrying Amanda—boarded the first car. Because the blinds had all been pulled on the other cars to disguise the presence of the soldiers, those men had no way of knowing that the Stocks were on the unprotected one. If Rudy and his mother barricaded themselves in that car, they would have control of the train—and they would have Amanda.

Seth hobbled down the alley, where Sam was trying to get to his feet once again. "You okay, kid?" he asked as he stopped to be sure his brother wasn't seriously hurt. He turned at the sound of footsteps and saw Jim Matthews coming his way.

"I'll take care of him!" he shouted, heading straight for Sam. "The train's moving out."

Sure enough, the train rolled forward, and as it did, Seth saw shades raised in the rear cars, even as soldiers dressed in street clothes stepped onto connecting platforms to find out what had gone wrong. He ran alongside as the train gathered speed, his ankle feeling like it was on fire. An officer leaned down and offered him his hand, and with a mighty tug, swung Seth onto the train.

As they rolled past the station and confused onlookers, Seth could still hear the musicians playing. And as he shouted to be heard above the rush of wind and the noise of the train, he fought for enough air to make it from one breath to the next.

It was a losing battle. The officer helped him inside the rear car to a seat where Jess glared at him as if this was his fault. Then he saw blood staining the bandages wrapped around his torso and shoulder.

❧

The minute Rudy dropped her on the floor and headed toward the locomotive, Amanda glared at Rudy's mother, who was making herself comfortable in a plush seat just inside the door. "You won't get away with this," she challenged.

The widow, who had seemed such a timid soul during their time together in the boardinghouse, laughed. "Honey, we already have." She raised the shade and nodded to the passing scenery outside.

The train was moving. Amanda saw the stunned faces of Ollie and Miss Dooley and Addie as the train chugged out of the station. She bolted for the door, only to be stopped by Rudy.

"Everything under control up front, son?" Mrs. Rosewood nodded toward the door that led to the engine.

Rudy grinned. "Yes, ma'am. Amazing what a handful of gold coins will buy you these days." Without pausing for further conversation, and dragging Amanda with him, he moved quickly to the back of the car, where he used an iron rod to barricade the door. Then he tied Amanda's wrists so that she stood stretched in the aisle between two rows of seats near the back, closest to the door that led to the rear cars.

"Let's see what them soldier boys do when they

come rushing through that there door and see you standing smack dab in their line of fire." He was giddy, clearly assuming he and his mother had won.

Having secured her, he retrieved the two valises he had heaved onto the platform after shoving Amanda to her knees. She could see how heavy they were and assumed they did not contain clothing. He placed them on the floor near his mother and collapsed on the seat next to her. Like a little boy exhausted from a long day of play, he rested his head on her shoulder as she stroked his cheek.

Amanda rolled her eyes and forced her attention on the door. *Think.*

She had not seen Jess among the passing faces of the crowd. Was it possible he had boarded the train? Was it possible that even now he was planning her rescue? She tried to see through the soot-covered glass of the connecting doors. She could see movement but not really make out individuals. The soldiers had their orders, and unless someone had seen the Stocks take her hostage, or ·maybe if Sam had been able to sound the alarm, or maybe if…

She stared harder at the silhouettes beyond the glass. Two men, clearly in a heated discussion. Two men whose body movements she knew all too well. Jess. And Seth! *Oh please, stop arguing and think,* she silently pleaded. She watched as a man in uniform stepped between them. Then she saw them peer through the glass, trying to see into the car where she was held captive. Jess wiped away soot with the sleeve of his shirt, then a minute later the door opened, and her brother and Seth stepped onto the platform.

No! Go back! She glanced over her shoulder—mother and son were still comfortably enjoying the ride, oblivious to her or whatever might be happening in the rear cars. They were confident they had won, and that made Amanda furious.

She tried her best to communicate with Seth and Jess through sign language, tilting her head to make them see she was tied, trying to maintain her balance as the train picked up speed, and then looking over her right shoulder toward the outlaws in the front seat. All she could do was pray they understood her signals.

Relieved when Seth and Jess returned to the other car, she turned her focus to escape. Sweat rolled down her neck, back, and arms. Her gown was stifling, and the energy it took to keep her balance in the moving car only added to her exertion. But then she realized she could use her discomfort to her advantage. Slowly, so she did not attract attention, she twisted and pulled, allowing the dampness of her skin to moisten the rope binding her wrists.

A flicker of movement caught her eye, and she saw Jess exit then climb to the roof of the car she occupied. Not three seconds later, Seth followed. She wanted to protest. He was in no shape for such exertion. He could fall. They could both be killed.

"Whatcha looking at, girlie?"

She hadn't heard Rudy leave his seat. For a big man, he was surprisingly agile. Realizing she had nearly succeeded in freeing one hand, she quickly shoved it forward so the ropes would appear secure. "Could we possibly open a window?" she asked.

Rudy ignored her and glanced at the car behind

them and grinned. "Looks like those soldier boys don't quite know what to do, Ma."

Amanda could see the soldiers milling about. Occasionally, one would come to the glass and peer through. Rudy pulled out his pistol. "Can I shoot, Ma?"

"Put that thing away."

"Aw, Ma, it would be like shooting fish in a barrel for sure." But he slid the pistol back in its holster. "I'll go check on the engineer. Seems like we're slowing down some."

"There's a tunnel," Amanda volunteered.

"Good thing them boys back there have realized you're standing in their way, then," Rudy said. "It would be a real shame if they decided to start shooting in the dark of the tunnel." He grabbed Amanda's face with one beefy hand and forced her to look at him. "That would be a damn shame, girlie, 'cause when this is over…? Ma says you're all mine, and I got plans—I got plans you can't imagine."

He was close enough that she could smell his fetid breath and see his bloodshot eyes. Amanda did the first thing that came to mind. She spat in his ugly, pock-scarred face.

Rudy moved his hand to her throat and squeezed. She couldn't breathe, and all she could think was that she didn't want to die.

"Rudy!" Mrs. Rosewood snapped. "We've no time for that."

The outlaw loosened his grip but did not release her as she gasped for air.

"I'm gonna take my time, girlie, and when it's over, you're gonna wish I had finished you now." He gave her a shove that served to loosen the ropes as he stalked toward the front of the car. "I'll go check on the engineer now," he muttered again, as he passed his mother standing in the aisle.

"What's happening back there?" she asked, standing and staring down the aisle, as she pointed in the direction of the car behind them.

"I don't know," Amanda lied. "I think they're confused—disorganized." *Please come closer,* Amanda silently pleaded. She had loosened the ropes enough so that both hands were free.

Just as they entered the tunnel, shots rang out from the front of the train. Mrs. Rosewood turned her back to Amanda, and seeing her chance, Amanda shoved the older woman to the floor and fell on top of her. Behind her she heard glass breaking as soldiers stormed through the barricaded door.

"No!" she shouted, afraid they might trample her in their zeal to do their duty.

"Hold your fire," she heard the officer command.

For an instant, everything stopped, and as the train emerged into daylight, Amanda turned to see half a dozen soldiers standing by the rear door as Mrs. Rosewood struggled beneath her.

Amanda ignored her as another shot rang out from the front. "Go!" she shouted to the officer. "I've got this." To prove her point, she grabbed the loosened ropes and used them to hog-tie the woman—always Mrs. Rosewood to her.

Clearly impressed, the officer directed his men to climb over the seats as they made their way forward. She stood to watch them go just as Jess came through the door.

"Stock shot the engineer and fireman, then turned on Seth and me. He got off a second round before I killed him, but we've got a bigger problem." Wild-eyed, he surveyed the men before him. "Anybody here know how to stop this train? Otherwise, the way that steam is building up, the thing's gonna explode." He dropped onto one of the seats, clutching his arm. Blood oozed from a wound above his temple.

Amanda pushed her way forward. "You've been shot."

"It's nothing." He pressed his hands to his head. "We've got to move everybody to the back or jump. Seth is…he was…" His eyelids fluttered as he passed out.

"You heard my brother," she said. "Help him, so we can all move to the rear."

When the soldiers gathered to tend to Jess, she slipped through the forward door and onto the platform, where she stopped. Below her the ground whipped by as the train rocked precariously from side to side. Between her and the locomotive was the tender. She had to get to Seth before the train ran off the tracks and crashed, or exploded as Jess had predicted.

She reached for the ladder on the tender. Behind her she saw soldiers carrying Jess and Mrs. Rosewood toward the back of the train. Clearly, no one had yet realized she wasn't with them.

Because her gown was weighing her down, she pulled off the skirt and let the wind carry it away. She did the same with her petticoat and, dressed in pantaloons and the top half of the brocade gown, she pulled herself up the five steps of the ladder, inched

her way across a short catwalk, and down onto the
coal pile used to feed the engine. Covered in soot, she
slid forward into the cab.

Seth's back was to her, and the noise of the
whistle, the racing locomotive, and the building
steam pressure was deafening. He was shirtless, and
his bandages had come undone and pooled around
his waist. He bled where the stitches had broken and
was covered in sweat. She saw how the muscles in his
back strained as he tried in vain to slow or stop the
runaway train.

"There's a steep incline ahead!" she shouted as she
touched his shoulder, and he spun to face her. "Maybe
that will work."

He shook his head. "You have to jump," he said,
"when the train starts to climb."

"Not without you!" She shook her head as the
wind tore at her hair that had come free.

Seth cupped her face in his palms. With his thumbs
he wiped soot from her lips. Then he kissed her. *I love
you*, he mouthed, and kissed her again, even as she
realized he had moved her closer to the door.

She wrapped both arms around his neck and held
on. "Then don't leave me!" She glanced over her
shoulder and saw the grassy landscape rush by, and
tightening her hold on him, she fell backward as the
train started its climb.

Seconds after they hit solid ground, Amanda
groaned and tried to sit up. Although she could still
hear the moving train chugging its way up the mountain, there was no wind, and she was surrounded by
an eerie silence. In the fall she had released her hold

on Seth, and now he lay facing away from her, as still as the air.

She'd killed him.

Imagining the worst, she crawled to his inert body. "No," she whispered as she touched his bare shoulder and saw blood oozing from the gunshot wound he'd suffered a day earlier. "Oh please, no," she whispered as she knelt next to him and looked around for help.

Behind her she was faintly aware of an explosion, and seconds later, she was pelted with what she thought must be ash and shrapnel. She covered Seth's head with her folded arms and face, determined to protect him from further harm, and felt his breath on her cheek.

He was alive! They were both alive. They could have a life together after all. She released a strangled mix of laughter and tears and stroked his face. But then she thought of the others—Jess had still been on that train.

"Stay here," she whispered to Seth. "I have to…I'll get help."

She struggled to her feet, and in so doing saw that they were surrounded not by ash and shredded metal as she had thought, but by scraps of paper money and bent gold coins. She blinked as the loot from the robbery blanketed the area. Then, through the smoke from the explosion, she saw movement and swallowed the fear that had built in her like the steam in the train when she saw soldiers emerge from the wreckage of the rear passenger car. It had been far enough away from the explosion to suffer only minor damage. They helped Jess down and supported him as they moved away from the wreck.

"You folks all right?" the officer shouted, waving to Amanda.

She waved in return as from the direction of town she heard the fire wagon and riders racing cross-country. She staggered back to where Seth lay and collapsed next to him. She cradled his head in her lap, noticing for the first time the blood pouring from her thigh and the metal shaft that had penetrated the skin.

"We're going to be all right," she whispered, and as she slipped into unconsciousness, she prayed it would be true.

Thirteen

SETH WAS PRETTY SURE HE'D DREAMED A GOOD DEAL OF what had happened once he followed Jess up that ladder and across the roof of the moving train. He recalled how he had struggled to keep his balance, how Jess had motioned for him to go back, how each had made the leap across the divide that separated the tender from the first passenger car—the car where Amanda had been held prisoner. He recalled the whispered argument he'd had with Jess about how best to overpower Rudy and take charge of the train. He recalled the sudden gunfire and the body of the fireman slumping at the foot of the coal pile.

Yet he was sure what happened next was real— Rudy spotted them and raised his pistol, the engineer tackled Rudy from behind and wrestled him to the floor, another shot, and the engineer staggered backward and fell from the open cab. All of that was real—especially the part where Rudy took aim at Jess, and Jess shot him.

But after Jess yelled at Seth to get off the train and then started back the way he'd come…that part was fuzzy. Seth only knew that he needed to stop the train, or else they were all going to die, and he had plans that did not include dying, and certainly didn't include losing Amanda.

Had she really been there? Had she really been there only half-dressed? It was a fantasy he'd entertained on numerous occasions. He just hadn't thought they would be hurtling through space on a moving train when that moment came.

"Seth?"

He couldn't really make out the person calling his name. It was a man, and therefore disappointing. At the moment, the only voice he wanted to hear was Amanda's. He forced himself to focus and saw Jess peer down at him. He had one arm in a sling and looked worried.

"Amanda," Seth managed to choke out.

Addie gently pushed her husband aside and smiled. "Well, look who finally decided to join us."

"Amanda," he repeated firmly, and tried to sit up.

"Easy there, cowboy," Addie admonished him. "She's resting comfortably, although she probably won't be walking down the aisle any time soon."

"I need to see her." Once again, Seth tried to get up.

This time it was Jess who restrained him with one firm hand. "Listen to the doc."

Seth glanced around and realized he was back in his room at the boardinghouse. And that might mean Amanda was across the hall. "Open the door." When Addie did as he asked, he added, "And hers."

Jess and Addie exchanged a look, but when Seth

seemed determined to leave his bed, Addie nodded. "All right. Just calm down."

He heard Addie cross the hall and an exchange of words between her and Amanda. When she returned, she was smiling. "You have to be two of the most stubborn people in the world when it comes to doing what's best to heal. Go ahead, then. She's listening."

"A little privacy would be nice," Seth said, glancing from Addie to Jess.

Addie burst into giggles. "Where do you think we can go that we won't…"

"Leave," Seth demanded, and Addie took Jess's hand and they left the room. He waited until he heard their steps retreat before speaking.

"Amanda, can you hear me?" He pushed himself to a sitting position and waited.

"Yes." Her voice was weak.

Seth held onto the iron post of the bed and pulled himself to his feet. Using the furnishings and the railing on the stairway as support, he stumbled across the hall. Every muscle in his body screamed to get back to bed, but he refused until he reached her room and could lean against the doorjamb while he studied her.

She was lying against several pillows, her hair fanned out around her. She was dressed in some frilly lace nightgown that covered her to her chin. She looked pale and weak, but she was beautiful—and if he had his way, soon she would be his.

She smiled. "You look terrible."

"Thanks. I kind of hoped if you felt sorry for me, you might agree to marry me." He kicked the door shut, covered the two steps it took to reach her, and sat on the side of the bed.

"You want me to marry you out of pity?"

He loosened the first ribbon holding her gown closed. "Whatever it takes." The second ribbon slipped through his fingers, and he saw her breathing quicken. "So, will you?"

"I might. Of course, there would be terms."

Opening the third ribbon gave him space to place his palm on her bare skin. "I'm listening."

"I do not want to live some quiet life in the country, so get that idea right out of your head."

He shrugged. "How about Chicago? Would that be lively enough for you?" He untied two more ribbons and spread her gown open as he ran one finger along her throat and the cleft between her breasts.

"How about we live here? You could run for sheriff—I hear there's an opening."

"Tucson's nice. What else?"

"And," she continued, "I want at least half a dozen children."

He chuckled. "Then maybe we'd best get started."

She put her lips on his ear and whispered, "Send for Judge Ellis, and let's do this now. I won't wait a day longer to have you make love to me as your wife."

Her words and warm, moist breath threatened to be his undoing. He raised his face to hers. "You're sure this is what you want?"

She nodded, cupped his face with her hands, and pulled him close for her kiss.

He shifted on the bed as he prepared to gather her in his arms and feel her whole body pressed to his.

Only when she winced did he realize he had hurt her. "Sorry. I…"

To silence him, she pulled him closer, and he saw that her eyes had filled with tears. "I almost lost you," she whispered. "What if…" Tears spilled over and trailed down her cheeks.

"Shhh," he whispered. "We're done with all that. It's over. All we need to think about now is the future—our future."

She swiped at her tears and smiled. "And yet, here you sit when it's already been at least two minutes since I asked you to send for Judge Ellis. Oh, and we'll need Addie and your brother as witnesses, and…"

Sam!

Seth sat up. "I haven't seen Sam. I mean, why wouldn't he have been there when I came to? If that kid has taken off again…"

"He must be resting. Addie told me he was pretty roughed up—broken jaw from Rudy hitting him, not to mention a bunch of cuts and bruises he suffered while on the run."

"I need to see him. He'd best be glad he's already banged up because his bone-headed action nearly got us both killed."

She took hold of his hand and kissed it. "Go call for Jess. We'll send him to get Sam and the judge, while Addie helps you put on a proper shirt and gets me ready to be a bride."

He stared. "We're really going to do this?"

She frowned. "Are you trying to back out now that you're the one who—"

He grinned, planted a quick kiss on her pouting lips,

and hobbled to the door. From the top of the stairs, he bellowed, "Jess? Doc? We need some help up here."

To his satisfaction, three sets of footsteps thundered up the stairway.

"What's happened?" Addie demanded, the first to reach the top, followed by her husband and Miss Dooley.

"You need to see Amanda," Seth instructed. "Something about getting all gussied up for the wedding. You," he added, turning to Jess, "need to fetch Judge Ellis and my brother. And you…" He paused a second as he considered a task for Miss Dooley. "We're gonna need some flowers, maybe some cake, if Bessie has something. Oh, and a ring."

"A ring?"

"We're getting married—Amanda and me." He felt something rush through his body and realized the only word for it was *joy*, so he said it again. "We're getting married."

Jess scowled. "Kind of rushing this, aren't you?"

"Your sister wants things this way," Seth replied, as the feeling ebbed. "It's what I want as well. We've already wasted too much time."

"Jess?" Both men turned at the sound of Amanda's voice. "Stop picking on Seth, and go find Judge Ellis. I'll send Mama a telegram to let her know we'll come back to the ranch for a real fandango to celebrate."

Jess slammed his hat on his head and headed downstairs, muttering to himself all the way.

"He'll come around," Addie assured Seth.

Seth nodded and started toward Amanda's room.

"Not so fast," Addie said, stalling him as she checked his stitches, and then tightened the bandages.

"You get yourself cleaned up and dressed. You'll see your bride in due time." Assuming he would do as she instructed, she turned to the stairway. "Miss Dooley, maybe we could get Ellie Baxter to help a bit? Amanda says it might lift her spirits."

It was one more thing he loved about his bride-to-be—his *wife-to-be*. She had a way of thinking how she might make life better for others. She would be a wonderful mother.

He realized Addie was talking to him as she returned to Amanda's room. "...clean shirt...comb that hair..." The door closed.

"Seth?"

He hadn't heard his brother come up the stairs. Sam's jaw was wired almost shut, so the word came out in a mumble. But it was Sam, and he was alive, and this time Seth didn't give a hoot about whether hugging another man was right. It felt right, and that was enough for him.

Like the kid he was, Sam broke down and cried, his thin shoulders shaking as he clung to his older brother. "Hey, stop that now," Seth said, pulling away enough so he could see Sam's face. "I'm in need of a best man for my wedding, and I was thinking you might fill the bill."

"You're getting married? Does Ma know?"

"Not yet. How about I write out a message, and you wire it to her while I get cleaned up and put on a shirt?"

"Sure thing."

Any sign of tears was gone as Sam waited for Seth to scribble a note to his parents and then took off for the telegraph office.

Seth watched him go as it hit him that the danger had passed, and they were about to start a new part of their lives. He smiled and then let out a whoop of pure jubilation.

※

Amanda could not stop smiling. Everything she had ever dreamed of was about to come true. And it was all neatly packaged in one person—Seth.

Over the next couple of hours, her room was alive with activity as Addie, Ellie, and Miss Dooley fussed over every detail. They filled vases with grasses and early-blooming wildflowers Ellie and Eli had gathered. Miss Dooley insisted on arranging Amanda's hair into a chignon with tendrils of curls framing her face. Addie helped her dress in a freshly laundered gown of white with lace trim around the neckline and cuffs of its long sleeves.

"It's almost a wedding gown," she declared. "With fresh cases on the pillows, you'll look like the princess you are."

The only disappointing news came from Jess, who reported that the judge would not be available until later that evening. The wait seemed excruciating, but Addie assured her Seth was every bit as restless as she was, and then settled into the chair near Amanda's bed to bring her up to date on what had happened since the explosion.

"Apparently, it wasn't so bad as to damage the rear cars, so Jess and the soldiers were not injured. Nor was that woman."

Amanda smiled at Addie's refusal to call Mrs. Rosewood by any name at all. "Did they arrest her?"

"On the spot, and took her back to the fort, since she'll stand trial for her part in stealing a federal payroll."

"And Ezra Baxter?"

Addie frowned. "I'm afraid he'll have to answer for his part in all of this, but Seth's brother has volunteered to testify on his behalf. Ezra was forced to take part or risk losing his livelihood and his children in the bargain."

"He's not a bad man," Amanda said. "Just not…"

Addie heaved a sigh of exasperation. "You find the good in everyone. That man threatened you, and if it hadn't been for him—"

"If it hadn't been for his need of a teacher for Ellie and Eli, where would I be? Back on the ranch? Bored to tears?"

Addie threw up her hands. "I give up. I'm going downstairs to get your supper. Try to rest. Whether you admit it or not, this has been a full day, and you want to look your best for the ceremony."

Trying not to disturb her hair or anything about the arrangements to have her looking bridal when the judge finally arrived, Amanda pressed her head to the pillow and tried to sleep when she heard a light knock at her door.

"Come in," she called and was surprised when Jim Matthews stepped inside the room.

"I won't stay," he said. "I just…Ginny heard you and Seth were…" He shrugged. "I came to wish you happiness."

She held out her hand, inviting him to come closer. "Thank you for coming."

"Are you all right?"

"I will be."

They stared at each other for a long moment. Amanda looked away first. "It would not have worked," she said softly.

"I know," he agreed. "Look, Grover is a good man, and now that everyone knows he was working under-cover for Wells Fargo, seems like he's quite the hero."

"I love him."

"Yeah, I know. He's one lucky man." He squeezed her hand then bent and kissed her forehead. "Be happy, Amanda Porterfield. No one deserves it more." He walked back to the door and turned.

Later, when she woke, the room was in shadow, and she realized that some time had passed. A soft knock at the door drew her attention away from the sounds of people gathering downstairs.

"Come in," she called as she scrubbed sleep from her eyes.

Jess opened the door. "Ready to get married?"

"We'll need some light," she said as she surveyed the room. "Do you think there might be some candles we could use?"

Jess grinned as he approached the bed. "Sure thing, Sis, but you don't really want to get married lying in bed, do you?"

"I…"

Before she could protest, he had thrown back the covers and gently lifted her into his arms. He carried her downstairs, where she saw a wheelchair waiting by the front door. She heard voices she recognized coming from behind the closed sliding doors of the parlor.

"That's Mama," she whispered.

Jess nodded as he set her in the wheelchair and wrapped a blanket around her knees. "Well, you don't think I'd let you get hitched without her approval, do you? And since Judge Ellis couldn't be here until now, we had the time." He rolled the chair toward the pocket doors and knocked lightly.

Her youngest brother Trey pushed the doors open as her sister Maria and her mother stepped into the foyer carrying a bridal veil that they arranged over her hair. The room was alight with candles and a glowing fire. Among the people gathered in the parlor, she saw their housekeeper Juanita and her family. Maria's husband, Chet, Ollie and Miss Jensen, Eli and Ellie, Jim Matthews and Ginny, and even their ranch foreman, Bunker.

And Seth.

He was dressed in a blue shirt, a bolo tie, and black trousers, his hair slicked back from his high forehead. He listened to something his brother was saying, but then he saw her, and she knew that for him, as for her, suddenly the room might have been empty. No one else mattered.

Addie and Maria led the procession as Jess rolled her slowly past the guests to where Judge Ellis waited. When they were halfway there, Seth left his place and walked to meet her. He shook hands with Jess.

"I've got it from here," he said, and as he guided the wheelchair the rest of the way to the fireplace, Sam set a chair next to it for Seth to sit. When he did so, he turned to her and took her hands in his, then turned to the judge. "Ready when you are," he said, and behind them everyone chuckled.

Amanda felt as if she were living in a dream, hearing Judge Ellis's words but not really hearing them at all. She was only aware of Seth—the way his hands covered hers, the warmth that filled her at his touch, the way his eyes focused only on her, and the way he made her feel beautiful. Then the judge called for the ring, and she was about to say there had been no time, that a ring didn't matter, when Sam passed Seth a small heart-shaped green velvet box—a box she recognized. It was the box where her mother had kept the thin silver band that had been her wedding ring before her father made his fortune and insisted on something far more grand.

She had always loved that simple ring, and she glanced over Seth's shoulder to where her mother stood with her beloved family. Constance Porterfield smiled and nodded, giving this union her full blessing. And as Seth slid the ring onto her finger, she knew they were bound to one another 'til death did they part. *And beyond,* she thought.

"You may kiss your bride, sir," Judge Ellis intoned.

Neither Seth nor Amanda needed permission. Their kiss was no doubt shocking to some, but Amanda wasn't about to worry about satisfying others. This was the man she loved, the man she had desired during sleepless nights, the man she would spend her days to come living with, no doubt arguing with, and celebrating life's wonders with. This was her husband.

Judge Ellis cleared his throat to remind them they had guests and said, "Friends and family, it is my great pleasure to present Mr. and Mrs. Seth Grover."

About the Author

Award-winning author Anna Schmidt resides in Wisconsin. She delights in creating stories where her characters must wrestle with the challenges of their times. Critics have consistently praised Schmidt for her ability to seamlessly integrate actual events with her fictional characters to produce strong tales of hope and love in the face of seemingly insurmountable obstacles. Visit her at www.booksbyanna.com.

Please enjoy the following glimpse of Rosanne Bittner's
The Last Outlaw, *coming September 2017:*

THE LAST OUTLAW

Prologue

June, 1897

THERE WERE NINE OF THEM THAT DAY. ALL HARD men—all on a mission. To get rich off of someone else's money, that is—money they would steal from the City Bank in Boulder, Colorado. Their horses panted and snorted from the hard ride, and a mixture of dust and sod rolled from under the horses' hooves.

The riders wore long canvas coats over shirts and jackets in the cool spring weather, and under it all they wore gun belts packed with cartridges. Some held one gun, some two, and everyone carried rifles on their saddles. Some were clean shaven, others were nothing but filth and beards and unwashed hair. All wore wide-brimmed hats against the bright, spring Colorado sun, and all were filled with anticipation for the ways they would spend the money they were going to take today. Women and whiskey—those were number one.

They rode up toward the foothills of the Rockies and right over farmers' fields, avoiding the main roads. They were coming from the Santa Fe Trail in New Mexico, leaving behind their usual freighters and what was left of the stagecoach lines. Trains were their specialty, and always they were trying to avoid the Pinkertons, the relentless railroad detectives who hunted them.

Their leader, George Callahan, figured Boulder to be a peaceful, unsuspecting, little-guarded mountain town. They wouldn't be ready for nine men to ride in and take over a bank. They wouldn't be ready for men who didn't care who might get killed in the process. Tomorrow they would ride out of Boulder with a fortune in railroad and mining money, and head for Mexico.

There was only one problem with Callahan's plan. He'd picked the wrong day to rob a bank in Boulder. Neither he nor any of his men knew Jake Harkner happened to be in Boulder, and he would still be there…tomorrow.

One

JAKE TRAILED HIS TONGUE OVER HIS WIFE'S SKIN, trying to ignore his fear that she could be dying. Her belly was too caved-in, her hip bones too prominent.

She'll get better, he told himself. The taste of her most secret place lingered on his lips as he moved to her breasts, still surprisingly full, considering, but not the same breasts he'd always loved and teased her about, with the enticing cleavage that stirred his desire for her.

He would *always* desire her. This was his Randy. She was his breath. Her spirit ran in his veins, and she was his reason for being. God knew his worthless hide had no business even still being on this earth.

He ran a hand over her ribs, which were too damn easy to count. Sometimes he thought he'd go mad with the memory of last winter, the reason she'd become more withdrawn and had nearly stopped eating.

He met her mouth, and she responded. Thank God she still wanted this, but something was missing, and he couldn't put his finger on it. He thought he'd made it all better, thought he'd taken away the ugly.

He'd feared at first she might blame him for what had happened, but it had been quite the opposite. She'd become almost too clingy, constantly asking if he loved her, not to let go of her, asking him not to go far away.

He pushed himself inside of her, wanting nothing more than to please her, to find a way to break down the invisible wall he felt between them, to erase the past and assure her he was right here, that he still loved her. How in hell could he not love this woman, the one who'd loved him when he was anything but loveable…all those years ago. She'd put up with his past and his bouts of insanity and all the trouble and heartache he'd put her through…this woman who'd given him a son and daughter who couldn't make a man prouder and who loved him beyond what he was worth…six grandchildren who climbed all over him, full of such innocent love for a man who'd robbed and killed, and worst of all…killed his own father.

He moved his hands under her bottom, pushing himself deep inside her, relishing the way she returned his deep kisses and pressed her fingers into his upper arms in an almost desperate neediness.

That was what bothered him. This had always been good between them, a true mating of souls, teasing remarks back and forth as they made love. But now it was as though she feared losing him if she didn't make love often, and that wasn't the sort of man he was. It had always been pure pleasure between them. He'd taught her things she would never have thought of, helped her relax and release every sexual inhibition. He knew every inch of her body intimately, and she'd loved it.

This was different. And it was harder now, because not only did he hate the idea of feeling like he was forcing her, but he was also terrified he would break something. She was so thin and small now. He outweighed her by a good hundred and fifty pounds by now; she couldn't weigh more than eighty or ninety.

He surged deep in a desperate attempt to convince himself he wasn't losing her. And through it all, he was screaming inside. Sometimes he wanted to shake her and make her tell him what else he could do to bring back the woman he'd known and loved for nearly thirty-two years. He missed that feisty, bossy woman, the only person on this earth who could bring him to his knees. He'd faced the worst of men as a lawman in Oklahoma, and run with the worst of men the first thirty years of his life. He'd spent four years in prison under horrible conditions. He'd been in too many gunfights to count, taken enough bullets that he had no right still being alive. He'd ridden the Outlaw Trail and defied all the odds. His reputation followed him everywhere, and a reporter had even written a book about him—*Jake Harkner: The Legend and the Myth*. *Myth* was more like it. And the legend wasn't one he was proud of.

And this woman beneath him...this woman he poured his life into this very moment...she'd been there for most of it.

He relaxed and moved to her side.

"Don't let go yet, Jake."

He pulled her against him. "Randy, I can't put my weight on you anymore. You're too damn thin. You've got to gain some weight back or we'll have to stop."

"No!" She shimmied closer, pulling one of his arms around her. "I like being right here in your arms. Don't stop making love to me, Jake. You might turn to someone else. You're still my handsome, strong Jake. Women look at you and want you."

Jake sighed, the stress of her condition making him want to tear the room apart. "You have to stop talking that way."

"That you're handsome and strong?" She turned slightly. "Since when does the magnificent Jake Harkner hate compliments?"

There it was—a tiny spark of the old Randy in her teasing. Every time he saw that spark it gave him hope. "I've always hated compliments. You know that. The only thing magnificent about me is my sordid reputation. I'd like to wring Treena Brown's neck for putting that label on me in her letter."

Randy traced her fingers over his lips. "Peter's wife was totally taken by you when they visited the ranch last summer."

"She's a city woman full of wrong ideas about what she considers western heroes. God knows I'm sure as hell *not* one, and right now your magnificent Jake needs a cigarette." Jake pulled away and sat up. "You okay?"

"Of course I'm okay. You just made love to me. How could a woman not be okay after that?"

Jake took a Long Jack from a tin on the hotel's bedside table. "You know what I mean." She didn't answer as he lit the cigarette. He took a long drag. "Did I hurt you?"

"Of course not."

Jake ran a hand through his hair. "Randy, I mean

it about your weight. If you don't start eating, I'm not making love to you anymore. Sometimes when I'm on top of you I envision every rib breaking. We made this trip to Boulder because it was time you started getting away from the ranch, doing a few things amid strangers without being glued to me."

Be patient. Don't yell at her. She might go to pieces.

He heard a sniffle, and it felt like his heart was breaking. He took another long drag before setting the cigarette into an ashtray and turned, moving back in beside her. "Baby, I've done everything I can to help you. When you're like this, it makes me sick with guilt. I should have realized what was happening when that barn caught on fire…the way it burned so rapidly. Lloyd suffers with the same guilt. We shouldn't have left the house unguarded."

"No! No! No!" Randy threw her arms around him. "Don't ever blame yourself. You blame yourself for *everything* bad that happens to this family, but you never asked for any of it, Jake."

He held her close, being careful not to use too much strength. "Randy, I want my wife back. The woman I'm holding right now isn't her."

"I will be. I promise. Tomorrow, Teresa and little Tricia and I will go shopping. I won't be quite so terrified without you at my side if I at least have Teresa with me. Thank you for bringing her along."

Jake was grateful for the Mexican woman who was such a help with the cooking as well as cleaning the big log home he'd built for Randy. It was still filled with noise at meals, some of the grandchildren or all of the family gathering, especially for Sunday meals.

Before last winter, Randy had been a vital part of those gatherings—the one most in control, who loved all the cooking, who loved teaching and reading with Evie and the grandchildren. Living on a remote ranch meant no schools nearby, after all.

Randy now left it all to Evie. She was no longer her joyful self at the dinner table, although she put on a good show. He knew her every mood, and he could tell she was still suffering inside.

"Tell me what you need, Randy. How else can I help? You aren't here with me when we make love anymore. I can sense it in your kisses, in the way you respond when I'm inside you. I won't make love to a woman who's doing it out of duty."

She buried her face in his neck. "Jake, I still love it when you make love to me. It's just…" She hesitated again. How many times had he come close to getting it out of her what was really bothering her?

"Just what? *Talk* to me, Randy."

She curled into a little ball against him. "That… ugly thing they did. That ugly thing. I can't…get past it. I'm so sorry, Jake."

Jake struggled against insane rage every time he thought about it. His precious Randy. Of all the intimate things he and his wife had done, asking her to perform oral sex on him had never been one of them. She'd never suggested such a thing or made an attempt, and he'd never asked. What they had together was enough for him. His first desire was always to give her pleasure, and that alone gave him pleasure in return. It would be disrespectful to ask this beautiful woman to do something he knew in his gut she wouldn't want to do. He still had the blazing memory of his father forcing himself on his mother that way right in front of her sons while she resisted. Sometimes, such childhood memories still made him wake up with screaming nightmares.

It all came down to his father...his ruthless, brutal, drunken father...the man he hated worse than all the dredges of humankind, more than the filth he used to run with when he believed he was the worthless sonofabitch his father had always told him he was.

"Don't be sorry." *God help keep me sane.* "We'll work it out."

"Don't stop making love to me."

"I won't stop."

"You do still love me, don't you?"

"Stop asking me that. You know better." He wiped at her tears with his fingers. "Get some sleep, Randy. Tomorrow is a big day."

"You won't ever be too far away, will you, even when I leave you to shop?"

"I won't be too far away."

"You'll watch for me?"

"You know I will." He'd never felt so alone. Ever since he'd found and fallen in love with this woman, he'd always had her to lean on, to keep him from the abyss of blackness that beckoned. Tough and able as he seemed to others, *she* was his strength. And now that strength was gone. The tables had turned, and he had to be strong for her. He secretly begged God to help him remember that. He wasn't sure he had it in him to last much longer this way. "Randy, when you figure out what more I can do, or what it is that will help you get better, you tell me. Don't ever be afraid to tell me—*anything*—all right? You know I've seen it all and done it all and nothing surprises me. And I love you. I'll do whatever it takes. Understand?"

"Yes."

"I can tell right now you're keeping something from me—something more than what happened last winter. You tell me when you're ready."

She clung closer, kissing his chest. "I will."

He kept his arms around her because she demanded it, every night until she fell asleep. He closed his eyes against his own silent tears. Without that closeness they'd always shared, it was as though he didn't even exist. Without this woman, who was Jake Harkner?

Please enjoy the following glimpse of Margaret Brownley's
A Match Made in Texas, *now available:*

A Match Made in Texas

Two-Time, Texas
1882

COULD SHE TRUST HIM? *DARE* SHE TRUST HIM?

The man—a stranger—looked like one tough hombre. Perched upon the seat of a weather-beaten wagon, he sat tall, lean, and decisively strong, his sun-baked hands the color of tanned leather. The only feature visible beneath his wide-brimmed hat and shaggy beard was a well-defined nose. The beard, along with his shoulder-length hair, suggested he had no regard for barbers. From the looks of him, he wasn't all that fond of bathhouses either.

"Need a ride?" the stranger asked, looking down at her with open curiosity.

She hesitated. It wasn't as if she had a lot of choices.

If she didn't accept his offer, she might have to spend the rest of the day, maybe even the night, alone in the Texas wilderness with the rattlers, cactus, and God knows what else.

"Where you headin'?" he asked.

This time she answered. "Two-Time."

"Same here," he said with a gruff nod, as if that alone was reason to trust him.

His destination should have offered no surprise. Two-Time was the only town within twenty miles. "Why there?" she asked.

Her hometown had grown by leaps and bounds since the arrival of the train but still lagged behind San Antonio and Austin in commerce and population. Most people, if they ended up in Two-Time at all, did so by mistake.

He shrugged his wide shoulders. "Good a place as any."

Moistening her parched lips, she shaded her eyes from the blazing sun as she gazed up at him. No sense beating around the bush. "You don't have a nefarious intent, do you? To do me harm, I mean?" A woman alone couldn't be too careful.

The question seemed to surprise him. At least it made him push back his hat, revealing steel-blue eyes that seemed to pierce right through her. What a strange sight she must look. Stuck in the middle of nowhere dressed to the nines in a stylish blue walking suit.

"Are you askin' if your virtue is safe with me?"

She blushed but refused to back down. The man didn't mince words, and neither would she. "Well, is it?"

"Safe as you want it to be," he said finally. His lazy drawl didn't seem to go with the sharp-eyed regard, which returned again and again to her peacock feathered hat, rising three stories and a basement high above her brow.

It wasn't exactly the answer she'd hoped for, but he sounded sincere, and that gave her a small measure of comfort. Still, she cast a wary eye on his holstered weapon. The Indian Wars had ended, but the possibility of renegades was real. The area also teemed with outlaws. In that sense, it wouldn't hurt to have an armed man by her side. Even one as surly as this one.

"If you would be so kind as to help me with my... um...trunk. I'd be most grateful."

He sprang from the wagon, surprising her with his sudden speed. For such a large man, he was surprisingly light on his feet. He was also younger than he first appeared, probably in his early thirties. He would have towered over her by a good eight inches had she not been wearing a hat gamely designed to give her height and presence.

Gaze dropping the length of her, he visually lingered on her small waist and well-defined hips a tad too long for her peace of mind.

"Name's Rennick," he said, meeting her eyes. "R. B. Rennick."

A false name if she ever heard one, but for once, she decided to hold her tongue. He was her best shot for getting back to town. He might be her only shot.

"I'm Miss Amanda Lockwood." She offered her gloved hand, which he blithely ignored. Feeling rebuffed, she withdrew it.

The man was clearly lacking in manners, but he had offered to help her, and for that she was grateful.

Thumbs hanging from his belt, he gazed across the desolate Texas landscape. "How'd you land out here, anyway? Nothing for miles 'round."

"I was on my way home from Austin when I…had a little run-in with the stage driver."

He raised an eyebrow. "What kind of run-in?"

"He was driving like a maniac," she said with an indignant toss of the head. "And I told him so." Not once but several times, in fact.

Hanging out the stage window, she'd insisted he slow down in no uncertain terms. When that didn't work, she resorted to banging on the coach's ceiling with her parasol and calling him every unflattering name she could think of. Perhaps a more tactful way of voicing her complaints would have worked more in her favor, but how was she supposed to know the man had such a low threshold for criticism?

She gritted her teeth just thinking about it. "Thought he would kill us all." He pretty near did. The nerve of him, tossing her bag and baggage out of the stage and leaving her stranded.

Mr. Rennick scratched his temple. "Hope you learned your lesson, ma'am. Men don't like being told what to do. 'Specially when holding the reins." It sounded like a warning.

Turning abruptly, he picked up the wooden chest and heaved it over the side of the wagon like it weighed no more than a loaf of bread. It hit the bottom of the wagon with a sickening thud.

She gasped. "Be careful." Belatedly, she remembered his warning and tempered his order with, "It's very old."

The hope chest was a family heirloom. If anything happened to it, her family would never forgive her. The chest had been handed down from mother to daughter for decades. She inherited the chest after the last of her two sisters wed. Since she had no interest in marriage, she used it mostly to store books. Today, it contained the clothes needed for her nearly weeklong stay in Austin.

He brushed his hands together. "Sure is heavy. You'd have an easier time haulin' a steer."

"Yes, well, it's actually a hope chest." While packing for her trip, she discovered the latch on her steamer trunk broken. The hope chest was a convenient though not altogether satisfactory substitute. For one, it was almost too heavy for her to handle alone—the most she could do was drag it.

"Don't know what you're hoping for, ma'am, but you're not likely to find it out here."

He gazed into the distance for a moment, then suddenly spun around and climbed into the driver's seat without offering to help her. "Well, what are you waitin' for?" he yelled. "Get in!"

Startled by his sharp command, she reached for the grab handle and heaved herself up to the passenger side.

No sooner had she seated herself upon the wooden bench than Mr. Rennick took off hell-bent for leather.

Glued to the back of the seat, she cried out. "Oh dear. Oh my. *Ohhh!*"

What had looked like a perfectly calm and passive black horse had suddenly turned into a demon. With pounding hooves and flowing mane, the steed flew over potholes and dirt mounds, giving no heed to the cargo behind. The wagon rolled and pitched like a ship in stormy seas. Dust whirled in the air, and rocks hit the bottom and sides.

Holding on to her hat with one hand and the seat with the other, Amanda watched in wide-eyed horror as the scenery flew by in a blur.

The wagon sailed over a hill as if it was airborne, and she held on for dear life. The wheels hit the ground, jolting her hard and rattling her teeth. The hope chest bounced up and down like dice in a gambler's hand. Her breath whooshed out, and it was all she could do to find her voice.

"Mr. R-Rennick!" she stammered, grabbing hold of his arm. She had to shout to be heard.

"What?" he yelled back.

She stared straight ahead, her horrified eyes searching for a soft place to land should the need arise. "Y-you sh-should s-slow down and enjoy the s-scenery."

Her hat had tilted sideways, and he swiped the peacock feather away from his face. "Been my experience that sand and sagebrush look a whole lot better when travelin' fast," he shouted in his strong baritone voice.

He made a good point, but at the moment, she was more concerned with life and limb.

He urged his horse to go faster before adding, "It's also been my experience that travelin' fast is the best way to outrun bandits."

"W-what do you mean? B-bandits?" It was then that she heard gunfire.

She swung around in her seat, and her jaw dropped. Three masked horsemen were giving chase—and closing in fast.

Two

"OH NO!" SHE CRIED.

"You better get down, ma'am," Mr. Rennick shouted. "They look like they mean bus'ness."

Dropping off her seat, Amanda scrunched against the floorboards. Her body shook so hard, her teeth chattered. "G-give me your g-gun," she cried.

"Know how to use it?" he yelled back.

"N-no, but I'm a f-fast learner!" She pulled off her gloves, which flew out of the wagon like frantic white doves.

Holding the reins with one hand, he grabbed his gun with the other. After cocking the hammer with his thumb, he handed it to her. The gun was heavier than she expected, requiring both hands to grasp. Keeping her head low, she balanced herself on wobbly knees and rested the barrel on the back of the seat. She held onto the grip with all her might. Still, the muzzle bobbed up and down like corn popping on a hot skillet.

Aiming at a specific target was out of the question. The jostling wagon made control impossible. The best she could do was to keep from shooting the driver.

She wasn't all that anxious to shoot the bandits either. She just wanted to scare them away.

Eyes squeezed shut, barrel pointed in the bandits' general direction, she pulled the trigger. The blast shook her to the core, and her arm flung up with the recoil. She fell back against the footrest and fought to regain her balance.

"Good shot!" he yelled, looking over his shoulder. "You stopped your hope-a-thingie from attackin'. Now see if you can do the same with the bandits."

Her heart sank. Oh no. Not the hope chest. Her family would kill her. That is, if the bandits didn't kill her first. Forcing air into her lungs, she fought to reposition herself. The horsemen kept coming. They were so close now, she could see the sun glinting off their weapons.

Bracing herself against the recoil, she fired again, this time aiming higher. The wagon veered to the right, and she fell against the side, hitting her shoulder hard. Her feathered hat ripped from its pins and flew from the wagon in a way that no peacock ever had.

"Oh no!" That was her very best hat, and the fact that it landed on the nearest highwayman gave her small comfort. His horse stopped, but the bandit kept going.

"Stay down!" Rennick yelled.

"But my hat…" It was one of the most elaborate hats she'd ever created. The peacock feathers matched the color of her eyes. "I loved that hat!"

"Yeah, well, too bad it didn't return your affection."

Of all the rude things to say. Blinking away the dust in her eyes, she hunkered close to the floorboards and struggled to catch her breath.

The wagon continued to race over uneven ground, jolting her until she was ready to scream. Just when she thought her battered body could take no more, the wheels mercifully rolled to a stop.

She shot Rennick a questioning look. "W-what are you doing?"

"Seems like our friends deserted us."

She raised her limp body off the floorboards on shaky limbs and flung herself onto the seat, breathing hard. All that was visible in the far distance was a cloud of dust that seemed to be moving in the opposite direction.

Relief rushed through her. "W-why do you suppose they gave up the chase?"

He lifted the gun from her hand and holstered it. "Guess the hat was enough to convince them that whatever chunk change we might have wasn't worth the trouble."

She glared at him. He didn't seem to notice.

Her hair had fallen from its bun, and she did her best to pin back the loose chestnut strands. She brushed the dust off her skirt and rubbed her shoulder.

"You okay?" he asked.

She nodded, though without her hat and gloves, she felt naked.

He drank from a metal flask and wiped his mouth with the back of his hand. "Here." He handed her the canteen.

She hesitated before bringing the spout to her mouth. The water was warm and tasted metallic; still, it helped quench her thirst. Pulling a lace handkerchief from her sleeve, she poured a few drops on it before handing the canteen back.

She dabbed her face with the moist handkerchief, but it offered little relief from the heat. The sun was almost directly overhead, and though still early spring, the temperature hovered in the high eighties.

"Do you mind if I retrieve my parasol from my hope…trunk?"

"I'll get it." Before she could object, he jumped to the ground and walked to the back of the wagon.

She tossed him an anxious glance and tried to remember how she'd packed. Were her intimate garments on the top or bottom of the chest? She'd packed in a hurry and couldn't remember. Shaking her head in annoyance, she blew out her breath. They had almost been robbed, maybe even killed, and here she worried about—of all things—a few pairs of red satin drawers and corset covers.

He returned to his seat with her parasol, his expressionless face giving no clue as to what unmentionables he had been privy to.

"Much obliged," she said, taking it from him.

He regarded her with curiosity. "What were you doin' in Austin?"

She opened the sun umbrella, casting a welcome shadow over her heated face. "I was at a Rights for Women meeting."

He made a face. "I should've known." He picked up the reins. "You're one of those suffering ladies."

She leveled a sideways glance his way. "They're called suffragists," she said. "I take it you don't much approve of women having the right to vote, Mr. Rennick."

"I have no objection to women votin'. But it's been my experience that you give women an inch, before you know it, they'll want the whole kit and caboodle."

"Right now all we want is the right to the ballot." She pursed her lips. "Are you married, Mr. Rennick?"

"Nope."

She narrowed her eyes. Had she only imagined his hesitation?

He met her gaze. "What about you? Got any marriage prospects?"

"None," she said, looking away. "And I plan on keeping it that way."